HER GOOD SIDE

REBEKAH WEATHERSPOON

RAZORBILL

RAZORBILL

An imprint of Penguin Random House LLC, New York

First published in the United States of America by Razorbill,
an imprint of Penguin Random House LLC, 2023

Razorbill & colophon are registered trademarks
of Penguin Random House LLC.
The Penguin colophon is a registered trademark
of Penguin Books Limited.

Visit us online at PenguinRandomHouse.com.

Library of Congress Cataloging-in-Publication Data is available.

Printed in the United States of America

ISBN 9780593465301 (hardcover)

ISBN 9780593696057 (international edition)

1st Printing

LSCH

Design by Rebecca Aidlin
Text set in Excelsior LT Std

For Ellee Dean –
Aka Debbie Door.
This is all your fault
and I can't thank you enough.

HER
GOOD
SIDE

1
BETHANY
(takes a very risky, yet brave, chance)

The way I see it, everyone has a type, and if you like thick Black girls of slightly above-average height with very clear, medium brown skin, dimples, and boobs just big enough to consider a reduction in the future, then I'm the girl for you. My type? Oliver Gutierrez, hands down. Problem is, I haven't figured out if I'm the kind of person he'd go for. He's had a few girlfriends in his sixteen years and there's been no pattern among them that I've been able to surmise. But today I am determined to find out if I fit into that randomness. Today, I'm gonna ask Oliver Gutierrez to homecoming.

"You want me to come with?" my best friend Tatum asks as we step out of Ms. Robinson's fourth period English class. We both have lunch next, with our other besties Glory and Saylor, and Tatum's girlfriend, Emily. I need to stop by my locker to grab my lunch. Oliver's locker is next to mine. He has fifth period lunch too. This is my moment to catch him and pop the big question. I'll push all my anxiety to the side. That weird, fast-talking mumbly thing I do when I get nervous will absolutely not happen. I'll flash Oliver a sweet, confident smile and ask him if he wants to join me on one of the biggest nights of the year.

It just sucks I have to do the asking in a crowded hallway and not on a quiet, starlit night on Venice Beach like I'd envisioned a million times.

"No. I have to do this on my own," I say as we stop at Tatum's locker. I wait as they swap out their books and grab their lunch. Then Tatum turns to face me. They put their hands on my shoulders and I hone in on the blue-and-silver glitter artfully streaked all over their beautiful honey-brown face. There's a football game tonight. Tatum has some very intense cheerleading to do.

"Bethany Greene, you are an irresistible goddess."

"She's right!" some random freshman agrees as she pushes by us.

"Thanks?" I say to the random freshman's back before I refocus on Tatum's glitter.

"You walk right up to that boy and you let him know that taking you to homecoming will be the best decision of his life. You can do this."

"I can do this."

"You're beautiful and I love you. Go get 'em, champ," Tatum says. Nothing uplifts you like a cheerleader telling you you're beautiful. I can do this. I'm gonna do this. Right now. I let out a deep breath and march down the hall. I turn the corner into the west wing and spot Oliver, head and shoulders over our classmates. He's wearing his royal-blue home jersey, with the number 87 ironed onto the shoulders. He looks good.

I'm what my moms call a *late bloomer*. I've always been more interested in other things that had nothing to do with boys, but sometime over the summer that changed. Actually, I'm lying. I know the exact moment things changed. I had my friends over to swim in my pool. Glory's boyfriend and the other juniors on the football team came by after they'd finished one of their preseason workouts. It was all fun and games until a splash fight devolved into something else. I was laughing, trying not to think about how long it was going to take me to blow-dry my knotless braids, when suddenly Oliver picked me up and effortlessly lifted me over his shoulder.

The air left my lungs, water flying all around us. Over the sound of my high-pitched screech, I could hear Glory telling Landon to put her down. I think their plan was some sort of backward chicken fight. I grabbed Oliver's thick waist and held on for dear life until he put me down. I couldn't find my breath, between the water running down my face and the odd laughter bubbling out of my lungs. He playfully pushed me out of the way, wrestling Landon into the deep end. The moment between us was over and so was my late bloomer status. Boys had officially entered the chat.

That night after my three-part skincare routine, I brushed my teeth, kissed the moms good night, exchanged the last few sisterly insults with Jocelyn and Trinity before they were due back to college in a couple days. I climbed into bed and instead of watching my favorite chef on YouTube, all I could think about was Oliver. How strong he was, his tan skin, the tiny pimples on the small of his back, and the few hairs on his upper lip laying the foundation for what would hopefully be a full mustache one day.

That moment in the pool changed everything. My eyes had been opened to how truly hot boys can be and I'm a little embarrassed to say this crush on Oliver has occupied too much of my mind since. I only have one choice. I have to ask him to the dance.

I walk a little faster and catch up with him just as he closes his locker door. He steps back a bit, his eyes flashing wide the second he sees me, and I know I've made my first mistake. I've come in a little too hot, but I can still fix it.

"Hey, Greene. What's up?"

"Hey," I breathe. "How's it going?"

"Good. You coming to the game tonight?" he asks. It's something so little, but he hikes his backpack over his broad shoulder and all I can think about is that afternoon in my pool. How he's built enough to support all *this*, all of me.

"Oh yeah. I'll be there. I gotta emotionally support Glory while she emotionally supports Landon. Cheer on Tatum while they cheer for you."

"Nice." He smiles, flashing his slightly crooked incisor, and I quickly wonder what we'll name our first child. "You heading to lunch?"

"Um, yeah. There was something I wanted to ask you first."

"Sure, what's up?"

"Well. I was thinking—I was wondering if you wanted to be my date to homecoming. To the dance. Landon and Glory are going together of course. So we could all be together."

Stupid, my brain immediately shouts at me. This is not a group thing. It's you and Oliver. Pure romance. "Not that it would be a double date thing. I mean, half the school will be there, so technically it's like a huge group date. But you and I would be there together."

I finally close my mouth and give him a chance to answer. As I look up at him, I already know what he's going to say. It takes about two seconds for all the stages of yikes to jump across his face. Shock, fear, a desperate need for an escape, bargaining, then finally acceptance. I'm holding out hope as he winces and starts scratching the back of his neck, but my body is already working on its own physiological reactions to the blow that my mind still hopes isn't coming. My face feels all hot and my throat feels like it's closing.

"Oh man, B. I don't think that's a good idea."

"Oh?" I choke out.

"Yeah, I was actually going to ask Poppy Carlisle after lunch." See, I can't blame him for that. Poppy Carlisle just transferred to our school last month, and beyond still having that new-car smell, she's like dumb hot. I mean, I'm cute, but if I weren't painfully straight, I would also have the hots for Poppy Carlisle. She's also newly single, having just kicked Jacob Yeun to the curb. I'm shocked she doesn't already have a date for the dance. But apparently she will. After lunch, when Oliver asks her.

"Oh" is all I can say.

"And I mean—aren't you scared of this?" he asks, motioning between us. "Lan said you'd rather chew off your own arm than let a boy touch you. Homecoming won't be much fun if you don't even want me to hold your hand." And there it is. Right there, my past just came back to beat my ass right in the middle of the hallway.

So yeah, fine, part of my being a "late bloomer" involved somewhat of a revulsion when it came to boys, but more importantly the concept of doing it with a boy. But that wasn't because I was scared, exactly. I just didn't understand it. And yes, maybe at the end of freshman year when Glory told us she and Landon had done it I burst into tears in the middle of the crowded lunch quad.

Unfortunately, a few people overheard my overacting and the news that the mere thought of someone else having sex was enough to make me cry spread through Culver City High School, and I'm sure the greater Los Angeles County, like an uncontained brush fire. So yeah, I'm a late bloomer as far as my family is concerned. But I'm paranoid and a bit prudish to the rest of my school.

"That's not what I said at all." Yes, it is, it's exactly what I said. "Plus, that was two years ago."

"Okay, but, like, I wanna have fun at homecoming and I think it's just a lot of pressure on me to be your first *everything*. And yeah, we can go as friends, but I don't really wanna spend the night after the big game with a *friend*." I let out a slow breath, trying to process the levels of this humiliation, but Oliver keeps talking. "And you know I'm trying to make it to the league. What if I don't live up to your expectations and you have a horrible time, and run back to tell your moms?"

Both my moms played in the WNBA. Now my mom Teresa

is an assistant coach for the Lakers and my other mom,
Melissa, has her own show on the National Sports Network.
You can catch *Before the Buzzer* weekday afternoons at
two p.m. "Yeah, they have connections, but neither of them
are the vengeful type. Besides, even if you make it to the
league, you won't be draft ready for a while. I don't think
our date will factor in."

It really hits me then that he's already said no, and I'm
still standing here, trying to haggle with him.

"Still, it's the Lakers, Beth."

"Yeah, okay." I muster up a hint of a smile. "Well, I hope
Poppy says yes. She seems pretty cool."

"Hey, thanks. We good?" He smiles back and I can just
see it: Tonight when I'm in bed wiping the world's most pathetic tears from my eyes, I won't be thinking of that afternoon in my pool and the way the water dripped down his
face. I'll be thinking of this pity smile. I'll be thinking of
the first time I ever got up the courage to ask someone out
and how they said no.

And then it happens, the true kiss of death. He lightly
nudges my shoulder. The bro nudge. I will never get a chance
to make out with Oliver Gutierrez. We are officially just
friends.

"Yeah, we're good."

"Cool. See ya at the game."

"Yeah, I'll see ya."

Oliver turns and walks toward the quad. In the distance
I hear the bell ring. My feet carry me a few yards to my
own locker. My whole body numb, I grab my three-tiered

isolated lunch box with the watercolor strawberry print. The highlight of my day. I put a lot of effort into my sandwiches. And I think that might be part of my problem. I need to focus a little bit more on showing boys, specifically Oliver, that I'm a new woman, capable of some really intense hand-holding and some quality end-of-the-night smooching. A new woman afraid of nothing. Kinda.

2
BETHANY
(inspired anew)

The homies are already at our table when I finally make it out to the quad. Like they can sense me, Tatum's head pops up and they flash me this sweet *Well????* grin. I shake my head and cross the patchy grass back onto the concrete patio. It's hot as heck outside, but at least there's shade over the lunch tables. Shade to hide my misery and pain. Saylor is midsentence, but she moves so I can take my usual seat beside her.

"It just doesn't need to be today. Like, chill," she finishes, before she turns to me and presses her lips to my cheek. "Hey, Bets."

"Hey," I say, sounding a little more pathetic than I mean to.

"What happened?" Tatum asks me. Their girlfriend Emily gives me a hopeful nod, her blonde ponytail bouncing around, encouraging me to spill the beans.

"He said no."

"Why?" Glory asks. The look on her face almost makes me laugh. It's pure disgust, like saying no to me is not only ridiculous, but a truly bad business decision.

"Apparently Crybaby Bethany left a lasting impression."

"Oh, come on," Saylor nearly shouts. A few people look over at us, but she ignores them.

"Who's Crybaby Bethany?" Emily asks. She's only been dating Tatum for a few months, so she's not caught up on all our personal problems, but that was my nickname for like a year straight, so I'm kinda shocked she never heard about it.

"It's nothing. I embarrassed myself and I paid for my crimes, but clearly Oliver hasn't forgotten about it. Also, there was some other nonsense about him trying to impress the moms at some point in the future. I didn't have the heart to tell him I have a better chance of making the Lakers than he does." Oliver and I play the same position in basketball. He's good. I'm better. We've played against each other. It's just facts. Doesn't change how cute I think he is.

"I feel like he could have just said no," Glory replies. That look of disgust is still on her face. I do appreciate the support, true Black girl solidarity. "Don't worry, Bets. We'll find you a date."

"I hope so. I just wanted that date to be Oliver," I admit. My friends know my crush is pretty hefty, but it's just now that I realize how much I actually liked him and how much thought I put into picturing us together. Rookie mistake, I guess. Maybe I do need more experience with all this.

"Well, now I feel bad for my news," Saylor says, her bottom lip jutting out.

"I mean, if it's good news I definitely wanna hear it. If it's bad news, sorry in advance, but I will use your pain to distract me from mine," I say. I open my lunch box and pull out the over-the-top sandwich I made. My friends don't say anything, but I see Glory's gaze immediately dart to the parchment paper holding the shaven chicken breast club sandwich that I've leveled up with mozzarella, pesto spread, crushed pecans, and a honey drizzle on a toasted ciabatta bun. I brought some Salsitas, the best chips ever made, and some green grapes the size of golf balls. Oliver's rejection was almost enough to make me lose my appetite, but not quite.

"That's true friendship." Saylor laughs. "No, it's good news."

"Let's hear it."

"Jake Yeun and I are a thing. Like a *thing* thing. He's my new boo."

"Oh, you did it!" Tatum squeals.

"Yup. Caught him after Spanish. I think after a week of flirting in the DMs it was time to put him out of his misery." Saylor sucks her teeth and does a shimmy with her shoulders. "Dats my man now."

"Nice," Glory says with a smile.

Just hearing Jacob Yeun's name reminds me I'm not the only person who changed over the summer. I used to sit across from Jacob in second grade. He was this teeny, really quiet kid I used to try to make laugh, but he never really said much. I do remember his favorite dinosaur was a triceratops. In middle school he went full goth skater, which seems to make sense since both of his parents are tattoo artists. He still doesn't talk much, but he makes up for it with how good he is with a camera, like a legit camera, and with a phone. He has the most TikTok followers in the whole school, thanks to the skating videos he posts. He's also on yearbook and whatever footage the school refuses to post on the official socials, he edits together and makes something five hundred times better for his own account. Smart, if you ask me.

Oh, and over the summer he grew like a foot and just got insanely hot. Long skater hair, sun-kissed skin, the black-on-black wardrobe that always seems to work for him instead of making him look like the drama club's stage crew. All of that is probably why Poppy Carlisle laser locked on him the first week of school. They dated for a bit, but the rumor is she dumped him because he wouldn't have sex with her. That sounds fake. Like, what boy wouldn't do it with Poppy Carlisle, but whatever the real reason they broke up is, they aren't together anymore. And now newly hot Jacob is with Saylor.

"What? What's that look?" Saylor asks.

My brain short-circuits and I realize I'm definitely making a face. I'm picturing Jacob, so my brow is all tucked up from concentration and my mouth is hanging open because I'm in shock. It's not that Saylor and Jacob are a thing now. If you think Poppy Carlisle is a ten, Saylor is a firm twelve. She's gotten "Most Photogenic" every year since sixth grade and we all know that's just code for certified hottie.

She's biracial; Black dad, white mom. She has her mom's hazel eyes and dark blonde hair, but unlike her mom, she and her twin sisters have these amazing big, long curls. She's tall and thin. People do fetishize her looks sometimes, but that doesn't change how beautiful she is. She plays two varsity sports, and is very personable and a friend to creatures big and small. Of course Jacob would say yes to being Saylor's boyfriend.

That isn't the thing tripping me up. I'm in very real shock because my bestie supreme, Saylor, already has a date to homecoming. Rhys Hayes, this white boy who plays the tuba and always has this wave of blond hair flopping in his face, asked her last Friday with a little help from the rest of the marching band's bass section in the upperclassmen parking lot. I knew she'd been talking to Jacob, but this new development is, well, new. I close my mouth. I should probably say something.

"No, I just—you inspire me. Not even the end of the week and you've locked down a boy for business and one for pleasure."

"I do like to cover my bases." Saylor laughs.

"Yeah, what are you going to do about Rhys?" Emily asks.

"Nothing. I told him straight up we were going as friends when he asked me. And Jacob has to be there for yearbook. He's not going as a dance participant, so if I wanna slow dance with Jacob once or twice, I think I can squeeze that in."

"Wow," I whisper. I think of Oliver's many reasons for rejecting me and how I'm the only one of my friends who doesn't have a date for homecoming now or a boo to call my own. This isn't gonna work. "I need a date for the dance."

"We'll get you one," Glory says before she takes a bite of her simple turkey sandwich. She deserves better lunch meats, but I don't say anything about that.

"Is it that easy though?"

"Uh, yeah. It's a date to the dance. It's not a kidney. So Oliver was your top choice, but there are a lot of people at this school."

"She's right," Tatum adds.

"Neither of the Gupta twins have dates. I heard them talking about it earlier," Emily adds.

"And B, I know this might be a lot for you to process, but . . ." Saylor turns to me and purses her lips together like she's about to tell me I do need a kidney. "Kayden Smith doesn't have a date either."

"No—"

"Just hear me out!"

"No, ma'am. Nev. Er. No. No way. No how."

"Why not?"

"Because I almost puked talking to Oliver, and he and I are, like, decent friends. I'm afraid to look directly at Kayden's face. He is . . . everything. All of it. I would actually die if Kayden spoke to me. I would leave this earthly plane."

If my crush on Oliver is something real and true, based on my knowledge of the softness of his back skin, my crush on Kayden Smith is the reason I get out of bed in the morning. The only reason he knows I'm alive is because I made a half-court shot that went viral freshman year. He wasn't at the game. Why would he be? But he saw a TikTok—a TikTok Jacob Yeun made, now that I think of it—and made a point to come up to me in the hall the next day and tell me how sick he thought it was. I just stared at him and made a bird noise that was supposed to be a thanks. He seemed to take it that way and went on with his day. He hasn't even looked at me since.

I don't consider that my true boy-crazy awakening only because Kayden isn't a boy; he's a sex god. Tall, actually dark, extremely handsome. Perfect teeth, just perfect. He smells like the ocean after a storm. His shape-up is always so crisp, he must have his barber on call. And the thing that really matters to me: His sneakers are always clean. It's weird, but it's hot. But he's too hot for mere mortals like me. Plus, he's a senior! Basketball season starts in a few weeks. We share the gym with the boys and if Kayden makes varsity again, which I'm sure he will, I'll have to figure out how to deal with the amount of drool I'll be producing with him just a few yards away.

"You do not ask someone like Kayden Smith to homecoming," I go on. "You build a marble pedestal and set him upon it. You don't touch it! You just look. From a safe distance where you have absolutely no risk of embarrassing yourself."

"I don't think he's *that* fine." Glory shrugs.

"Because you have Landon vision. You don't think anyone is as fine as him," I say, letting my eyes roll extra hard. Landon is actually the freaking cutest, but he's no Kayden.

"I vote AJ Gupta. He's shy, but he's super sweet. I like that he always holds doors for people," Tatum declares.

"You do have a point. Okay." I shake myself and push the

lingering sting from Oliver's no down with all the rest of my repressed feelings. "AJ Gupta. I'm gonna do it. I need like twenty-four hours to recover, but I'm gonna do it."

"We believe in you," Tatum says. Emily nods enthusiastically. Glory adds her old-church-lady nod. I'm glad we're all in agreement. All hope for my pathetic love life is not lost.

"Perfect. Can we talk some more about Jacob?" Saylor asks.

"Yes. Please," I reply. I unwrap my sandwich and pop one of the loose honey-drizzled pecans into my mouth. I might have zero skills when it comes to boys, but at least I know how to make myself a delicious sandwich.

3
JACOB
(has no clue what he's doing)

"I just want to know how? And why? Why? Why would you do this to me?" Heaven groans.

"I didn't do it *to* you," I say, leaning against the wall next to her locker. School's over, but I have about fifteen minutes to get to yearbook. There are two games I have to film this afternoon, and I was supposed to hang out with my best friend Heaven after, but I kind of have new plans. Plans with my new girlfriend.

This time last year I got exactly zero attention from girls. Now we're a month and a half into our junior year and I am in my second relationship this semester. At first, I had no idea why the new girl, Poppy Carlisle, was even looking in my direction, but after a week sitting next to each other in chem she just flat-out told me I should be her boyfriend. In retrospect, it was a mistake. For one, I got dumped. Two, Poppy made me realize I have no clue how to interact with girls, in the romantic sense. That's why she dumped me.

And now I'm dating Saylor Ford, probably the hottest girl in our grade, if not the whole school. Trust me, I have no idea how I ended up in this situation either, but I get why Heaven is pissed about it.

"Are you sure? 'Cause at this point it feels personal. We already lost Axel to this relationship BS. And just when I get you back from Poppy's evil clutches, you run back into the arms of love. Gross." The gagging noise she makes really drives her point home.

"I've been dating Saylor for three hours. I don't think we've gotten to the point of love just yet," I say.

"Oh, but I know her and her little IG-perfect family. She's gonna suck you in with her perfect smile and her mom's professional lighting kits and you'll be the worst kind of couple."

"What kind of couple is that?" I laugh, ignoring the part about the lighting. Lighting is important.

"I don't know, but it's gonna be bad. You're gonna start wearing matching beige-and-white outfits. And khakis. Khakis, Jacob." I try not to point out that Heaven and I are currently dressed alike in our black Carhartt pants and black Vans. My black T-shirt has the logo from my parents' tattoo shop, Ink & Pearl. Hers has the TWICE *MORE & MORE* album collage across her chest, but from behind we're definitely matching. But that's not the point.

Saylor Ford is Saylor Ford. She's really into school sports and, I don't know, stuff like being perceived as a human by the general public. Skating means a lot to me, and that's technically a sport, but I prefer to be behind the scenes, behind my camera or my phone, whichever the situation calls for. I don't need to be seen. Saylor is like her own marquee, bright lights and a catchy title in tall bold letters. Her whole crew is like that, which is cool.

They are all pretty nice, especially Tatum Fujikawa and Bethany Greene. Heaven joked about starting a Blasian book club with Tatum once, but it never happened. Glory Johnson has forty-year-old-trapped-in-a-teen-body, real serious put-together energy, but she sticks up for people, which makes the world a better place. Emily Pruitt is the only white girl who hangs out with them thanks to whatever is going on between her and Tatum. She seems happy. Saylor's friends are cool. We just don't run in the same crowds. Until now.

"Am I being selfish?" Heaven goes on. "Yes, I am. I have two friends, Jacob. Well, *had*, but now I have to sit around while the *two* of you play kissy face instead of playing *Gran Turismo* with me. Do you understand what it's like being a third wheel? A fifth wheel? It's a special kind of hell I wouldn't wish on anyone."

"Are you really mad at me?" I ask, because now I'm starting to feel bad.

"No," she huffs out.

"Good. Besides, Valentina does play *Gran Turismo* with you."

"Yeah, and she sets a timer so she doesn't miss a moment of her face-sucking time with Axe. It's unjust is what it is. A violation of terms of friendship. You know I was there when they both dropped the L-bomb the first time? I just stood there while they had their noses pressed together like this." She presses the palm of her hand against her nose. I laugh at her demonstration though it's completely unnecessary. I know how things are with our best friend Axel Diaz and his girlfriend, Valentina Barzola. It was a lot to get used to.

And yeah, I felt the same way Heaven does now, I just kept it to myself.

It's been the three of us for as long as I can remember. We met in kindergarten. Axel's wild energy balanced out my quiet side. Our moms used to joke that he used to do the talking for me and that worked out just fine. My mom and Heaven's mom met at a Korean mom meet up and even though they couldn't be more different—my mom has tats on her face and Dr. Maurene Goo-Campbell is Culver City's most respected dentist—that didn't stop them from becoming friends. We only got closer during the start of the pandemic when we bounced between our houses and our houses only.

I thought we'd be inseparable, just the three of us until graduation finally forced us apart, in physical proximity at least. And then Axel and Val just sort of collided at the beginning of the summer. She can't skate, but she found a way to be with us every day all summer long, and yeah, it was a bit of an adjustment. She's cool though, and Axel's happy so I can't really complain, and at least I had Heaven. We could look the other way or leave together when Axel and Val decided to give each other a thorough oral exam.

Axel becoming part of a two-pack wasn't the only thing that changed over the summer. I changed a lot. I grew a freakish amount and according to half the girls in our school, that seems to have upped my stock value. My nose is now in proportion with my face, but that's just 'cause my head got bigger. Because I stretched out it feels like I'm skinnier than before, like a light breeze could blow me out to sea. My arms and legs feel like they might get tangled up any second if I'm not watching where I'm going.

But I get the true power of the heightist society we live in now. I'm taller than my dad and I can actually see down the hall instead of looking at everyone's backs. A *late bloomer*, my mom called it. People are treating me differently. Still, I like to think my personality is the same, but I'm more self-conscious. Maybe shier. I'm so aware of myself in an uncomfortable way. I'm still adjusting.

None of that has stopped girls from asking me out though.

Heaven closes her locker, clutching her skateboard in her right hand. Then she lets out this killer sigh. "Why'd you have to go and get hot?"

"I'm not hot. I'm just tall."

"Oh, you sweet fool. They're the same thing."

"What about Ash Becker?" I ask. "She's short as hell and you had a crush on her."

"Oh, I'm talking about the world of the straights. Not lesbian rules."

"Fair enough."

"Just promise me something," Heaven says, suddenly dead serious.

"What's up?"

Heaven steps forward and puts her free hand on my shoulder. "Just don't wear beige."

"You have my word."

"Good. I'll meet you at Axe's after the football game?"

"Ah, yeah. About that. Saylor invited me to go—"

"Ugh!" Heaven grips her board over her head and starts walking away from me. "Goodbye, Jacob!"

I laugh nervously at her dramatic exit because it is funny, but now I'm wondering if I'm making a mistake. I head down to the yearbook office, trying not to talk myself out of the consequences of my current romantic situation. It'll be fine. Heaven is annoyed and I don't think she and Saylor will suddenly become best friends, but Heaven wouldn't kill *our* friendship over this.

I've been monitoring how much I've been letting Saylor run through my mind all day. Now that I'm alone it's like she comes sprinting back to the front of the line. Saylor Ford is really my girlfriend. It's pretty wild. She knows that Poppy dumped me because I wasn't ready to lose my virginity yet and doesn't care at all. That's a plus. Apparently it's one of the reasons she wanted to go out with me. Saylor's ex Tagger Evans was "intense." More like a candidate for an FBI watch list. One of those white boys who carries a little too much unjustified rage around. Anyone seems like a better choice than Tagger, but Saylor's words were "Poppy said you were sweet." Too sweet is probably what Poppy really said. Too sweet and too inexperienced to be her boyfriend.

But the too-sweet thing sounded good to Saylor, I guess, because she just laughed this cute-as-hell laugh that kinda scrambled my brains before she whispered, "I get the sex thing. I wasn't ready to do it with Tagger either. I'd like to be with someone I can take it slow with."

That fried my brain completely, mostly 'cause when I told

Poppy I didn't think it was a good idea for us to do it after only dating for a week and a half, she kinda scoffed at me. And then when I explained that I was still a virgin, she actually laughed in my face. She said she'd be happy to help me fix it, but she definitely laughed.

The gut punch of that conversation hits me again as I head over to my edit bay in the yearbook office. I'm on sports and helping out our senior digital editor, Noah Killgore, with the digital component of the yearbook. We've shot some pretty sick stuff so far.

"You gotta tell me how you did it, Yeun," Troy Barry asks me the second I sit down. I turn around and jerk back. He's wheeled his chair two centimeters from mine.

"Gimme some space, dude. Geez."

"Sorry." He wheels back enough for both our comfort and I turn back to my computer. "You gotta spill though. Poppy, then Saylor? Holy hell. Are you paying them?"

"I gotta know too," Birk Wilkins says. News travels fast, I guess. I sigh and try to ignore them, but then Madlyn Lowell joins the party.

"I heard why Poppy dumped you, so I definitely have questions," she says. I'm not sure if she actually knows, but Madlyn loves other people's business.

I roll my eyes and turn around. "I don't know what's so confusing about it. Someone asks someone out. They say yes or they say no. Sometimes people get dumped. What's the big mystery?"

"I just want you to admit the puberty thing is really working out for you," Troy grumbles. He's pissed at me because we both used to be shrimps. He's still short and kinda scrawny, but his voice dropped a lot. I'm still terrified that mine's gonna crack at any moment. He definitely sees the height thing as a betrayal.

"Well, thanks for letting me know I have no other redeeming qualities," I say sharply. For me at least.

"I didn't even know you and Saylor knew each other," Madlyn adds.

"We sit by each other in Flores's Spanish class."

"Oh. Okay, then."

"So, it's okay?" I ask, still annoyed. "You guys aren't too surprised that someone would like me?"

"Chill, man. You're just lucky. That's all," Birk says. "She's hot. So is Poppy. We're just confused. You barely talk."

"As a close professional associate, I do want to know if you're cool with the fact that Saylor's already going to homecoming with Rhys? Why wouldn't she ask you first?" Madlyn says, like she's really concerned and not digging for dirt.

"Yeah, we'll see if he's still with Saylor by homecoming," Troy says, and for a split second I think about our school's nonviolent conflict resolution policy.

"They are just going as friends. Besides, I'm already going so Noah can spend the night with his girlfriend. I'll be there with her; I just won't be her date. It's not that big of a deal," I say. Which it isn't. Saylor was up front about the Rhys thing and clear that she has no interest in him whatsoever. I believe her. I have no reason not to.

"Let's all stop harassing Jacob and huddle up, please,"

Mr. Wolfson says, walking in with his afternoon Starbucks. Noah's right behind him. I grab the tablet and hand it over to Noah as he sets down his stuff next to mine.

"You check your grade for Wei yet?" he whispers as he takes the tablet from me.

"What? No? He said he was getting them back on Monday."

Noah shakes his head. "I just saw mine in the portal." I pull out my phone as I follow him over to the empty round space in the middle of the room. I go right to our school's online grading portal. Advanced Placement: FILM III. Instructor William Wei. Script Assignment 2: C–

"Fuck," I say. Not quietly enough though.

"Yooo," I hear Mr. Wolfson say. I glance up and he and the rest of the yearbook staff are looking at me. "With the language, Yeun. Pull it back a bit."

"Sorry," I say, feeling my face going bright red. I'm psyched to have a new girlfriend, but maybe I need to worry a little less about the Saylors and the Poppys and focus on getting this grade up.

4
JACOB
(needs to focus)

I stare at the C minus again and look at Mr. Wei's note. *Dark humor is one of the greatest art forms, but make sure you take yourself seriously. Happy to talk with you about it.* My short script sucked. I know it did. I worked on it for hours. Missed two trips to the skate park, one with Heaven and Axel and one with our dads and my little sister, Esther. Still, I couldn't crack it. I knew it was crap when I handed it in, but I was out of time. It's not a huge percentage of our grade and if this was any other class I wouldn't be too stressed out, but this is Mr. Wei's advanced film lab. It's only open to juniors and seniors, and even then getting in is hard as hell.

Not for me though. Mr. Wei took one look at the reel I submitted and held a spot for me. And now I'm blowing it and getting in the way of my own plan. Here's my plan:

Step 1: Kill it in our school's film program.

Step 2: Submit the best student project anyone has ever seen.

Step 3: Get into my top choice film school, USC.

Step 4: Become the world's best cinematographer.

Step 5: Win my first Oscar at twenty-seven.

But I have to pass his class first.

This semester we're studying theory, technique, and story. We watch a lot of films—of varying lengths—and practice writing them for a grade. Next semester we focus on genre and specific directors, before we pick a genre and director to emulate for our final project. The fall semester is mostly important for seniors. Mr. Wei has gotten a lot of people into their film program of choice. The stressful part for juniors comes from the fact that if you get into the lab and you blow it, Mr. Wei doesn't have to let you back in next year.

There's a lot of solo work and we are assigned to each other's crews for each project. I thought I had this whole year in the bag, until it came to the actual writing. I can't write for crap. I have an eye for the perfect shot, and the skills to be one of the best Steadicam operators to do the job. I have ideas, but not a full story in me. I got a C on our first script sample about a homicidal tattoo artist. My mom agreed to play the killer, but I need Mr. Wei to sign off on it down the road.

This time I tried to write about a skater trying to rob a bank. Heaven already agreed to be my robber. I didn't want it to seem like I was copying *Point Break* (1991), the best movie ever, but by the time I handed it in, I knew the pacing was off. I could picture the action, but not the emotion or the motivation. Maybe because I'd never be ballsy or crazy enough to pull off a robbery. I knew this C minus was coming, but I guess I was just hoping by some miracle I'd nailed it or at least gotten a B. I was wrong.

"Jacob," I hear Mr. Wolfson say. I snap out of my panicked thought spiral and focus back on the staff meeting going on around me. "What's the news?"

"Oh, uh. Gonna go shoot varsity girls' volleyball and then I'll be at varsity football tonight. And I was able to recover the footage from last week's cross-country meet. The drives got swapped."

"Excellent and even better. Let's keep an eye on our labeling before and after. Thank you."

"On it," Noah adds, nodding at me and Mr. Wolfson.

"And Coach Fuller keeps trying to get our drives," I say. Our football program is one of best in the state, which means the school gives Coach Fuller whatever he wants, including a professional to shoot their game tape. I only cover home games and I'm not really covering the game itself. I'm filming the players, looking for the moments, the memories. Not the touchdowns, but the seconds after. The end zone celebration and, if I'm lucky, those rare tears of joy. Fuller still wants the raw footage I get though, I think for himself.

Mr. Wolfson rolls his eyes. "I'll talk to him."

"Thanks."

"Clubs?" he goes on. Callum Matthews fills us in on where he is with the official club photos and that's where I zone out. I need to talk to Mr. Wei and I need to figure

out how to turn my crappy writing around. I'll get an A on
every technical project, but a B in the class is not going to
get me into USC.

o o o

I have a quick debrief with Noah, then grab my gear and
head down to the gym. The volleyball team is playing
Hamilton today. I have no clue who will win, but I'm sure
I'll get some good stuff. The hallways are basically empty,
but there's noise buzzing around the whole school. Concert
band practice. Concert choir. Play rehearsal. This year they
are doing *Little Shop*. I asked Mrs. Brenner if I could put a
camera in Audrey II's mouth, but she said no. Then I asked
if I could film opening night with a drone. A small one.
She's thinking about it.

I turn the corner to the gym and spot Bethany Greene at
the end of the hall talking to AJ Gupta outside the locker
room. I have to walk right by them, so I should probably say
hi. Poppy was kind of weird with my friends. Especially
Heaven, and I don't want it to be like that with Saylor. I'm
maybe halfway down the hall when AJ pats Bethany on the
shoulder and takes off into the boys' locker room. I watch
her as she stands there for a second, her expression dropping at first, and then I see it. Her whole face just crumbles.
She turns and rushes down the hall.

I probably shouldn't, but I go around the corner after her.
I have a feeling I know where she's going. It takes a second
for me to catch up, but I find Bethany near the emergency

side exit no one really uses between the teachers' lounge and the library. She's crying. She has her black-and-blue varsity basketball jacket tucked under her arms.

"Hey, you okay?" I say carefully, but my voice still makes her jump a bit. She looks at me for a half a second, before she lets her head fall back against the wall with a thud.

"Oh Jesus. Not you," she groans. I don't know why, but the way she says it makes me laugh. Like I, specifically, really effed up her whole day.

"What? What did I do?"

"Nothing. You're probably the third to last person I want to see me cry right now."

"Who's the first?" I'm genuinely curious and I want to distract her.

"Nope. That information is coming to the grave with me." She sniffles, dabbing under her eyes with the side of her knuckle. She has blue-and-silver glitter on her cheeks and her temples. She's careful not to smudge it.

"Well, I can't fight at all, but I'll give AJ a piece of my mind if he hurt you."

That makes her laugh. "He didn't do anything. I just embarrassed the shit out of myself."

"I bet it's not that bad," I say.

"Oh, it is. But nothing I can't handle. Or get used to, which I guess I should." Her shoulders drop when she looks up at me with this sad smile. I know she said it was nothing, but now I really feel bad. "I'm gonna suck it up real good and go watch this volleyball game."

"I'm heading that way. Come on."

"I need one second." She blows out a deep breath, then dabs under her eyes again. I don't know what AJ said to her, but she looks sad as hell and something about that seems unfair.

"Sure you don't want to talk about it?" I ask.

"It's not that serious. I'm just a crybaby. You might have heard."

"You mean Crybaby Bethany?" I tease her.

She laughs harder this time, like a short wheezing noise. A few more tears spill out, but at least she's definitely smiling. "That's me."

"You got a much better nickname now though. Number thirty-four, Bethany 'the Beast' Greene. Only player in Minotaur history to hit a shot from half-court as a freshman and your first season back after the stay-at-home 'Rona time?"

"Yeah, I really owe you for that TikTok, even though some people thought it was fake. Really helped my street cred with my sisters."

"I'm glad my parents were cool with me being a terrible artist. Must be tough, following up all that star power," I say. Her moms are legit names in sports and both her sisters play D1 ball. I didn't know her oldest sister, but her sister Jocelyn was a senior last year. I got a lot of great footage of her and Bethany playing varsity together.

"Lucky," she says quietly. I'm not sure I heard right, but I figure it's better if I don't ask. She sniffles a few more times and then seems to have shaken it off. "Okay. Lead the way."

I turn back toward the gym but walk slow enough for her

to fall in step beside me. My legs are too long now, my sister keeps telling me. I walk too fast. I try to think of something else to make her laugh, but when I look over her smile's gone. She's in her head. I get it, so I keep my mouth shut. The gym is pretty packed when we get there. Back-to-back games on a Friday and most people stick around.

My brain automatically starts looking for a place to set up.

"There's Saylor," Bethany suddenly says. I look to where she's pointing at the top of the bleachers. I smile the second I see Saylor waving at me. I wave back and then look down as Bethany lightly pats my shoulder.

"Good talk," she says.

"Yeah, no problem," I chuckle back. I stand there by the edge of the court until she makes her way to the top of the bleachers and drops down next to Saylor. My girlfriend. Shit, I should have gone up there. I almost do, when both teams start to gather on the sidelines. I rush to the other side of the gym and start mounting my camera to my rig. And then I pull out my phone and send Saylor a text.

> Let me get set up and I'll come talk to you at halftime.

> Okay! xx
> Thanks for being so sweet
> to my Bethy Boo.

No problem.

I look back up at her one more time before the anthem starts. Focus on this game and then the next one and then afterward I'll try to get a handle on this being-a-good-boyfriend thing.

5
BETHANY
(is ready to throw in the towel)

I stand by my window seat, looking down at the party kicking off in my pool below. Saylor's on the edge of the deck still in her clothes, clasping Jacob's hand. He's still in his jeans and T-shirt too. They're talking to Landon and Oliver. Yes. Oliver is back at my house, after he rejected me with the old no thank-you. He said hi to me, made sure to suck up extra hard to my mom Melissa about her framed jersey in the hallway, and then was first in the pool. He scored the winning touchdown, so I guess he earned this celebration. In my pool. At least he didn't bring Poppy.

I watch as Oliver jumps into the pool again and Landon follows. I realize then I'm kind of staring blankly at Saylor and Jacob while they're still standing on the pool deck. Saylor says something to Jacob. He nods. She smiles. He tries to smile? He looks a little out of sorts. Maybe he has a crush on Oliver too. Saylor kisses him on the cheek and then I see her coming back inside. Probably to change. Jacob looks around for a second before he sits down in one of our deck chairs. I wonder for a second if he can swim and then my eyes and my thoughts drift back to Oliver. What a bummer.

With a sigh, I adjust my own bright pink swimsuit, then turn around and flop down on my window seat. I look over at Tatum sitting in my desk chair in their bikini. They glance up from their phone for a sec and smile at me, before their phone has all their attention again. Emily had to go home, but that's what texts are for.

I almost look out the window again when a bikini-clad Glory comes out of the bathroom connecting Jocelyn's and my rooms. I miss my sisters. They'd know exactly what to say.

"Okay, spill. Stupid play practice. I feel like I missed everything," Glory says.

"Hey, stage production is important," I reply. I could have filled her in during the football game, but I spent the whole volleyball game trying not to cry. No way I was risking the return of Crybaby Bethany at the fifty-yard line.

"Yeah, yeah, whatever. What happened?"

"Yeah, I wanna know. I miss everything on the sidelines," Tatum adds. They did do a lot of cheering today.

"I mean nothing. I found AJ before he skipped off to cross-country. I asked him. He said no. He heard Madlyn Lowell is gonna ask him."

"He turned you down for a hypothetical?" Glory asks.

"Yup."

"Well, that's bullshit."

"What about Isaac Cross? I mean, you love a short king. He's so funny," Tatum suggests.

"He asked Heather Sinclair before the game. He posted a TikTok about it," Glory replies, sealing my fate. So many single boys in my school and somehow there is literally no one for me to ask to homecoming. Not that I want to do the asking anymore. I've had enough rejection and humiliation in that department to last me a long time.

"Maybe I'll just skip the dance," I say as Saylor flings my bedroom door open. She has a slightly deranged smile on her face. The three of us look at her before Glory turns back to me.

"No. You are not skipping the dance. You're gonna be more upset if you stay home," Glory says.

"Definitely don't skip the dance," Saylor says. "I have an idea."

"About what I can do while you are all at the dance?" I ask.

"Tsk, no. Go to homecoming with Jacob." The idea just kinda hangs in the air for a second. I glance over at Tatum, then my gaze skips over to Glory. A half second goes by before she realizes I'm looking at her. She shrugs, the corners of her mouth turning down and her eyebrows going up in the universal gesture of *eh, not a terrible idea.*

"Hear me out," Saylor says.

"I'm listening," I say, but already my stomach is starting to churn. It's one thing to cast your own dramatic doubt on a situation. Being dramatic is how I process things. I can't help it. But something changes when your friends also admit defeat on your behalf. Then you know it's truly a hopeless situation. My best friend's dateless boyfriend is my best option. Bleak. Still, I'm listening.

"So, you're a little smitten with Oliver. I get it. Love takes

time. AJ said no, and no always burns a little, but you didn't
have a thing for AJ."

"True."

"So, homecoming is one thing; it's only one night. An
Oliver-level love is something else."

"Go on."

"Take a break from the date hunt. Go to the dance with
Jacob. Take ah-dorable pictures together. Enjoy your night.
We'll make memories, all of us," Saylor says. She's talking
a lot with her hands, her whole face animated, full of hope.
"And all while you have time to consider who at Culver City
High School is truly the man for you. It's a win-win, baby."

"She's right," Glory says. "I like it."

Tatum flashes me a huge smile and nods their head. It's
not a bad idea. Missing homecoming because I can't find a
date is pretty humiliating and I'm embarrassed to say: The
crush on Oliver hasn't completely gone away. It will, but I'm
gonna need a little time to convince myself to get over him.
But there's one small issue.

"What's wrong?" Tatum asks.

"I don't know. Maybe Oliver was right. May—"

"Yeah, I'm gonna stop you right there," Glory cuts me off.
"Oliver's great. That's Lan's bestie, but he's wrong about
like eight different things a day."

"No, I know." I laugh. "I just mean he might have been
onto something. Maybe I do need more experience when it
comes to dating and stuff."

"Listen, you're looking for a boyfriend who wants you

and not every guy is boyfriend material," Glory replies. "You're looking for one yes from the right boy, not all the boys. We just need to find you the right boy."

"Oh no. I want *every* boyfriend. *All* the boyfriends. Hey, Tatum, give me your girlfriend too."

"Nooo, she's so cute," Tatum whines.

Glory rolls her eyes. "Anyway, Saylor's right. We'll all be there together. You'll have someone to dance with and take pictures with. It's just one night. And we have plenty of time to help you in the actual romance department. I'm thinking makeover."

"No makeovers. I'm cute as fuuuck. What does Jacob think of this brilliant idea?" I ask. Saylor's dramatic side is one of the reasons we get along. It's like her to get ahead of herself. Watch: Jacob has no clue about any of this.

"He's in. He's happy to help make it the most magical evening of your young life," Saylor assures me. In theory, going to homecoming with Jacob would solve my most urgent problem, but I can't say the thought of it is a real self-esteem booster. I know there's no use in sulking about Oliver. I just wish my best option wasn't my best friend's boyfriend. I can still skip the dance or go alone. Neither sounds like an ideal choice. I let out a deep sigh and give in to Saylor's brilliant idea.

"Hmm, okay. I guess I'll go with Jacob, then."

"Great! You'll have a magical time. I promise," she says.

"How's the magic going with you and Jacob?" Glory asks Saylor.

"Okay. I think? I forgot how shy he is. I haven't really

talked to him since like fifth grade, but he really showed up for our Bets today." Glory and Tatum look over at me so fast I almost laugh.

"Jacob witnessed my post-AJ breakdown and came to the rescue," I tell them.

"See, all-around good guy before I even asked him to step up." Saylor beams.

"Go get changed," Glory tells her, nodding toward my bathroom.

"Oh, right." Saylor hustles into the bathroom. I glance back out the window to catch a glimpse of Jacob, my maybe homecoming date. But he's not out there anymore. I hope all the football energy splashing around in my pool didn't scare him away.

6
JACOB
*(believes that hiding and observing
are two different things)*

step out of the Greenes' bathroom just as I hear voices coming down the stairs. Letting out a quick breath doesn't help with the low-grade panic rushing through me. I'm out of my element. I had all day to get ready for this moment. The second I said yes to Saylor, I knew what being her boyfriend would mean. I'd have to go places and do things with her. Things like splash around in Bethany Greene's pool with half the football team. In theory, that's all good. In reality, it's freaking me out a bit.

Not that Saylor's freaking me out. She's cool. Nothing like Poppy, who wanted to spend all our time outside school just the two of us, doing sex stuff, but wasn't affectionate or into PDA or anything. The second I met Saylor in the parking lot after the game she was right next to me, kissing my cheek. Kissing my cheek and holding my hand. It's different but good. Great. But, again, scary as hell 'cause I'm not actually sure how I feel about PDA yet. It draws attention and attention isn't really my thing. Also, I forgot the only swim trunks I have that fit are bright green with neon sharks on them.

I come around the corner into the kitchen where Saylor and her friends are standing by the back door. Saylor comes right to my side and takes my hand.

"Oh, look at that pop of color," Glory says. "You look good, Jake."

"Thanks," I reply, but my voice sounds weird. I clear my throat and try again. "Thanks." Tatum just smiles at me and follows Glory out to the pool. And then there's just me, Saylor, and Bethany. My new girlfriend and my new date for homecoming. Unless she doesn't want to go with me.

"Those are some sharp shorts," Bethany says.

"Thanks. I like your suit." She's wearing one of those suits with the cutouts on the sides. Bethany has really big boobs that are hard to ignore. I try not to be a creep though and focus on the color. I look down at the black bikini Saylor is wearing. "You look good too."

She smiles up at me and squeezes my hand. "Thanks, babe. So I told Bethany my idea and she's into it," Saylor says.

"Don't say it like that," Bethany replies. "It sounds like I agreed to have a threesome with you guys."

"Yeah, no. Definitely not a sketchy sex invite, but an invitation to fun."

Bethany tries to hide her laugh by rolling her eyes before she looks back at me. "You're cool with this? Us going to the dance together?" she asks.

"Yeah. I'm going anyway. I just figured it would be me and my camera. Having a human date sounds like a better option," I tell her.

"Okay, cool. Well, I'll get the tickets, I guess."

"Nah, I got them. My dad would kill me."

"Mr. Yeun is raising a real gentleman, is he?" Saylor says. I just shrug.

"Come on. I wanna swim." Saylor tugs me outside. I slide into the pool with her and her friends. It's hot as hell out, so getting in the water is definitely a good idea. Usually I'd be down at the beach skating with Axel and Heaven, sweating our asses off. Now I just kind of exist in the water, not really saying anything while the party happens around me. Saylor doesn't seem to mind. She's busy talking to Tatum and Bethany for a while, but she does climb all over me, hanging off my back, hanging off my front, using my shoulders as a diving board. She kisses me a bunch on the mouth. Her friends don't seem to mind the kissing, especially Glory and Landon who take serious make-out breaks every six minutes or so.

The whole time I keep wishing I brought my camera. The Greenes installed this great blue light around the inside of the pool and the fake rock wall lining the small hill the goes up behind the house. I can do something with my phone, but I could shoot some really cool stuff back here if I had my Canon.

"Hey, Jake, do you have one of those underwater setups?" Landon asks me, and I swear I could kiss him. Finally, something in my wheelhouse. He and his boys have been talking about football and people at our school I know of, but don't really know.

"Yeah, I left it at my house though. I have my phone."

"Get your phone, man," Oliver says. "Your TikToks are tight as hell."

I look back at Saylor, who's on my back, her legs wrapped around my waist. "Is that cool?"

"Yeah, of course." She floats off into the shallow end and I head inside to grab my phone. My mom tells me ten times a week to put my phone down and give my eyes a break, but as soon as I fish it out of my bag, it's like my heart stops trying to jump out of my body. There's nothing to be anxious about—I know that. But I'm definitely not relaxed until I unlock my phone.

"Everyone act natural," I say as I walk back onto the deck.

"You taking photo or video?" Glory asks before she starts posing. Saylor and her friends rush behind her and start posing too.

"Both," I laugh. I spend the next while taking video and pictures. We shoot two quick TikToks. I send them to Landon so he can post them on his account. I go back inside to actually use the bathroom and then stop in the kitchen and start looking at everything I shot. The vision is already coming together.

"You're good." I turn around as Bethany walks inside. She wraps a towel around herself and goes right for the fridge.

"Good at what?" I ask. I take the bottled water she hands me.

"Slowly backing into a high shrub and disappearing."

"Yeah." I laugh a little. "It's my superpower."

"I get it. I wanna curl up in a ball under my covers, but it's my house."

"Why? These are your friends. I don't even know these people," I joke. That makes her smile and I really wish I had my camera. Bethany has a great smile. She has dimples.

"Oh, Saylor didn't tell you?"

"Tell me what?"

Bethany glances over her shoulder, then lowers her voice. "I asked Oliver to homecoming this morning and he said no. His reasons were kinda brutal," she admits.

I look out at the pool too, cringing as I catch a glimpse of Oliver strutting to the end of the diving board.

"Oh man. That sucks. I figured it was just AJ."

"Nah, he was rejection number two of the day," she says, and then lets out a heavy deep breath. I've never been rejected, because I've never asked anyone out before, but I'm sure it hurts. I don't think I would feel all that great about the person who rejected me showing up at my house to hang out a few hours later.

"I think it's for the best. Madlyn Lowell is in love with AJ. She might have run you over with her car," I tell her, and she laughs, those dimples popping. I'm not great at poolside small talk, but at least I can cheer Bethany up.

"You don't have to do this if you don't want to. Go to homecoming with me," she says suddenly, her smile dropping. "I know how persuasive Saylor can be. And yeah, I appreciate the effort, but this is kind of embarrassing. Having to borrow a date and all."

"No, I want to and you shouldn't be embarrassed," I say,

and I realize I mean it. Bethany is pretty easy to talk to and I'm not scared of blowing it with the boyfriend duties around her. "You get a date and I don't have to feel weird watching Saylor and Rhys all night. I'm not jealous or anything—"

"No, I know. Clearly you and me aren't like super tight or anything, but it doesn't seem like jealousy jives with your whole . . . thing," she says.

"I guess, yeah."

"Well, I'll distract you from that weird situation and you can distract me from Oliver and Poppy." As soon as the words leave her mouth her eyes pop wide in horror. "Shit, sorry. I forgot you and Poppy—"

"It's okay," I say.

"Oliver asked her. She said yes."

"It's okay." I don't know how to explain it. Getting dumped sucked, but I don't exactly miss Poppy and I'm definitely not stressed out about who she dates next, unless it's Heaven or Axel. That would be weird. "We had a clean break. And now I'm Team Saylor."

"Hey, it's a fun team. Her mom always makes sure there's catered snacks."

"Really?" I ask. Saylor's mom is a professional influencer, but I know that stuff can be all smoke and ring lights.

"Oh yeah. Cristine Ford is fancy. You might want to keep a tux or, like, one of those fancy eye things in your camera bag just in case."

"A monocle?" I laugh. Bethany snaps her fingers, smiling back at me.

"Yes!"

"Look at you two already getting along." Before I can turn around, Saylor is next to me with her arm around my waist.

"Truly a dream team," Bethany says.

"What I miss?" Saylor asks. I unlock my phone and show her the first picture I took of her with Tatum. "Ooh, we look cute. Send that to me."

"I will," I say. And then she kisses me again. It's like our tenth kiss already, but it's the first one I feel present for. The first one where I'm not caught off guard. It's good. I hope she thinks so too.

7
BETHANY
(is stuck between a rock and a basketball)

I need to go to sleep, but I can't turn my brain off. Swimming was a good idea. I'm tired and the moms firmly believe in sleeping in on Saturday as long as my room is clean, which it is. So I have a good nine hours ahead of me if I play my cards right. I have the YouTube channel of my favorite chef, Chef Evie, on my tablet. She's making some braised short ribs. I've watched this recipe like ten times. For some reason it relaxes me. Still, I glance back at my phone. The website for LA Cooking School is staring back at me. Tuesday 6:00 p.m.—Knife Skills keeps catching my eye.

I drop my phone when my door cracks open.

"Bethany?" my mom whispers. "You wanna say hi to Mama T?"

"Yeah."

Momlissa slips in the door and sits down on my bed. She hands me her phone and hits pause on my tablet. The NBA preseason has already started, so Mama T will be on and off the road for months. I miss her, but when she's away I get a little break from the pressure, the crushing weight of responsibility—we are Greenes and Greenes know how to hoop. My mom Teresa can't help but remind me and my sisters every chance that she gets. Even our donor dad, Omari Jackson, has three championship rings and now works in the Celtics' front office. Basketball is in our blood and we're all good at it. And I'm the only one who hates it so, so much.

To be honest, I hate playing all competitive sports. Around fifth or sixth grade it stopped being fun and all that mattered was winning. I don't like that. Not that I want to lose, but seeing adults crying over twelve-year-olds losing a basketball game really puts things into perspective. Like, if it's that important to you, why don't you get out there on the court and win some titles yourself and stop putting that pressure on your kids. I play softball in the spring and that's only semi-enjoyable because our coach, Mr. Taylor, is really chill when we lose. Coach Miller, who is expecting Lady Minotaurs basketball to go undefeated for the second year in a row, is not.

This new distraction with boys, crushing on Oliver and gazing longingly at Kayden Smith from across the parking lot, has been a blessing, even if my hopes of making one of those things real were just dashed. It has given me something else to think about, something that isn't basketball. And no, I haven't mentioned my hatred of playing the sport to anyone, and definitely not my moms. Basketball is the reason we have that lovely pool out back.

"Hey, Mama."

"Hey, my Bethany. How was school today?"

"Good. I got an A on my English paper and Mrs. Hamilton

gave me some of that good applied-knowledge extra credit on my history homework."

"Nice." She smiles back at me. "I love applied knowledge."

"She also locked down a homecoming date, so we need to go shopping for a dress. Cris already texted me her vision for the photos," Momlissa says.

"She did?" I ask. My friends left an hour ago. Damn, Mrs. Ford works fast.

"It's Cris." She shrugs.

"Who's this hot date?" Mama T asks.

"Just a friend date. It's Jacob Yeun. You know his mom," I remind her. His mom tattooed Mama T before.

"Kelly. Right. Well, that'll be fun. Nothing wrong with a friend date," she says in that tone, that it's-fine-you're-a-dateless-loser tone. My sisters have always been in relationships. Trinity just started dating this girl Lucianne and Jocelyn has been dating this sprinter named James since the first day of freshman orientation. I'm looking forward to a hot night of nothing with Saylor's annoyingly cute boyfriend.

"Yeah, we'll have a good time."

"Did you get a workout in?" Mama T asks, and I consider rolling across my bedroom floor and jumping out the window. The fall won't kill me, but I'll mess up my ankle pretty bad. A trip to the ER will stop this conversation right in its tracks. Might take me out for the season.

"No, but I will tomorrow."

"Okay, good. The season starts in three weeks and I still feel like you didn't do enough running over the summer."

"I swam a lot though," I say. Which I did. Swimming is great exercise.

"Oop," Momlissa says suddenly. I look over as she reaches under her butt and pulls my phone out. I try not to choke as she looks at the screen. "We might have to buy Bethany some new sandwich knives," she teases before she locks my phone and sets it down on my nightstand.

"Well, get the workouts up and I'll spring for a new bread maker and a whole set of knives," Mama T replies. She's not serious. My moms are chill about my weight. I'm the only fat person in my family besides my uncle Jarred, but he's not my moms' responsibility. Still, I can tell when Mama T is just itching to tell me to eat more vegetables. I eat plenty of veggies, but I also eat a lot of other things. I like food 'cause good food tastes delicious. Did that cause me to gain weight? Sure did, but I'm pretty sure it didn't turn me into a bad person. It didn't stop me from making varsity as a freshman and didn't stop me from hitting that half-court shot.

My weight doesn't bother me and I don't think it should bother other people either.

My moms are fine with the fancy sandwiches I like to make myself for lunch, but they definitely aren't gonna buy me a bread maker, and there's no way they are gonna let me take any kind of classes at LA Cooking School.

"I will get in a run tomorrow morning."

"And run some shooting drills this weekend," Mama T

insists. "There are plenty of balls in the garage. Have Saylor come over. You can do it together."

"We'll go look for dresses and then you two can practice," Momlissa says.

"Sounds good," I say, choking on my own sarcasm.

"Good. Okay, my girls, I gotta hit the hay."

"'Night," I say. Momlissa kisses my forehead and tells me not to stay up too late before she disappears back into her bedroom. I roll onto my back and stare up at my ceiling. If I start walking now, I can get to Mexico before the season starts.

My phone buzzes on my nightstand and I thank the heavens for Saylor or Tatum's itchy text finger. I snap it up and see a text from Jacob.

> Saylor gave me your number for home-coming stuff. Thought you might like this.

I look at the picture he sent along. It's me sitting on the steps in the shallow end of the pool earlier, my elbows on my knees. I'm smiling at something Tatum said. I look good, like really good. The blue light from our pool is lighting me from below. The water is beading on my skin. My dimples are popping. I look happy. I photograph pretty well, but I've never had someone take a picture of me like this. I feel my cheeks go hot with that good kind of embarrassment. I didn't know Jacob was even paying attention to me out there, but looking at this picture I'm glad he did. I text Jacob back.

Wow. Thank you!

No problem. Have a good night.

It's silly, but I'm kinda bummed by his abrupt goodbye and I have no idea why. Maybe I just want someone to talk to after that not-fun conversation with my mom. It's probably a good time for me to finally go to bed. My phone vibrates in my hand again just as I reach for my charge cord.

I groan at the screen. It's a message from Oliver.

Thanks for being so cool tonight.
Lan said youre going to the dance
with Jake.

I'm in hell. Actual hell. I have no idea what to say back. So I don't say anything. Maybe I'll text him back tomorrow. But as far as he knows, I'm asleep. I plug in my phone and go back to Chef Evie. I gotta stop letting Oliver use my pool.

8
BETHANY
(needs more than a vision)

don't sleep in. I wake up early and go for a spite run. I
realize how bad of an idea this is around the first-mile
mark, but I still have to run back to my house, so I can't
really quit when I want to. I do take a long shower and
make a waffle the size of my head before Momlissa asks me
if I'm ready to meet Saylor and Cris at the mall. I am, but
I'm still cranky as heck by the time we get over there. Running is a terrible way to start the day.

"Are you okay?" Momlissa asks when she cuts the engine to her SUV. It's barely eleven in the morning but the
Century City parking garage is already starting to fill up.

"Yeah, I'm fine. I just woke up on the wrong side of the
bed."

"I love her, but I know how Cris can be. You give me the
signal and we'll cut this whole mission short."

"No, I want to at least look. Even if I don't find anything,
I can get inspiration to order something online."

"I love that attitude," she says, flashing the smile that got
her her own show in my direction. We head inside and she
only gets stopped once for her autograph and a selfie before

we make it to the first store. Saylor and her mom are waiting for us at the entrance. I know that look on Cris's face.
This woman is ready to shop.

"I want to apologize in advance." Saylor chuckles. "She's
had two cold brews already."

"Psht, whatever. You two will thank me when you look
ah-mazing. Okay," Cris announces as she pulls her tablet
out of her massive brushed-leather tote bag. My eyes shoot
toward Saylor as Cris starts swiping.

"I told you," she mouths.

"Here's what I'm thinking." Cris hands my mom the tablet. She takes it and looks over the full presentation Cris has
put together.

"Listen, babe. I love your taste," Momlissa says. "I love
what you're trying to do. But we're getting real close to
bridesmaid territory here." I look over my mom's arm at the
screen. Cris is really stuck on the idea of us wearing jewel
tones. Saylor mentioned she already ordered the step-and-
repeat backdrop she's planned to set up in their front yard.
I appreciated her dedication. Ever since we were little, Cris
has made sure all of our special moments are extra special,
but she's getting a little carried away here.

"You're talking about how many young people?" Momlissa says.

"Uh, total? Five. Emily said she's going to wear a jumpsuit. No, four. Glory already has her dress," I say.

Cris looks at me completely scandalized. "What color
is it?"

"Oh my god. Mom," Saylor groans.

"It's dark blue, I think." I bite my lips to keep from laughing.

"Oh, that'll work."

Momlissa isn't letting up though. "Okay, so Cris, you want four or five teenagers, different body types, wearing similar dresses."

"Yes. Yes, I do."

"Just close your eyes for one moment and think about Tif's wedding and the lovely jewel tones she had her bridesmaids wear," Mom says. This time I do snort a little.

Cris rolls her eyes and closes them. "Yes, everyone looked so beautiful. I don't see your point."

"Yes, beautiful and matchy-matchy, and thirty. I don't think this is the look teenagers are going for."

"It's not," Saylor says. "Mom, just let Bets pick out her own dress. Tatum is gonna pick whatever they want too."

"Fine," Cris huffs. "But you have to give me something. Your oldest daughter only goes to a homecoming dance once."

"Mom, this is literally my third time going and they are gonna have homecoming again next year."

"How about this? We see if we can get the boys to coordinate some part of their outfits with whatever you all are wearing," Momlissa suggests.

"That's perfect!" Saylor says. "Emily and Tatum are going to coordinate but not match exactly."

"I knew I liked Tatum and their girlfriend," Mom says.

"What do you say, Cris? We let the kids pick what they want. Take the pressure off a little."

"Yeah, yeah, fine," Cris replies.

"You and John decide to renew your vows and we'll all show up in jewel tones. I promise."

"You better."

Mom turns to me. "Okay, my baby girl. What are we thinking?"

"Something that fits." I've pinpointed every retailer with a decent plus-size section, but almost every time I find something I like, the arm holes are too small or the dress fits everywhere but my chest.

"A low bar," Mom says with a wink. "We're going to find you something perfect." We settle on a divide-and-conquer strategy. We head in one direction and Saylor and Cris head in another.

I know it's only store number one, but Mom and I both start losing hope pretty quickly. "Ugh, this is all very mother of the bride. What were you thinking for shoes?" she asks me.

"Shoes that don't make my feet hurt." My wide feet are not made for heels, not that I could walk in them even if they were.

"We can do crisp white 1s or some Converse. They'll go with any color and if Cris has anything to say about it, just send her my way."

"I like that," I say as my phone buzzes in my pocket. I pull it out and see a notification from Jacob. I glance up to look for Saylor, but I don't see her.

> Hey Bethany.
> Saylor said we're matching.
> Let me know what dress you get.
> I'll get the same one.

I can feel myself smiling as I read the message again. I still haven't messaged Oliver back.

> Ha. Ha.
> I'm talking to my mom
> about shoes right now.

"Who's that?" Momlissa asks.

"My super-hot date."

"Ah, yeah, about that. You didn't mention he was Saylor's boyfriend. Cris told me this morning."

"Yup."

My mom looks around like she needs the coast to be clear before she lowers her voice. "Is that cool with you?"

"Yeah, it's fine. Jacob is really nice. It'll be fun. Saylor already had a date when she asked him out." Saying it out loud does feel a little weird, but it's all good. I'm going to homecoming with someone else's boyfriend. It's a perfectly fine plan.

"Impressive on Saylor's part, being all double-booked, but okay," Momlissa replies.

My phone vibrates again and a picture of a pair of slippers that look like trout fill the screen.

> Look no further.
> I found the perfect pair.

I send back a coffin emoji.

> Those with my alligator onesie.
> I'll be the hottest girl there.

I look up from my phone and see my mom standing there holding what looks like fifty pounds of sparkling pink and gold.

"Sorry." I slip my phone back into my pocket and take the dress. It looks like it could fit, but the color combination is kind of hideous. "Nah," I say, shaking my head. We put that one back and start our quest anew. A few minutes later I get another text. It's from Saylor.

> Dude. Dressing room now.

"I think Saylor wants our opinion on something." Momlissa follows me to the rear of the store. Saylor's standing just outside the dressing room with a blue-green dress draped over her arm.

"I like the color. Very mermaid," I say. "Did you try it on yet?"

"Not for me, baby. For you. It was in a pile of go-backs and it was just calling to me. It's perfect."

I'm skeptical, but I take it out of her hands. Knowing my

luck, it won't fit at all. I hold up the short-sleeved dress with a low-cut V-neck and a high waist. The top half is sparkly and the skirt is made of layers of fluffy tulle that'll go all the way to the floor. The neckline looks a little low, but it's cute. I look at Momlissa.

"Try it on," she says.

I'm sweating by the time I find a fitting room attendant to open a room for me. I shuck out of my clothes and gather up all the fabric so I can pull it over my head. My heart starts thumping when I look in the mirror. My arms fit in the holes. I'm wearing the wrong bra for it, but the low neck looks . . . It looks really good. I stick my head out the door looking for my mom.

"Can you zip me up?"

"Of course." Momlissa steps inside for the moment of truth. I suck in like it'll somehow make my bones smaller and pray the zipper goes up all the way. But I don't need to suck in. The zipper glides up nice and smooth. It fits perfectly.

"Like butter, baby," Mom says. "What do you think?"

I fluff out the skirt, turning so I can see myself better in the mirror. I have to resist the urge to pet the dress like it's my prized possession. "I love it."

"I do too. You want to show Saylor?"

"Yeah. I'll need a fancy bra." My sports bras and brown-and-black granny bras won't cut it.

"I got you covered, my baby girl. Don't worry." Momlissa opens the dressing room door and holds it for me and my fluffy skirt to pass through. Cris is waiting there with Saylor. The both of them gasp, big smiles spreading across their faces.

"Oh my gosh. It looks so good," Saylor says. "You have to get it. Jade is definitely your color."

"What did I say?" Cris gives Momlissa a look that screams *I told you so*. Then she whispers, "Jewel tones."

o o o

Saylor leaves the mall empty-handed. Only because the purple dress she wants wasn't available in her size, but they have it online. All in all, a successful day. We stop for lunch and then Saylor comes back to our house. We shoot around for about an hour before I hit my limit.

I line up at the top of the key painted on our driveway and drain an easy three. "That's it. I'm done."

"Tell Mama T to chill. We have this season in the bag. I'm good. You're great. Emily's fast as hell. Dylan Smith is already being scouted. We're gonna win a whole lot," Saylor says. I watch her as she slips to the ground in the shade and leans against the garage door. I walk over and slink down beside her.

"Do you think Jacob likes me?" she asks out of the blue.

"What? Of course. He put up with Landon's million questions about underwater camera lenses just for you."

"I know, but he didn't really talk to me."

I lean my head back and try to picture how last night went. Every time I looked at them, Saylor was all over Jacob, which is peak Saylor. And just as the thought crosses my mind, she leans her head on my shoulder. "You guys were talking a lot."

"I was talking. He was nodding."

I'm not Saylor, so if she says he didn't say much, I have no reason to think she's wrong. He did talk to me though. He wasn't super chatty, but there was talking.

"I mean, he is shy," I offer. "Maybe he was just overwhelmed. None of his friends were there. Try hanging out with him and his friends. I bet when he's in his element you'll be able to peel back all the many, many layers to his inner workings or whatever."

"True. I'll ask him if he wants to hang out tonight. With his friends. Or alone."

"Excellent plan. Glad I could help. I'd hate to see you unhappy with my homecoming date. That would truly ruin everything," I joke.

"Ha. God, he's so hot," she groans before she stands and tugs me along with her. We go inside and hydrate and then I drive her back to her house. She has to go discover the depths of Jacob Yeun.

9

JACOB

(is going for an A for effort)

"What's up your bum?" Axel asks me in the worst British accent.

I close the email I'm drafting to Mr. Wei on my phone and look up at him. He's got his shirt off, tucked into the back of his pants. I'm hot too, but I don't think the whole skate park needs to see my skinny chest. I had enough shirtless fun in Bethany's pool yesterday. I look across the park at Valentina. She's on one of the benches reading on her phone. I figured hanging around us would be boring as hell for her, but she seems genuinely happy to be a part of the team.

"I think I biffed it last night. With Saylor," I tell Axel.

"I thought you had a chill time. I saw the stuff you posted earlier." I stayed up half the night editing all the stuff I shot at Bethany's pool. It came out pretty good and I found the perfect sound to go with it too. Last I checked it had a lot of likes and comments. Which is good for my account and stuff, but it doesn't change how I feel about the night in general.

"I mean, we had a good time," I lie. I had an okay time. I like being with Saylor. I do. I just—"I didn't really talk to her."

"What was the problem?"

"I don't know. You know me."

"Yeah." Axel shrugs. Most of the time he and Heaven do the talking, and we're all fine with that. It might not fly with Saylor though. "Just tell her, man."

"Tell her what?"

"That you like her, you're just a quiet dude. She can't be mad about that. I mean, I'm sure Val wishes I would shut up."

"Nah. She's thinks you're hilarious."

"Good, 'cause I am."

"I think Saylor makes me nervous."

"I mean, it is Saylor Ford. She makes me nervous," Axel says.

"I know, but she's nice and she was, like, all over me. And her friends were cool. Nothing was wrong. I just froze up. I'm also worried about her and Heaven not liking each other," I admit. Our third musketeer is over waiting her turn on the quarter.

Axel sucks his teeth. "Heaven will get over it. You're not breaking any laws by having a girlfriend."

"I know. I just know they aren't gonna vibe."

"For real. Don't worry. Heaven's just annoyed it's not the three of us anymore. She'll be pissed for a few days and then Saylor will start talking her face off and Heaven will see she has no real reason not to like her. Yeah?"

"Yeah. You're right." *Heaven would actually like Saylor if she gave her a chance*, I think and then see how much of a hypocrite I'm being. I need to give myself a chance to get things right with Saylor.

"If you'll excuse me." Axel makes a squawking noise before he kicks and pushes to the other side of the park. He goes right for Valentina and it's hard to miss the way her face lights up the second she realizes he's coming her way. She's smiling before he kisses her and smiling after. I unlock my phone and go to my texts with Saylor. I missed a couple messages from her about a half hour ago.

> Hey there, hot stuff.
> Wanna hang tonight?

> Hey sorry.
> I was skating super hard.

I take a picture of the crowd by the half pipe and send it to her.

> Yeah, let's meet up.

> Great, you wanna come pick me up at 7?

I'll have to swing by the shop and get my mom's Yukon.

> 7 sounds good.

She drops me her address. I text my mom. She's cool with me taking the car. I tell my friends I'll catch them tomorrow for our Sunday skate with our dads. I get the car. I go home and shower. I actually brush and blow-dry my hair, put it up in a ponytail. I pick Saylor up and we go get pizza and then we walk down the street and get Cold Stone. She talks a lot, but I listen. I ask her questions. I knew she had little sisters, but not that they were tiny demons. I remind myself to ask Esther about them. They are in her grade.

I tell her how I learned to skate and I show her part of the reel that secured my spot in Wei's film lab. I remind myself to finish that email as soon as I get home. She talks some more, shows me a picture of the dress she's gonna be wearing to homecoming. She tells me about the dress Bethany got too. She doesn't have a picture of it, but she shows me the color and tells me to get a matching tie for the pictures. I'll need my mom's help with that for sure.

We take some selfies together and before we know it, it's time for both of us to go home. I drop Saylor off at her house and she kisses me. I tell her Sunday is our family-skate day, but I'll see her on Monday. She seems cool with that. She smiles at me as she waves goodbye. And then she texts me a bunch of times before I go to bed. I'm not sure I nailed it, but I think I did better this time. It's gonna take some practice, the whole talking thing. But I like Saylor and I think we have a pretty good shot.

o o o

Ten days later, Saylor Ford dumps me.

10
BETHANY

*(is wearing the wrong dress
for this sort of news)*

\|\|\| "You did what?!"

"I broke up with Jacob," Saylor says as we head
to lunch. This whole situation is made all the more ridiculous because she is in a full Elsa costume, complete with an
extremely realistic platinum lace front. I'm in a full Tiana
custom gown, a little sparkly tiara tucked into my braid
bun and all that. There's a little stuffed frog Velcroed to my
shoulder. Like I said, ridiculous. Tatum just ran to the restroom in a full Snow White getup. The whole Disney princess theme for All Hallows' Eve was Cris Ford's idea, but
even she would agree all of this would be easier to process
if Saylor and I were both in our normal clothes.

"Why didn't you tell me this morning?"

"I tried to FaceTime you last night, but you didn't pick
up. So I called Glory," she says as we step out into the quad.
Glory is waiting for us in her chocolate-chip-cookie costume. Landon is walking around school somewhere in a
full Cookie Monster getup. Cris tried to rope them into her
Disney scheme, but they said nah. So did Jacob. I saw him

earlier in a black T-shirt that says THIS IS MY COSTUME. He had a pair of vampire teeth in his hand.

Emily meets us halfway across the quad in her Dopey costume. We'd truly win a costume contest this year if we were involved in one.

"When did you dump him?" I ask as we sit down.

"You dumped Jake?" Emily asks.

Saylor nods. "After Spanish." That was after I saw him second period in stats. Oh, this is bad.

"What happened? What did he do?" I ask. Tatum arrives just in time to get the deets.

"Nothing. He's so sweet and he knows how to make me look ah-mazing in all forms of visual media. But I think Poppy was onto something. He's super sweet and nothing else."

Okay, now I'm officially confused, but Glory shrugs as she lets out a deep sigh. "I mean, that's reason enough. He is nice, but she wasn't feeling him."

"It's not even that. I can't explain it. I don't think I was even getting to know him, and I don't think I will. He just— the kid is a vault. He never opens up about anything. He just looked at me and smiled. I wasn't into it and honestly, I could never tell if he actually liked me or if he was just being polite. There was no heat."

I blink, trying to process this all. The last couple weeks have been fine. I settled back into being the single friend. I also spent a disgusting amount of time looking at pictures of Kayden Smith on his Instagram. And the pictures his sister Dylan tagged him in on her profile. And then one picture he was tagged in on the Minotaur Insta. It was a good picture.

On the weekends I've had to decide if I want to hang out with my mom or if I'm in the mood to be the seventh wheel. Mostly I've been focusing on maintaining my GPA and pretending I love getting ready for basketball to start this coming Monday. I'm also bummed I missed the Knife Skills class, even though I was too scared to ask my moms if I could go. I might ask Omari for a knife set for Christmas though.

Anyway, when we all hung out, Jacob was there, being perfectly nice and just chillin'. We talked a couple of times. Once when he asked me what shoes he should get for the dance and once at Glory's house about *Star Trek: Discovery*. He had a DISCO CREW shirt on and it just happens to be Momlissa's favorite show. And then another time he sent me a picture of Tatum styling my braids while we were sitting in Saylor's backyard. It was another really good picture. The last time we talked, he just texted to tell me his jade tie had finally arrived.

Oh crap. Homecoming. I groan and let my head fall forward. The dance is in three days.

"Are you mad at me?" Saylor asks.

"No, no. I just remembered I'm supposed to go to homecoming with him."

"So, you can still go," Glory says. "It's just the dance."

"If he even still wants to go with *me*."

"Just talk to him, Bets. I'm sure it's fine," Saylor replies.

"Are you okay with him coming for pictures?"

"Yeah, of course. He didn't cheat on me or, like, kick a puppy or anything. We just aren't a good match. I mean, it's my fault. I shouldn't go man shopping with just my eyes. He's so hot and sweet, I didn't stop to think that we might not have a single thing in common. Every hottie isn't for me and that's okay. I just need something between Tagger's anger issues and Jake's next-level introverted thing."

"I'm sorry it didn't work out, Say," Tatum replies. "I like Jake."

"I do too. Just not in a romantic way. He did nothing wrong. It just wasn't right between us. Actually . . ." There's a dramatic pause and then Saylor turns in her seat to face me. "While I was stressing over all of this, I was thinking how good you and him would be together," she says, like that's a completely normal thing to say.

"Wha— No? Why would you say that?" I need to know because *what???*

"Because I saw you two together when he was around. He actually talked to you."

I look down at my lunch box, this sour feeling dropping into my stomach. Tears start to sting the backs of my eyes. "You don't think that, do you? That he likes talking to me instead of talking to you?"

"No, not like that. I don't think that Jacob was, like, macking on you behind my back, but yeah, he seemed comfortable enough to talk to you."

"I mean, I guess, but in an ultra-friend-zone-y way. And he knows about Crybaby Bethany. Trust me, me and him is not the move," I reply.

"Okay, I'm just saying." Saylor shrugs.

I glance over at Glory and her eyebrows are arched up in that way where I know she really wants to say something, but she's biting her tongue. I almost ask her to just say it, but I have this feeling she's gonna side with Saylor.

We drop the conversation then. Saylor and Jacob are no longer a thing and there's not much more to say about it. Tatum has some hot gossip about something that went down at the last away volleyball game. I try to listen, but all I can think about is the conversation I have to have with my homecoming date. It's gonna be so awkward.

○ ○ ○

I don't see Jacob for the rest of the day. After the final bell I go right to the yearbook office. It's where I know he'll be for sure. I wait for what feels like a long time, but he doesn't show up. Finally, I poke my head in and get Madlyn Lowell's attention. She comes out in the hall.

"Hey, what's up?" she says.

"Have you seen Jacob? I need to talk to him."

"I heard he went home after third period. Your friend gave him the boot."

"Crap. Thanks."

"Are you gonna ditch him too?" she asks in this weird

whisper, like she's digging for dirt. Not like she actually cares about Jacob. I don't like that.

"No. I just wanted to talk to him."

"Oh, well, he left."

"Got it." I turn to head back to the student parking lot. I pull out my phone and send Jacob a text.

> Hey can I come by so we can talk?

Later maybe.
I'm helping my mom put up some decorations.
She'll be gone later.

> Yeah sure sounds good.

He sends back a thumbs-up emoji. Man, this sucks.

11

JACOB

*(is wondering how this
happens to the same guy twice)*

My phone vibrates in my hand. For some weird reason my heart does this weird triple beat when I look at the screen. It's Bethany.

Hey I'm outside.

I hold in a pathetic groan and toss Heaven the Apple TV remote. "I'll be back in a second."

"That Bethany?" Valentina asks from her spot on Axel's lap.

"Yeah."

"We're here if you need backup," Axel offers.

"We're just gonna talk. Not street fight."

"Hey, you never know. Saylor might have sent an unassuming assassin to finish the job."

"I'll scream if I need help."

"You want me to pause it?" Heaven asks. I look at the kid version of Michael Myers starting to unravel on the screen.

"Nah, it's cool. I've seen this like twenty times."

Heaven shrugs and turns her attention back to the TV. She's doing a good job of being there for me post-breakup, but I know she's low-key relieved she doesn't have to hang out with Saylor anymore. Turns out she did not win Heaven over.

I should have stayed at school. I know everyone thinks I had some emotional breakdown over Saylor dumping me. I guess I did technically, but I didn't actually give it that much thought. I just walked straight to the office and called my mom. I was in a haze the whole way home. I'm still pretty numb.

I grab the huge bowl of candy by the front door and head outside to keep the deal I made with my mom. I could skip school if I stayed home and handed out candy while she helped out at the middle school carnival. Fair trade-off, if you ask me. Saylor's at the carnival.

Bethany is carefully making her way up our driveway right as I walk down the steps to our porch. She's still wearing her massive Tiana gown. She has a Lakers zip-up hoodie on over it now though. I got a pretty great picture of her, Tatum, and Emily in their costumes in the student parking lot this morning. Saylor was running late. Or that's what she told me. I'm pretty sure she was avoiding me until she was forced to see me in Spanish.

"Hey," I say to Bethany. "Still rocking the look?"

"We went to see the original *Scream* down on Melrose. Tickets were half off if you came in costume."

"Oh, nice. My mom loves that movie."

"It holds up. I could see Tagger Evans going nuts and knifing half the school because of something his dad did."

I can't help but laugh. "That tracks."

"May I?" Bethany motions to the stairs.

"Oh yeah. Come up here. The stairs are kinda dirty. Don't want to mess up your outfit." I set down the candy bowl and move the scarecrow my mom built off the porch swing so she can sit down.

"Thanks." It takes her a second to get her dress situated, but she sorts it out. "You guys really went all out with the decorations. My mom just hung up this cute ALL OUT OF CANDY sign on our gate."

"Yeah, both my parents really get into it. You look great," I tell her.

"Thanks. I only got called Fat Tiana once today, so I'll take that as a win."

"By who?" I ask. I didn't picture Bethany as someone who got bullied, but I guess I was wrong.

"Who else? Tagger Evans."

"Fuck that guy."

"Amen." She laughs a little and then she gets quiet. I watch her as she starts toying with the zipper on her sweatshirt. I guess this is awkward for us both.

"You can say it," I tell her.

Her head snaps up. "Say what?"

" 'I'm sorry.' 'Tough break.' 'It's for the best.' Same stuff I've been hearing all day. Even Landon texted me his condolences."

"Oh, well then I'll just skip that part. I came over here to give you an out. You are officially off the hook for the dance. You're free," Bethany says.

"Wait, why?"

"I mean, you only agreed to go with me because of Saylor. Seems silly to make you stick to it if you two aren't together anymore."

"I said yes because of her at first, but it's not like I don't want to go with you. Besides, the tickets are paid for and I have my suit and my shoes and everything. I have a jade tie. We'll go and have a sufficiently awkward time." I try to joke, but Bethany just looks back at me. No laugh, no smile.

"Are you sure?"

"Yes. I'm not— There's no bad vibes here, with me and you. What happened between me and Saylor happened between me and Saylor. However I feel about it, I'm not going to take that out on you."

"Hmm, okay," she says before she focuses back on her zipper. *That should be the end of it*, I think. We'll go to the dance together and then go back to seeing each other in stats. It's fine. Pretty much back to the way it was before. Kinda. Bethany goes on, "Can I ask—I mean, you don't have to tell me if you don't want to, but can you tell me why you guys broke up?"

"She didn't tell you?"

"No, she did," Bethany says. "I just—I'll be honest. From her perspective, I don't get it."

"What do you mean?" I ask, 'cause I don't get it either.

"Oh, wait," she says, nodding over my shoulder. I turn around and see this lady with her little kid dressed in a duck costume walking up our driveway.

"Are you open for business?" the mom asks.

"Yes."

"Can I tay it?" the little ducky asks with a slight, but adorable, lisp. I grab the candy bowl.

"Go for it, honey," the mom replies.

"Twick or tweat," the baby duck says. The kid is so excited, holding up their pillowcase, I grab a huge handful of candy and dump it into their bag.

"Oh wow. She's gonna be high on sugar for a month. Say thank you, sweetie."

"Tank you."

"You're welcome, small duck." I wave bye and then they head back down the street.

"That was the cutest thing I have ever seen," Bethany says. I turn around and it looks like her eyes are tearing up.

"Are you crying?" I ask.

She dashes her finger under her eyes. "This is just something you gotta know about me. I cry at everything. Happy tears. Sad tears. Oh-my-god-that-was-so-cute tears. Doesn't matter. I'm a cryer."

"Nothing wrong with that."

"Mmmm yeah, you try it for a day. It's embarrassing as hell. But we're talking about your problems. What happened with Saylor?"

"Right." I hold back a sigh and just tell Bethany my own embarrassing truth. "She said things felt a little one-sided, like she was into me and I was just nodding along."

"She said that?" Bethany asks. She seems shocked and I guess she knows Saylor wouldn't say something that way.

"No, not like that, exactly. But that was what she meant. She said that she thought maybe our communication styles didn't work well together and that she wasn't comfortable with the whole relationship being about her. I guess I didn't really open up that much." I try not to think about the look on her face when she said it or the way I felt like I was gonna barf hearing it. Let's just say I've had better conversations.

"Hmm, okay."

"What did she say to you guys?" I ask. "If you can tell me. Heaven explained girl code to me a few times."

That makes Bethany laugh. "No, I would never violate the sacred code of friendship. She didn't say anything bad. She just said you were too sweet."

"I'd love to know what that means and why it's such a bad thing." Bethany is quiet for a few long seconds and I can't help but think she's about to violate the girl code any minute now. "What is it?" I ask.

"I don't—I don't know if I should say it, but screw it. I don't understand why she dumped you. And like, this is definitely a me thing. Saylor is grown and she seemed pretty secure in her decision. But boys won't even look at me. I can't imagine someone being really sweet and listening to you when you talk being a bad thing. It sounds pretty good to me. I'm sorry. I definitely shouldn't have said that."

"Why? It's just you and me talking."

"I know, but this isn't about me."

"I mean, it kinda is. I'm your homecoming date. The most sacred bond two people can form."

"Funny," she replies, rolling her eyes at me.

"No, for real. You can tell me."

She twists her lips up, thinking again, and I feel like this time she's gonna drop a pretty big bomb on me. "Do you know how I got the Crybaby Bethany nickname?" she says.

"No, I don't." People were pretty serious about calling her that, but it seemed pretty self-explanatory. Like she said, she's a cryer.

"Freshman year, Glory told us she'd lost her virginity to Landon. No big deal, right?"

"Right. They seem pretty solid."

"They are. Landon is in love with her. She's smitten with him. Always has been. And I should have been happy for her, but no. I burst into tears. Like weeping, in the middle of the quad."

"Why?"

"Because at the time I was afraid of . . . you know." She motions in front of her, her eyes going wide.

"Sex?"

"Yes, but more specifically . . . penises," she whispers the last part. It takes every cell in my body not to laugh. "I can't believe I'm telling you this."

"Hey, you know why Poppy dumped me. I'm not one to talk."

"Wait, so that was true? You wouldn't have sex with her."

I shrug and shake my head.

"Wow. Wow."

"What?"

"I don't know. I just thought that was what hot people did. You meet each other and just, like, bone. I thought it was part of the hot people code of ethics."

"Well, I'm not hot, so I haven't received that handbook in the mail," I tell her.

"Oh, okay. Yeah, you're, like, super ugly. Shut up, Jacob."

"What?" I laugh.

"Don't make me say it. You're so hot it's borderline annoying."

"I'll take that as a compliment. I guess." I've been hearing that a lot the last few months, but I don't think I'll ever see myself that way. I'm just me.

"Anyway. All of this is just really confusing for us normal-looking undesirables. Not that you needed to, but I can't picture a world where any straight boy wouldn't— You're straight, right?"

"Yeah, so far."

"So yeah. I guess from my perspective I don't get why anyone wouldn't hop into the sack with the likes of Poppy."

"I just wasn't ready. Sounds like you understand that," I tell her honestly.

"Fair. That's very fair."

"But there's more?" I ask her.

"Nah." She shakes her head and I think we finally crossed into the no-sharing zone. I don't pressure her to say, but I still want to know.

"I think you think you're the only person who doesn't have this all figured out," I say.

"What do you mean?"

"I said yes to going out with two girls this year because I was afraid to say no." The shocked look on Bethany's face matches the way I suddenly feel inside. I can't believe I said that out loud, but it's the truth. "I guess you have a point about the power of hotness. I was too shocked to say no, so I didn't, and then I thought it would develop into something and both times it didn't. I guess Saylor was right. I was just nodding along. I spent our whole relationship just asking her questions and saying yes to everything she suggested. And I'm gonna stop you before you even say it. Yes, I still want to go to homecoming with you."

"Thanks." She chuckles a little. "But why? I mean to all the yesing. Saylor is my best friend. We disagree all the time and that's still my homie. She's not a human bulldozer."

"I didn't know what else to do. You know her and I have nothing in common?" Bethany opens her mouth and then closes it. She opens it again, her eyes darting to the side. She's trying really hard to come up with an example, but I know she knows I'm right. "I didn't tell her about my *Star Trek* obsessions 'cause I brought it up once and she said she wasn't really into sci-fi stuff. *I* almost started crying."

"Right. I remember what you said about loving *Discovery* and *Strange New Worlds*."

"It's not like *Star Trek* has a small following, but of course I say yes to someone who isn't interested in it at all. Not that we have to like all the same things, but if I really open my mouth, my feelings about the Prime Directive are gonna come spilling out and I'm pretty sure Saylor would have died of boredom."

I watch Bethany as she sighs and leans forward on the swing. "I guess that settles it. You two weren't a good match."

"I thought if I just smiled and nodded at Saylor it would all work out fine. I just have to learn to be myself with girls, I guess."

"Not a bad idea. And I'll be in my corner waiting for the legend of Crybaby Bethany to die once and for all. Then maybe a member of the opposite sex will actually look in my direction." She stands and walks over to me.

"Wait, is that why Oliver said no to you? To the dance?"

"Oh yeah. He figured I'd be too scared to even hold his hand, so I'd pretty much be wasting his night. I wish there was some sort of, like, dating school you could go to with classes like Bethany, A Penis Won't Surprise Murder You 101 and AP Jacob, This Is How You Talk Confidently to Girls about Your Undying Love for Spock."

I burst out laughing, just picturing the syllabi. "That would make things a lot easier."

"Alas, we're doomed to learn the hard way, filled with the ego-bruising experience of winging it. Anyway, good talk. See you in stats tomorrow." She pats me on the shoulder and then maneuvers her gown down my front steps.

I watch her and her puffy green dress, thinking about how this weird and crappy day has played out and everything she just said. I wouldn't even know who to ask about girls. Axel and Valentina are a unique match, so I don't think he could help me there, and I'm definitely not talking to my parents about this. Winging it sounds like the worst idea ever.

She's almost to her car when I call after her. "Bethany, wait!" The plan formulating in my head is a bad one, but it just might work.

12
BETHANY
*(knows she's making a huge mistake,
but she's gonna do it anyway)*

All this oversharing definitely calls for a speedy retreat, but of course Jacob has more to say about round one of the humiliation games. I plaster a smile on my face and turn around. "Yeah, what's up?" I take an involuntary step back as he rushes down his porch steps.

"I have an idea," he says.

"Okay . . ."

"Well, the beginnings of an idea. We should date each other," he says, like that's a completely normal thing to say.

"What? Why would you say that?" I ask him, stumbling back another step. I almost trip on my dress, but Jacob grabs my wrist just in time. I correct my footing and remember this is not the outfit for doing anything backward. "Thanks."

"No problem." He lets go of me and shoves his hands into his pockets. It's dark out, but I can still see that his face goes bright red. I thank god every day for my brown skin and how it hides that flavor of embarrassment. I would have been crimson all night.

"So, you were saying something really ridiculous."

"Right. I think we should date each other."

"Yes, but why?" I ask again. Sure, two single people can date each other, but Jacob doesn't actually like me, and while I think he's hot enough to melt a few pounds of butter, I don't actually *like him*, like him. We're acquaintances. Maybe extremely casual friends-in-training at best.

"You need to shed the Crybaby Bethany persona and I need to learn how to be myself while having a conversation with an actual girlfriend. I'd also like to show people I can get someone to date me for more than two weeks. We could date each other and, like, help each other out with the hard stuff. Fake it 'til you make it, right?"

I just stare back at him, my eyebrow arching toward space.

"We both need practice," he goes on. "You didn't just show up on the court crushing buckets and setting rebound records, did you?"

"Well, kinda."

"Okay, fine. You're really good, but you still have to practice."

"Right . . . ?"

"So how are either of us gonna get good at this whole boyfriend/girlfriend thing if we don't practice?"

"I don't know. I was just gonna pick a random day in my thirties, go to a city hall, and hopefully a man would just show up and marry me," I tell him.

"I guess you can wait that long."

I look over at the cluster of jack-o'-lanterns on the edge of their yard, mulling over everything Jacob is saying. He's

not wrong: Practice does make perfect, and when it comes
to legit experience, it seems like we're both lacking a lot of
what we need. It could be wild enough to work. "You might
be onto something," I admit. "It would take the pressure off
if we're on the same page, helping each other out. But Jacob,
you gotta be more specific here. If we go out, even as practice, you'd have to do stuff like kiss me and hold my hand. Is
that something you'd want to do?"

"Yeah. I think I'll survive."

I look back at him like he's truly lost the plot. I repeat:
I am cute as hell. It's just that the Saylors and the Poppys
of the world and I just attract a different kind of guy. They
attract hot guys. I attract zero guys. Absolutely no guys,
whether I am ready or not. And even if he can't see it, Jacob
is so cute, I'm shocked I haven't fainted once during this
conversation. Logic dictates that his next girlfriend should
be a literal model or the daughter of one. I know how he'll
react if I tell him that though, and there's no need to rehash
the hot-people-code-of-ethics portion of this conversation.

"Okay. Say I do go along with this plan? How will it
work?" I ask.

"Let's say for like a month we go out. In public we are
boyfriend and girlfriend, and then behind the scenes—"

"We kinda debrief and give each other notes?"

"Yeah, yeah!"

I can't help but snort. I've never seen Jacob jazzed about
anything. "I can tell you if you're being a little too pushover-y,
give you a little what-girls-want tutorial, and you can help
me show that punk Oliver, and any other boys watching,

that Crybaby Bethany is long gone. Super mature, not-afraid-of-wiener Bethany has arrived."

"I wasn't going to say it exactly like that, but yes."

"Yeah, I see the vision now," I say. "This might work."

"So, you wanna try it?" he asks, his expression lighting up.

"Why are you so excited?" I laugh.

"Because I feel like crap and I don't know how to fix it. I can't explain how . . . weird it is to get dumped twice for being quiet and too nice. It's not a good feeling."

"Yeah, I can see that." I realize then that maybe I was a little angry with Saylor. Not that she wasn't right to dump him. She wasn't happy, but it still doesn't make sense to me. Doesn't matter now, I guess. Right at this moment, it's just me and Jacob, both single, both kinda clueless and available to help each other out. I sigh and squeeze my eyes closed. There are so many ways this could go wrong. "Yes. Okay. Let's do this."

"So, we're going out now?" he says.

"Slow down there, cowboy. Plans like this need a little bit more finesse." I turn to do some pacing and my dress catches on the bottom of his mailbox. I really should have changed out of this thing before I came over. "Okay, okay, okay. How about this—" I say just as Jacob's front door swings open.

"Everything okay out here?" Axel Diaz yells across the yard. Heaven Campbell pokes her head out behind him.

"Yeah, everything's fine. Go back inside," Jacob replies.

"Hey, Bethany. Just wanted to make sure there was no knife fighting going on out here."

"Nah, I left my blades at home," I say, confused.

"Bummer," Axel says, before they both slip back inside.

"They've been in there this whole time?" I ask.

"Yeah. We were watching *Halloween*."

"Oh. Well, I'll let you get back. We can talk later."

"Nah, it's cool. You were saying?"

"Uh." I'm still wondering what any of this had to do with knives. "Um, yeah. We go to the dance and use that as our cover. We show up at school on Monday and say we had such a good time at the dance together we decided to give it a try. That way there's at least a few days between you and Saylor breaking up and we have a concrete romantic moment to use as a starting point."

"I'm in," Jacob replies. "That's genius."

"We can't tell our friends though. That would kind of defeat the whole purpose."

"Right. I probably should have asked if your friends would freak out over this."

I don't know how to tell Jacob how over him Saylor is or that she thinks I should ask him out for real. He doesn't need to know all that. "No, they'll be cool. They'll be happy for me and for us."

"Okay, cool. So we have a deal?" He holds out his hand for a sec before he takes my elbow and moves me to the right. "Watch out."

I move onto the grass just as a large black SUV pulls into the driveway. A few seconds later a little kid who I can only assume is Jacob's little sister climbs out of the car. She's in a full-white Starfleet medical officer's uniform and a white wavy wig.

"Nurse Chapel?" I ask her.

"See! She gets it, Mom," the kid says before Jacob's mom comes around the front of the car. She's in a skeleton onesie with really elaborate skull makeup painted on her face.

"Not a lot of members of Starfleet tonight." She shrugs. "Is this the famed Bethany, the homecoming date? Or should I say Princess Tiana?"

"Yes, ma'am. That's me."

"Bethany, this is my mom, of course, and my sister, Esther," Jacob says.

"Nice to meet you both. Uh, I think you tattooed my mom once. Teresa Greene."

"Oh yeah. She's great," Mrs. Yeun replies. "Sits like a champ."

"She says getting tattooed is her quiet time."

"If only all my clients were like that. Well, I guess we'll see you on Saturday. I've been told the photo call is at four-thirty sharp."

"Oh yeah. Cristine Ford has a very serious plan for photos."

"We will be on time. Come, E. Jacob, not too late."

"All right. Heav and Axel are inside with Valentina," he tells his mom. I don't know how I feel about his whole clique being fifty feet away while we've been plotting and scheming.

"Ooooh. I look forward to kicking them out," Mrs. Yeun says. "Good night."

I glance at my phone and it is kind of getting late. "I should go. Um, I'll text you?"

"Yeah, cool," he says. "But we're doing this?"

I reach over and grab his wrist. I hold up his hand and give it a firm shake. At that moment my brain decides to do the worst thing ever. It decides to direct my eyeballs up so I'm looking right at Jacob's stupid-hot face. I'll be honest: I'd tried not to stare at him too much the whole time he and Saylor were together. Not in a weird way, but I think in the back of my mind I wanted there to be absolutely no chance of me accidentally checking him out and adding him to the wrong boy file in my brain.

But of course I'm looking at him now, the nice shape of his lips and his dark eyes. He has a beauty mark on his neck and—I force myself to stop looking and focus back on where our hands are touching. I can ignore the fact that he has nice fingers. "We're doing this," I say.

"Cool."

"Cool. Well, 'night." I flash him an awkward smile and walk back to my fairly new, fully-loaded Kia Sorento. Let's hear it for NBA sponsorships.

○ ○ ○

I beat Momlissa home from the studio. It's kinda funny when they ask her to fill in on NBA game night, especially when Mama T is coaching. A Greene everywhere you look. The Lakers are on their last night away in Houston and then Mama T will be back home for two games. This means

I have the house to myself, giving me plenty of time and space to freak the hell out.

What in the world did I just agree to? And did I really suggest that we keep it a secret from our friends??? If there was ever a moment that called for an emergency sprint to the group chat, it's the spontaneous relationship pact I just hatched with Jacob Yeun.

I go right up to my room and catch myself in the mirror. Too much has happened in this dress. I peel out of it and start my shower.

My sisters. They can help, I think, but then I remember exactly who Trinity is. By the time I was five, it was apparent that if we had a family snitch, it was Trin for sure. And if I breathe a word about this to Jocelyn, she'll tell Trin and Trin will tell the moms. And then it'll get back to Cris. Momlissa likes to act like Cris is over the top, but that is her gossip buddy 'til the end. I really have to follow my own suggestion. This is gonna be hard.

I can talk to Jacob, I realize. He's my confidant in this now, right? I'm tempted to message him, but his friends might still be over. Even if he's alone, I just left his house. It might be too soon to reopen the lines of communication. I hop in the shower instead. I have zero experience with boys, but something tells me if you are desperate enough to text a boy you should at least count to ten before you start drafting. The shower is lovely and scorching, but my heart rate is still through the ceiling after I dry off and lotion up. I put on my jimjams, then grab my phone and send the pics I took with my friends to the family chat.

> Trin: Super cute, Bets. Best Tiana ever.

> Jocelyn: Yes, Girl! I should have tried a little harder. 💀

She sends back a picture of herself with simple cat whiskers and cat ears on. She is still wearing her Stanford basketball hoodie.

> It's the thought that counts.

I hear the garage door and sprint downstairs like a lunatic. Mom's home. Just the distraction I need. I flop down in a chair and try to play it cool as Momlissa comes through the mudroom.

"Hey, sweetie." She looks very glamorous, still studio ready. I know she peaced out the second the cameras went off. Two shows in one day is a lot.

"Hey," I say, real natural like. "How was the game?"

"Good." She sets down her bag, then looks around the kitchen like she's just now remembering this is, in fact, her house. "Lakers lost though, so I'm expecting a very annoyed call from your mom in about thirty minutes. But you'll get to talk to her tonight. How was Halloween?"

"Good. Good. We had fun."

"Good. Oh!" She stops halfway to the fridge and turns to look at me. "I got a text from Cristine."

Shit.

"About what?" I ask.

"Jacob and Saylor broke up?"

"Yup. They did. Earlier today." Playing it cool. Playing it very, very cool.

"Are you okay still going to the dance with him?"

"Oh yeah. We talked. It's fine."

"Okay. Homework all done?" Momlissa asks. I know she's wiped and ready for her own bed.

"It sure isn't. Let me go do that." I hop off the stool and head for the stairs.

"Hold on."

Shiiiit. I don't know what I did, but now that I actually have a secret, I feel like any false move could lead to the beans being spilled.

"Come back here."

I turn and cross the kitchen. Mom wraps her arms around me and kisses my forehead. "Oh, you smell good."

"I do like a good shower."

"Good. I'll come to say good night in a bit."

"'Kay." I head up to my room and pull out my English reading. This stuff is getting skimmed. There's no way I can focus. And, as if the universe isn't done with it's evening of cruel jokes, it sends one more my way. My phone chimes. It's a text from Jacob and a few pictures too.

> I thought you might want these.

There's a picture of me and my friends all dressed up and then two pictures of me in my full Tiana outfit. I don't know how he does it, but I look *good.*

13
BETHANY
(is doing so much stress sweating—so much)

I t's homecoming day. Game day. Not dance day. And I would
give anything for a reliable poker face. Anything. For the
last couple days, I've kinda had to avoid Jacob. As far as
everyone else knows, we are just dance dates and nothing
else. His business with Saylor has come to its natural con-
clusion, so that means mine has too. We play it cool and just
say hey in stats. I see him a few more times in the hall, but
that's it. Still, I'm on edge. Our plan has completely con-
sumed my mind.

By the time I make it to lunch, my friends have already
asked me four times if I'm okay. I finally make up some lie
about being nervous about the upcoming basketball season. Basketball comes with more feelings of annoyance and
dread than anxiety, but they don't need to know that.

"It's just my first season playing without Jocelyn, and
Mama T is putting on the pressure extra thick," I say.

"She is," Saylor agrees. "Even Big John doesn't make me
practice that much." Saylor's dad played five seasons for the
Steelers before he retired and went to law school. Now he's a
very well-paid family lawyer. The man knows the meaning

of work, but he lets Saylor and her twin sisters do whatever they want.

"No need to stress, Bets," Tatum says. "You're amazing."

"And we're a team. Right?" Emily adds. "We're all in this together. Forget about the *me* in *team* for a second," she says with a wink. The wink makes me laugh and the laugh is enough to get the girls off my back. Glory starts talking about our plans for the weekend before and after the game, and before and after the dance, and they all forget the way I'm sweating like I'm on the run from the law.

I just can't stop thinking about Jacob. Not in a sexy way. It's just now that we have this plan and I know that his hands are soft, but not too soft—but also warm and dry, but in the right way—it's like I'm *allowed* to notice him all of a sudden and that's all my brain wants to do. Jacob Yeun is suddenly running laps through my mind. I guess it's a good distraction from the fact that Poppy and Oliver are not just going to the dance together but are, in fact, *together* together.

By the time the game comes around, I'm in full-blown panic mode. Thank god my friends aren't paying attention to me. Tatum's on the sidelines, Glory's focused on her man on the field, and Saylor is focused on Rhys and his tuba on the sidelines.

We win the game. By a lot. How great. How wonderful. What a time. I miss half the game because I keep looking over at Jacob where he's filming near the end zone. He has one of those handheld mounts and really knows how to use it. As soon as that thought passes through my mind, I focus right back on the field. After the game, I lose him in the crowd spilling into the parking lot—not like I was going to say anything to him, but still.

We go over to Landon's house and party into the night. And for some awful reason, I spend the whole time wishing Jacob and I had decided to start our little plan early. I wish he were here, partly because all of my friends are paired off (Saylor brings Rhys) and kinda because I just want to talk to him because he's the only other person who knows about the plan. Maybe I'm just anxious to get it started, I realize. It's a big plan and it seems kinda cruel to make ourselves wait three whole days to get the plan rolling. I stop myself from texting him and asking him to come over anyway.

After the party, I get us safely back to Saylor's house where we crowd into her den and finally get a chance to talk without the prying ears of the lunch quad or the noise of a football game. Tatum and Glory have some hot goss to share, and I tell them the story about catching Sweeney Marks and Noah Killgore getting into a blowout near the bathrooms during halftime, and Saylor excitedly shows us the bonkers porn she found online. I try to peer over Glory's head as we gather around Saylor's laptop when my phone vibrates in my hand.

It's a text from Jacob.

And a couple pictures.

I stare at the screen for a second, swallowing slowly so I don't give my shock away. "Um, I'll watch it again in a sec," I say. "Gotta hit the tinkle tent."

"Eww." Tatum laughs. I give them an overly bright smile before I almost run to the bathroom. My whole body is warm as I shut myself inside. It's not the same as a face-to-face conversation, but it's contact. I need it. I unlock my phone and read the text.

> I thought you might like this.

They're pictures of me and Emily in the stands during the game. I'm trying to teach her the basics of patty-cake and failing miserably, but it was still pretty funny. We're both laughing, wearing our black-and-blue Lady Minotaurs Basketball jackets, blue-and-silver glitter all over our faces.

I text him back.

> How do you do it?

He's responding before I have a chance to lock my phone.

> Do what?

> Make me look so good in every picture.

> I'm a good photographer.
> And that's how good you look.
> Sorry. You'll just have to deal with it.

14

JACOB

(is all dressed up and a little bit stressed)

"Can't we just show Dad the pictures? I'll take extra video just for him," I say to my mom as we pull up to Ink & Pearl. "We're going to be late."

"Not if you hurry up."

I glance at the front of the shop before I turn back to my mom. "Let's just FaceTime him from Saylor's yard."

"Jacob. Please. Just go inside. Your dad hasn't seen you dressed up like this in ages. Let him be proud of you for like five seconds."

"I got an A on my ancient history test. He can be proud of that without parading me in front of whoever's on his table," I say, leaving out the part where I am still completely blowing the storytelling portion of film lab.

"Jacob."

"Fine. But you have to break the sound barrier to get over to Saylor's in time."

"I know. Cris sent all the parents *another* email reminding us of the timetable. We'll get there. Just go."

My parents still require all guests wear masks inside Ink & Pearl, so I pull one out of the glove box, then hop out of our Yukon. The second I step inside, Laury, our shop manager, pops up from behind her desk. "Welcome to Ink and—Jake!"

"How do I look?"

"Freaking amazing, kid. Definitely big-dance ready." I thought it would be hard to find a suit that fit right, but my mom and my Aunt Patty came through with a nice black one and Aunt Patty's tailor only needed to see me for a few minutes to get the adjustments right. Between the suit, my blue-green tie that's supposed to match Bethany's dress, and my brand-new white Air Force 1s, I think I dress up pretty nice.

"Thanks. I'm about to be in four hundred photos and an Insta Story or two. I have to look good."

Across the shop, my dad excuses himself from his client. He makes his way over, peeling his black gloves off and tossing them into the trash. He comes around the divider and stops a few feet away. Hand on his hip, he gives me that rare dad nod of approval.

"I have nothing left to teach you. My boy is a man."

"Nothing?" I laugh. "I have no idea how taxes work. Also, this was all Mom. She's out in the car if you want to go take credit for how good my hair looks right now."

"Turn around," Dad says. I hold out my arms and execute a slow spin move.

"Nice, slick man bun. Pop of color with the tie. Nice crisp Nikes. Bethany's a lucky girl. Bethany, right?"

"Yeah, and we're just going as friends," I say, even though I feel my face get hot the second he mentions her name. I know my dad notices, but he doesn't say anything. I'm in over my head. I can admit that to myself. Ever since Bethany drove away in her Tiana gown, I knew I'd made a mistake. As I'm pretty sure I have a crush on Bethany.

The last few days have been a special kind of hell, just waiting to put our plan into place. We barely talked to each other at school, and I had to stop myself from texting her like fifty times. The two pictures I sent her from the game were just two of the twelve I took. I was tiptoeing close to stalker behavior, but she looked really cute. I had to document it. Plus, one of those pictures is perfect for the yearbook. I was doing the whole school a service really. And I'm just anxious to see her. Like, now.

"She's lucky her friend looks good in a suit. You're staying over at Axel's tonight?"

"Yeah. Mom's letting me take her car though. I'll have it back in the morning."

"Sounds good. Be safe. Call us if you need anything. Come home if shit gets weird. No drugs, no drinking, and if you and Bethany decide to—"

"Dad. Just friends. Seriously." Laury is still standing right there. This is not the time for a last-minute safe sex talk, especially when there will be absolutely no sex. Period.

"All right, all right. But if you think things might go that way, man? Your mom always has emergency condoms in her bag. Ask her."

"Ugh. Gross."

"What? You want another little sister? The hormonal shit is only like ninety-five percent effective."

"It's like ninety-nine percent, but two forms of birth control are always better than one," Laury says with a shrug.

"Bye, Dad."

"Hold on. Laury, get a picture of us." Dad hands over his phone, then pulls me close with an arm tight around my shoulder. Even though we're still wearing our masks, I do my best to smile.

"Perfect."

"Okay." I step back and straighten the sleeves on my suit jacket. "I have to go. Mom just wanted you to see all this in person."

Dad gives me a double thumbs-up. "You look good. And I mean it—if shit gets weird, just come home."

"I will." I say goodbye to Laury, then book it back out to the car. I make a dramatic show of throwing the door open and jumping into the passenger seat. "Drive! Drive! Drive!" I yell through my mask.

"Shut up." My mom laughs. "No more than ten over the speed limit. We'll get there."

We're late. And I feel like a complete jerk because Bethany is standing off to the side talking to her mom while Saylor's mom, Cristine, is busy lining up the rest of the couples in front of this custom-made HOMECOMING backdrop setup. Bethany catches my eye as our car passes by the house. I can't read the look on her face, but I think it's happy.

"Crap."

"We're five minutes early!" Mom practically screeches. She pulls into a spot two houses down and I wait until the car is actually stopped before I jump out. I don't run, but I walk fast as hell right for Bethany. She peels off from her mom and meets me partway.

"Sorry I'm late. We had to stop by the shop to see my dad for a second."

"It's okay. Cristine was ready to go last night," she says.

"Oh. Well. You look good. Really good. You look amazing." Hot is what I want to say. She looks really, really hot. The blue-jade dress. She's wearing makeup. Her hair is half up in this twisty bun with a little crystal band around it. And her dress. I tell myself to be a gentleman. But wow. Her boobs look really nice too.

"Thank you. I'm glad we found this dress." She runs her fingers over the fluffed-out skirt. "I kinda love it." When she looks up at me, she has this soft smile on her face, like she hasn't been this happy in a really long time, but this dress is finally the thing to do the trick. Something about that smile does something to my chest.

"Jacob," my mom says, snapping me out of my trance. She's holding up the white-rose corsage I'd left in the car and my gear bag.

"Oh, sorry. Thanks, Mom."

"Here." She opens the box for me so I can grab the small bundle of white roses. When I slip it onto Bethany's wrist, my fingers brush her skin and I can't help but notice the way goose bumps spread up her arm. They are tingling up the back of my neck too. I clear my throat. "Should we hop in the photo madness?"

Mrs. Greene waves us back together. "Wait! I want to get a few of just the two of you."

Both our moms take a few dozen pictures before Mrs. Ford calls us over to join the group.

"Ready?" I ask Bethany, holding out my hand. She clasps her fingers with mine and that weird feeling I've been fighting is back. *Just follow the plan*, I tell myself.

"Let's do this." Bethany smiles up at me.

I thought it would be weird being with all Saylor's friends like this, but it's not. Landon high-fives me and Glory says hi like she's actually happy to see me. Same with Tatum and Emily. And Saylor isn't weird. She did apologize to me again last time I saw her in Spanish, but she's more normal this time when she says hi and tells us to jump in beside her and Rhys. Mrs. Ford adjusts us eight different times and finally I'm standing there with my arms around Bethany. That odd warmth in my chest boils straight to heat.

"One second," Bethany says. She lightly moves my arm and steps away from me, but just for a second. She readjusts, pressing closer with her back to my chest. It's the worst time for me to notice she's the perfect height—her head is notched right under my chin. It doesn't mean anything, but I do like the way we fit together. She smells nice too. Fresh and light, like this fancy soap I'd used at this beach house I went to with my cousins. I don't mind when she presses closer to me and lets out a deep breath.

We take pictures for almost forty-five minutes. All the girls. All the *enby babes*, as Mrs. Ford says. (I pull out my Canon for those rounds.) All the boys. A ton of photos for all the couples separately. Solo sessions so we can capture the details of everyone's formalwear. Close-ups, funny faces. Saylor's mom is going for some kind of record. She keeps coming up with new things for us to do. I'm pretty sure she takes fifty pictures of

Bethany's and my matching sneakers from different angles before Bethany's mom finally speaks up and saves us all.

"Cristine," Mrs. Greene calls out. "Not. A. Wedding. Let these poor kids get to the dance. We're losing light anyway."

"Okay. Okay."

Mom walks over and hands me the keys to the Yukon. Bethany's mom is right behind her. "Drive slowly and call me when you get to Axel's."

"I will."

"You two have fun," Mrs. Greene says.

"We will. You ready?" I look over at Bethany. I can't gauge what she's feeling, but I know *I'm* dying to get two seconds alone. The last few days of acting normal have been brutal. We need to talk. We say bye to our moms and head over to my car.

"Can I turn up the AC?" she asks once we're inside.

"Yeah." I start the engine and crank the cool up.

"Thanks. I was getting warm doing all the shuffling and posing, and I didn't want to start sweating before we even got to the dance."

"Oh, but we're gonna sweat tonight. We're gonna crush that dance floor."

"I thought you were on yearbook duty?"

I nod toward my gear bag in the backseat. "I have my head rig for my GoPro and everything. What kind of cinematographer would I be if I couldn't get some action shots right in the middle of it all?"

"A dry one. And remind me to magically go missing when you put that GoPro on."

"Why?" I laugh.

"Have you ever seen your face in a GoPro?"

"Fair. Everything else cool?" I ask her.

"Of course not," she says, frowning at me.

"You want to back out of our plan?" I ask her, secretly praying her answer is no.

"What? No? It's a risky, but solid, plan. I need to do this. I'm just—I'm gonna be honest with you since you already know my most embarrassing secrets."

"Sure, tell me."

"I'm nervous, okay. I can't explain why. I'm just nervous."

"Well, if we're not explaining why, I'll just say I'm nervous too," I tell her.

"Okay, well then we're even. We have our mission and now we just need to go through with it. We get to the dance, fall magically in love, and then Monday we tell everyone we're a thing."

"Yup, that's what we're doing," I reply, the realness of it all making my palms sweat a little. Or a lot. I gotta do something about this crush between now and then. I gotta focus on the mission parameters, our own Prime Directive that has nothing to do with the way she looks in that dress and the way it's making my heart beat double time.

"Great. Shall we?" She motions to the line of cars already driving down Saylor's street. I pull out behind Tatum's car and follow them and Emily. Later, much later in the night, I'll ask Bethany if maybe we should seal the deal with a kiss. Later.

15
BETHANY
(is a big girl and she can absolutely handle this)

Technically, the moment we started taking pictures, the plan was in motion. But it doesn't really hit me that the game is truly afoot until Jacob parks his mom's car in the student lot. He turns to me and I can tell he's thinking the same thing.

"Okay, as your boyfriend in training, when I get out of the car should I hold your hand or let you hold my arm?" he asks.

"Oh man, that's a good question."

"Try not to overthink it. Just give me your honest answer."

"Sir, overthinking is my middle name, but if I'm going with my gut here? Hold hands. We should hold hands," I say, mostly because I want to hold his hand, but I'm not telling him that. I need the holding practice, that's all, and it's good for the plan. "Holding the arm is a little formal. Holding hands will plant the seed of a seed being planted."

"You're kinda weird." He laughs.

"Thanks. I try."

"Trust me. I'm used to weird. Spend twenty minutes with Axel."

"Oh, I know," I reply. "He offered me some paste to eat in art class last year."

"That sounds like Axel." He shakes his head. "Let's do this."

I watch as he climbs out of the truck and comes around to my side to open my door. I try my best to remember how to breathe. We should have come up with a less-stressful plan. I carefully slip down and hold my dress out of the way so I don't step on it, and then I take Jacob's hand.

Walking from the parking lot toward the gym, all I can think about is if my hand should be feeling this way. Well, not just my hand. The back of my neck is tingling in this strange way, a good way, and my cheeks are starting to get hot. My fingers laced with Jacob's feels good. It feels right. Maybe Oliver was kinda right. I had no clue what holding a boy's hand was like.

"Do you like holding hands?" I ask him, like the weirdo I clearly am. "What is it? Love languages or whatever? I also need to know if this is you being yourself."

"Yeah. I like it," he says. "Arm holding is actually kinda awkward for me, especially with shorter people."

"Okay. I'll file that away," I say just as we fall into step with Emily and Tatum.

"I'm digging the bun, Jake," Tatum says. They've silk pressed their own curls. It looks perfect with the red slip dress they picked out. Emily looks just as great in her black jumpsuit with little red rosebuds on it. They make a cute pair.

"Thanks. My mom used eighteen pounds of mousse."

"I love it."

"You do look good," I say quietly.

"Thanks," Jacob replies. When I look up at him, his cheeks are bright red. I'm taking that as a good sign. We make our way inside and it's like a party supply store opened up in the middle of the hall.

"Dance committee went all out," Jacob says.

"Ooooh! That's cute," Tatum agrees.

I look down the hallway. Most places got rid of their little floor decals, spread out six feet apart, but the line of sparkly stars leading the way to the gym are cute. I look up at the hand-painted banner hanging over the doors to the gym.

A NIGHT TO REMEMBER . . .

In a good way, I hope.

The gym is decorated floor to ceiling in blue-and-silver streamers and balloons. Go Minotaurs. The DJ is going, music blasting through the speakers, and there are already a couple dozen people on the dance floor. We make our way over to an empty table. Jacob turns to me and nods toward the back of the gym.

"I set up a camera over by the DJ booth. I got a time lapse of the setup and everything."

"Oh, cool! I never would have thought of that," I say, maybe a little too enthusiastically. Jacob just smiles.

"I'm gonna go check on it and then wait by the door just to get some close-ups of people coming in."

"Do you need any help?" I offer.

"Nah, I got it," he says before he looks over at my friends. "Can I leave my date in your hands?"

"Of course!" Tatum says. "Bethy, come dance with us."

"Just give me like twenty minutes. I'll be back," Jacob says.

"'Kay," I say, letting go of his hand. I try not to stare after him as he takes off for the DJ booth, but when I turn back around, I am completely busted.

"Ahem. Is there anything you want to tell us?" Tatum asks, their eyebrows arching up nice and high.

"What? What do you mean?" I reply, taking the clueless route.

"Um, I see you looking at him. I think you have a little crush on Jacob. Say won't care if you go for it, ya know?" Tatum motions with their chin to the middle of the dance floor where Saylor and Rhys are already getting pretty cozy, even though an upbeat Lizzo song is playing. "She's definitely moved on."

"Tatum, my darling. I am not looking at him any kind of way. I was just admiring the slickness of his hair, the crispness of his suit. He went to a tailor, you know?"

"Whatever, twenty bucks says you're madly in love before the night is over. The both of you."

"Ahaha, don't be ridiculous."

"Come on. I wanna dance." Tatum grabs Emily's and my hands and pulls us out onto the dance floor right near Say and Rhys.

"All good?" Saylor asks me, shaking her free thumb up and down. Her other arm is around Rhys. Neither of them can dance. It's really something.

"All good," I say back, giving her a thumbs-up. I start

moving to the beat with Tatum. We try to help Emily find the beat. It's a struggle, but she's doing her best. Glory and Landon show a few seconds later and to my horror they have Oliver and Poppy with them. I grab Emily's hand and spin her so she's between me and Oliver. Glory shoots me a look and completely fails at covering her snort.

I have fun dancing with my friends, but after a while it's starting to feel like that seventh-wheel scenario is actually coming true. Jacob's still not back from his yearbook mission.

"Where's your man?" Glory says a few songs later.

"Not my man. And I'm not sure. He was by the door, but he's not anymore." I look around and see his friend Heaven sitting at one of the tables, looking at something on her phone. His other friend Axel is on the far side of the dance floor doing a really interesting interpretive dance while his girlfriend Valentina just stands there watching. She looks like she's enjoying the show though, so who am I to judge.

I scan the bleachers, the snack table, and the DJ booth. He's not by the picture booth either. "Hope he didn't leave town," I joke, kinda. I know he had an actual yearbook thing to do, but an annoying part of my brain is a little worried he might be getting cold feet on the plan. And me.

"He'll be back," Tatum says. I'm cool waiting a little longer for him to reappear, until a slow song starts playing. I don't even give my friends a chance to convince me to stay on the dance floor. I wiggle by Saylor and Rhys and head right to the snack table. I finish a cup of water and grab another. Still no Jacob. I think about that first time he came over to my house and how I found him hiding in the kitchen. Maybe he's hiding from me now. Maybe I make him just as uncomfortable as Poppy and Saylor did.

The slow song ends and a more depressing thought crosses through my mind—maybe I should have come alone. I'd still be spending the night on the dance floor with my friends. It wouldn't be much different. I scan the dance floor one more time. No sign of my date, but I do spot Kayden Smith looking as fine as ever with his arms around Hannah Williams. That lucky bitch.

I turn back to the bowl of pretzels on the snack table and consider taking a handful of what is clearly leftover Halloween candy and going to hide in the library. Just as I come to terms with the fact that the bowl holds no Peanut M&M'S, I see Jacob walk back into the gym. He gives me one of those nods boys do and a little wave as soon as he spots me. I'm balancing my disappointment with the fact that he looks so good, especially with his gear bag hanging off his shoulder. Very professional. Even though he looks kind of annoyed. He comes right over to me.

"Sorry. Noah and I had a kind of heated debate about the time lapse," he says.

"Did you figure it out?" I reply.

"Yeah." He looks down at his sneakers for a second and then, like he's changed his mind about something, he looks back at me. "You wanna hear what we came up with?"

"Yeah," I say, smiling back at him.

"Okay, so he wanted me to stay until everyone was gone, but I kinda want to drive my date home. So we're gonna cut this with the winter formal and then I'll go to prom, stay 'til the end and finish that out, and then we can edit it all together. I sweet-talked him with the idea of also doing a transition of whoever wins prom king and queen, from being crowned to them walking across the graduation stage."

"Okay, that's kinda genius."

"Thanks. I won Noah over. Did I miss anything?"

"Just the first slow dance, but I'm sure we'll get a few more chances to show off our magical chemistry."

"Crap, my bad."

"It's okay. I thought you were hiding," I tease, like I wasn't about to go eat my feelings among a stack of books.

"Nah, tonight's too important for me to hide. We have a plan, remember? You wanna dance?"

"Yeah, let's do it."

I let Jacob take my hand and he leads me out onto the dance floor.

16
JACOB
(thinks he has a handle on things)

'm having fun with Bethany, but when another slow song comes on, it's pretty clear I still need some work in the playing-it-cool department. I put my hands on her waist as she drapes her arms over my shoulders. I do my best not to look at her boobs, but it is kind of hard. I have two left feet for sure, but I do my best to follow the way Bethany is swaying to the music. Being with her is much easier, maybe because of the plan or maybe 'cause we're just friends and I don't feel that kind of pressure to get every single second we're together perfect.

Still, I need to get used to having my arms around a girl. Any girl.

"I wonder who invented slow dancing," she says.

"Axel did."

She looks over to where he and Valentina are doing some hip movement that has to violate the school's code of conduct.

"So much friction." She giggles. "Did Heaven not want to come with a date?"

"She didn't want to come at all, but her mom is giving

her shit about not being more socially active. She wants her to come out of her shell more. This was their compromise. She's here, but she's been reading fic on her phone this whole time."

"Not a bad idea." Bethany shrugs and then a scowl comes over her face as she looks harder in Heaven's direction.

"What?" I ask.

"Nothing. It must be weird that half the school has your mom as their dentist, but I love Dr. Goo-Campbell."

"She's my dentist too. Heaven tries not to think about it, for a bunch of reasons. Her mom is very . . . classy. That's the word. She loves me and Axel, but I don't think she pictured her daughter being a gay goth skater who only hangs out with a quiet kid who is glued to his camera and however you would describe Axe."

"Hmm," she says. Then she looks up at me and lowers her voice. "We still need to figure out a time limit on this whole thing."

"Oh, with the plan?" I ask before I lean down a bit so I can hear her. I ignore the goose bumps that spread out over my skin when she whispers in my ear. But I can't ignore the way her fingers seem to hug my shoulders a little tighter.

"Yeah. If we do it for too long, people will be all devastated when we break up. If we break up too soon, people *will* think you have some sort of short-relationship curse. How about December tenth?"

"That's a super-specific date," I say. "Anything special about December tenth?"

"Well, if we break up before Thanksgiving, that will be

about as long as you dated Poppy, which will kinda defeat the purpose of what you need—to show people you can make something last longer than two weeks. If we do it too close to Christmas, people will expect some sort of dramatic show of sadness 'cause we broke up near the holidays. If we wait longer than that, then we're looking at Valentine's Day pressure and then really we can't break up until St. Patrick's Day." She stops talking suddenly and pulls back a little, looking me in the eye. She doesn't pull back that much though. Our faces are really close together. Like kissing close. And maybe she's thinking the same thing, 'cause her gaze definitely focuses on my lips and I focus on hers. Her tongue darts out and wets her already glossy lower lip. A voice in my head says I should definitely kiss her. But I don't.

"Sorry," she says, her voice still quiet against the music playing around us. "I have this thing where I ramble."

"It doesn't bother me," I tell her. "I was just listening. Keep going."

"I'm just saying we cut it too short, and you haven't solved your problem. We wait too long, we might as well get married by high school terms."

"No, that makes sense. December tenth, it is. I'll dump you so good."

"Ack," she gasps. "I mean, can't I dump you?"

"Then I'll be three for three. That would kinda blow the part of my plan where I try to save a little bit of face."

"We'll say it was a mutual thing and we decided we were better as friends."

"Yeah, that works. Good."

The slow song ends and the DJ cranks up some bass-shaking song that has everyone around us jumping up and down.

"I'm gonna briskly walk to the restroom." She laughs as Landon bumps into her.

"'Kay. I'll, uh, hop in line for the photo booth. We need some official night-to-remember photos," I suggest.

"Sweet. Meet you over there."

We both take off for our intended destinations. I make it maybe three feet before I bump into Saylor. She's been around all night, but pretty much glued to Rhys, so I haven't said much except hi.

"Having fun?" I ask her.

"You know I am. I'm enjoying watching you two love-birds finally come together."

"Ha, yeah, thanks for the setup."

"You know, I don't want to take too much credit for the universe's divine intervention, but you're welcome," she jokes.

I glance back toward the gym doors where Bethany has disappeared. "Hey, can I ask you something?"

"Yeah, what's up?"

"I know we just, you know. But I was wondering if you'd be cool if I asked Bethany out?" This was not part of the plan, but it seems like the right thing to do. For myself, for Bethany, and for Saylor. And for the plan. What did Bethany say it was, planting the seeds that need to be planted? I also don't want people thinking I snaked around Saylor's

back to get to her best friend. I definitely don't want Saylor
thinking that.

"I knew it!"

"Knew what?" I ask, shocked.

"That you two would be good together, like for real,"
Saylor practically squeals, like this is the good news she's
been waiting for all year, but it's news to me.

"Since when? Did she say something to you?"

"No, but I see it. Especially tonight. You guys look so cute
together. She's kinda shy with boys though, so just take it
easy with her, okay? She has a very soft, gooey center. That's
why we love her."

I would not put shy and Bethany in the same sentence,
but I guess Saylor has Best Friend intel I wouldn't know
about. And I can see the gooey part. She did mention the
crying. "I promise to handle with care."

"You need any help? You want me to put in a good word?
Though from the way you look all snazzy tonight, I'm not
sure she'll need much convincing. Me and the homies can
run to the store and get some rose petals for you to spread
out on the parking lot or something."

"No, thanks." I laugh. "I just wanted you to be cool with
it. I'm not gonna ask her here. Crowds aren't really my
scene."

Saylor just nods, this little smirk spreading across her
lips before her expression lights up. "Oh, here she comes.
Act natural."

I turn around just as Bethany makes her way over to us.
"That was fast," I say.

"The teachers' lounge was open. They have Bath & Body Works soap in there. Did I miss anything?"

"Nope. Just telling Jacob how snazzy he looks," Saylor says, doing her best to play it cool.

"I was gonna go with hot as hell, but sure, snazzy works. Where's Rhys?" Bethany says. I don't miss the way she avoids looking directly at me when she says it.

"Also bathroom. Apparently he didn't think to break into the teachers' lounge."

"I didn't break in. I calmly walked through an unlocked door. We were gonna get in line for the photo booth, but you want us to wait for Rhys to get back?"

"Nope. I'll go square dance with Glory and Lan. Off you kids go," Saylor says, shooing us away with all ten of her fingers.

I watch as Bethany playfully glares at her for a second before I follow her over to the line at the photo booth. "You guys have a good talk?" she asks me.

"Yeah. Just kinda squashed it once and for all. We're good."

"Good. Um, this is gonna sound really weird, but smell my hands." She holds up her palms. Axel has played this trick on me one-too-many times, but I'm trusting that Bethany and Axel have a different sense of humor. I take a cautious whiff and, thank god, her hands smell really good.

"Oh wow. That's nice," I tell her.

"Lemon soap and this fancy lotion. I'm definitely gonna have my moms complain about the soap in our bathrooms." She chuckles. Before she turns around, I take a calculated risk and put my hands on her shoulders. She freezes for a half second and relaxes.

"Is this okay?" I ask her.

"Yup. Plan perfect." She smiles at me over her shoulder before she faces forward again. We don't really talk while we wait in line, but neither of us seem to mind. When it's finally our turn, I sit down on the small bench inside the booth. It takes some convincing, but I finally get Bethany to sit on my lap.

"Your parents are gonna sue me if I break both of your legs," she says as I wrap my arms around her soft waist. She really isn't that heavy. The real hard part is getting her whole skirt inside the booth.

"I'm sturdier than I look. Come on." I loop her arm over my shoulder just as the first flash goes off. We blow that one but make up for it with the next few. I'm not sure how the plan is actually going to work out, but from the way a few people look at us when we come out of the booth, I think it might be working already.

17
BETHANY
(and the first of firsts)

can admit it; I'm having fun with Jacob. We dance some more and then when they announce that they are about to crown the homecoming court, I follow Jacob up into the bleachers. He pulls out his fancy camera and starts taking pictures. He hands the camera to me and shows me quickly how to use it. Apparently, the camera they are using for the time lapse belongs to the yearbook department. I snap a few photos of our king and queen, Lucas Ro and Tia Matthews, as they slow dance in the middle of the gym, basking in all their royal glory.

I hand the camera back and watch Jacob as he looks at the digital display. "These are really good," he says.

"I have many hidden talents," I tease before I nudge his white sneaker with mine. He nudges my foot back and I nudge him again and, yes, I know exactly what we're doing, and I don't care.

Soon the song goes back to something fast. "You wanna bust a move? I think they are gonna wrap this whole thing up soon," Jacob says.

"Sure, let's do it." I wait for him to secure his camera around his neck, then he helps me down the bleachers. It's a small miracle I haven't tripped on this dress. I love it, but it's very poofy. When we make it safely back to the gym floor, Landon comes running up to us. Glory is walking to catch up with him.

"In-N-Out. In-N-Out," he chants as he grabs me by the shoulders. "In-N-Out! In-N-Out! In-N-Out!"

"Landon wants to go to In-N-Out before we head to Saylor's," Glory says.

"Ugh, I don't know, man," I groan.

"You're not cool with In-N-Out?" Jacob asks me.

"Not on a Saturday night. Half the school is gonna go over there. The line will be wrapped all the way around to Exposition. Sensible people will be in the line for Wendy's, or better yet, Taco Bell."

"Jacob, take our girl somewhere she wants to eat," Glory says, rolling her eyes.

"I will."

"Cool. We'll see you back at Say's." I say bye to Glory and Landon and then Tatum and Emily as they rush by.

"Let me just go grab the other camera and give it back to Mr. Wolfson."

"Okay. I'll go wait with Heaven." I nod over to her table where she's still sitting. I don't think she's danced all night.

"Cool. I'll be right back."

I make my way over to the tables, and I'm almost there, just feet away, when Oliver steps in front of me.

"Hey, Bets," he says. He's sweat out his blazer and tie. The top three buttons on his shirt are undone. I tried to ignore him and Poppy all night, but they were dancing pretty hard.

"Hey."

"Looks like things worked out," Oliver says. "Tonight."

"Sure?" I have no idea what he's talking about.

"I mean with you getting a date. You and Jake. I heard he's more your speed."

What's on the tip of my tongue is something about Oliver's mother and *her* speed, but Momlissa would file comments like that firmly under *No, ma'am, not nice.* So, I settle for the truth. "I've never been insulted like that before. Thank you."

"That's not what I mean." He laughs. *He laughs.*

"No, it's okay. You and Poppy have a good night." I walk away before he gets a chance to shove his foot into his mouth any further. The sad part is, even after that thoughtless comment, I still have a crush on him. I truly need help.

I sit down at Heaven's table and she ignores me. Until she doesn't.

"Who gets to date him next?" she says.

I look over. She's still looking at her phone, but I'm pretty sure she's talking to me. "What?"

"Who in your posse of Real Housewives of Culver City gets Jake next? Is there anyone left?" She sets down her phone and stares at me. I stare back. This is Jacob's best friend. Saylor said she was hard to get a read on, but I have to think of something that doesn't involve me cussing her out.

"You really hate my friends, don't you?"

"I hate everyone."

"That's sad. I'm pretty fun at parties," I say with a shrug.

"I hate parties," Heaven says.

"Well, I think that's okay 'cause I'm pretty sure parties hate you. Like a lot." That does the trick. Heaven smirks and picks up her phone. I'm about to ask her where she got her check print skater dress when Jacob comes over.

"You ready?"

"Yup," I turn to Heaven. "This experience you and I just had, five stars. Top tier. Loved everything about it. We must do it again sometime."

"Girl, shut up." She laughs. I smile at her and then take Jacob's hand and lead him out of the gym. "What was that all about?" he asks.

"She was just trying to scare me away from you. It didn't work."

"Good." He opens the door to his mom's SUV. I gather up my skirt and climb in, grateful I made it the whole night without a fashion emergency.

"What did Oliver say to you?" Jacob asks as we join the short line of cars leaving the student lot. "I saw you guys talking."

"Jacob, it's too early for you to be jealous. I'm kidding. Nothing. But we might have to fight him and Poppy in the hallway on Monday."

"Yeah, I can't fight. Axel can though."

"Good to know. I have to say I'm shocked how little you had your phone out tonight. I figured you'd be TikToking all night long."

"Nah, there's this fine line of capturing the moment and missing the moment. I had a date. I didn't wanna miss out on *you* by taking TikToks of Landon and the rest of the football team all night. I did get some good pictures though."

"Good." The weight of the night finally hits me. The hours getting ready. The pictures, so many pictures. All the dancing. Going toe-to-toe with Heaven for a few minutes. It takes a lot out of a girl, but I did it. I survived homecoming. With a date. And I think some people are already ready to buy the plan. Even Oliver.

I could really use a nap. I settle back into the seat and let out a sigh a little louder than I mean to.

"Music or no music?" Jacob asks.

"Music's fine." He turns on the radio to the classic alternative station and turns it down so it's just loud enough for us to hear, but it's not blasting us out of the car. Perfect.

o o o

We drive to Taco Bell, but the line is down the block, so we go to Wendy's. There's a line all the way back to the Trader Joe's, but it's moving quickly and at this point we've committed.

We order Frosties, spicy nuggets, and fries. I convince Jacob he hasn't lived until he tries every flavor of their lemonade, though we both agree it's a shame the Taco Bell line was so long because nothing beats a Baja Blast. I have a fleeting thought about Mama T hearing this conversation and her head just exploding. Who cares about sugary beverages this much? Me. I do.

"Axel and I spent last summer trying every flavor of

Mountain Dew we could find," Jacob tells me, and I think I might have truly found my new best friends. We beat Saylor and the rest of my friends back to her house. Cris and Mr. Ford are home, so I could go in, but Jacob tells me he'll wait with me in his car. Besides, we have a few more things to iron out before Monday.

"How are you feeling about the plan?" I ask him.

"Pretty good. How did I do tonight? On a quality-of-date scale," he asks. "Be brutal. I need to know."

"Oh wow." I think for a second. I need to be honest, but fair. "All things considered, no notes so far. You were present and attentive. We need to talk about you clapping on the two and the four, but you really did give it your all on the dance floor, which I didn't expect from you. So you get bonus points there. You shocked me. But the question is: Did you have fun or were you doing all that stuff for me?" I turn in my seat so I can really look at him when he answers.

"Yeah. Yes. I had a good time. I was a little out of my element, but not in a bad way."

"Okay, good. Let me know if the bad way ever comes up."

"Deal."

I take a sip of my sunburst melon lemonade and then let out a deep breath. Here comes the hard part. "I think we need to kiss."

"Okay," he says without hesitation, but my brain is already ready with my explanation, so I keep talking.

"If people are gonna buy this, we have to be comfortable and in order—"

"Bethany, I said okay. I get it. We don't need to make out

in the middle of the halls at school, but we should get used to being . . . close."

"Okay. This is gonna be my first kiss so I just want you to know up front that I might not be great at it."

"That's the point of this though, right? I help you get some of these 'experiences' out of the way, shame free. And then we break up and I tell Oliver you're the best kisser ever."

I stare out the windshield at the streetlights dotting their way down the hill and wonder for a quick second how Oliver would process that piece of information. More importantly, how much I need this information to be true.

"You just let me know when you're ready and I'll kiss you."

I look around the car and assess the setting. The AC gently blowing, the ambient light coming from the dashboard. I check out the size of the center console and the way I'm having to twist in my seat. "This isn't gonna work. We have to get out of the car."

"Huh?"

"Come on. Turn off the car though." I don't waste any time. I open my door and hop out. It takes Jacob a second to catch on, but he eventually meets me around on the sidewalk. I turn my back to the car. Jacob faces me. Saylor's neighbor has this huge tree that covers this part of the street, so we're hidden from random people taking their dogs on late-night walks, but we can still see each other just fine. It's perfect. "Better, right?"

"Yeah."

"Okay. So since you have done this before, I'm just gonna

let you handle this. Kiss me." I close my eyes, tilt my head up, and wait.

"No pressure, then, I guess," he mutters. I almost tell him to relax and just do it, but a second later his lemonade-chilled hands are cupping either side of my neck. I flinch a little, but I'm glad he doesn't hit the reset button on this moment. Jacob presses his lips to mine. So many things run through my head: how soft his lips are, how new and different it is to have someone literally touching your face with their face, and how not weird that is. It's not scary, I realize. The part of me that remembers every single sensation of Oliver hoisting me over his shoulder is running in circles cheering, pumped we're back in the boy game, for real this time. Even if it's part of a plan.

I feel Jacob pull back from me and I open my eyes. "How was that?" Jacob asks. He takes another step back and moves to shove his hands into his pockets but stops himself when he realizes he's still in his suit. He seems nervous, like he's waiting for me to ruin his life. Lucky for us both, it's only good news.

"No, that was good, good," I say. "Uh, kiss me one more time. I just need to be sure."

"I'm not sure what that means, but okay."

He steps closer again. I feel kind of like a pervert focusing on his mouth, but it's what my Boy-Crazy Brain is telling me to do. *His lips. Aren't they nice? Focus on his lips.* I do, until he's so close, his face goes blurry. I close my eyes again. This time is different. This time is better. Much better. His lips part just a little and somehow my lips know to follow his lead. It doesn't get all nasty with tongue or anything, but it's more. This is the kiss I've been wanting. On a tree-shrouded street, after a really fun, kind of perfect night, with a really hot boy.

One day, it'll be with a boy who isn't in on some sort of scheme with me. One day, I'll share this kind of perfect kiss with someone who likes me as much as I like them. With someone who likes me for me.

18
BETHANY
(has a new perspective)

ike a woman starved, I almost ask Jacob for a third kiss.
Thank god the two sets of headlights coming up the hill
snap me out of the spell kissing has clearly cast over me. I
suddenly get why Landon and Glory do it all the time now.

"That's them," I tell Jacob as soon as I notice the first car.
Saylor's SUV pulls into the Fords' driveway. Tatum's parks
in an open space a couple houses down. I take that as my cue
to reach into the car and grab my phone and my bag.

"The rest of my fries are all yours," I tell him.

"Thanks. Should we—"

"What?" I ask. I don't know why I sound so panicked. But
I don't think I can handle another kiss. Not like a normal
person. I think I'm ready to do some making out and I know
now is definitely not the time.

"I was gonna say: Should we make this official now or do
you want to wait 'til Monday? Get Heaven and Axel to hold
up a sign? I could call in a yearbook favor and get concert
choir to sing you a song," he says.

I feel my eyes narrowing as I look at him. "Is that something you'd want to do?" I could just tell him that big public

displays make my skin crawl, but now is as good a time as any to see if he's that kind of guy.

"No. No way."

"Okay, so how would you want to do it?" Jacob opens his mouth to answer, but we both hear Saylor yelling for Tatum and Em to hurry up and I am so happy for her neighbor's tree. My friends haven't spotted us. We don't have an audience. A front door opens. Saylor announces that they are home. Glory says something I can't understand and then the door closes again. "Okay, go."

"No, I was just saying I'd do it like this. I'd ask you if you wanted to be my girlfriend right here when it's just the two of us. You know? Quiet, private. Quiet."

"It was kind of a loud night." I chuckle.

"It's cool. Do you want to be my girlfriend?"

"I mean, I guess so. I'm kidding. Yes, I want to be your girlfriend."

"Okay, cool."

"Well, that was easy," I joke so Jacob doesn't know my insides have basically turned into a butterfly exhibit. My phone vibrating in my bag saves me from saying anything worse. I pull it out and see the text from Saylor.

> Saw Jake's car.
> Hope you're not in there doing it.

> Yup. Doing it so good.
> We gonna make this baby.
> Be right in.

"They know I'm out here somewhere," I tell Jacob.

"Come on. I'll walk you to the door." This time I just assume he offered because he wants to. I let him take my hand and we walk across the street. "I'll text you later?" he says.

I nod and suddenly things feel real. He looks at me a few seconds too long and I have this urge to kiss him that has nothing to do with research. I'm gonna have to remind myself every time I look at him, this is just for practice. Just for the experience. I don't have true-love feelings for Jacob and he definitely doesn't have them for me.

The fact that we're suddenly kissing again means nothing at all.

o o o

I think I'll have a few seconds to get my mind right before I have to talk to my friends, but when I walk into the kitchen where they are finishing their In-N-Out, all eyes are on me and I know playing it cool just won't work.

"Spill it, Greene," Glory says, shoving a fry into her mouth.

"Spill what?" I go for playing stupid instead, taking a long sip of my lemonade.

"Yeah, nah. We saw you two all night and we know you've been posted up outside in his mama's car for at least thirty minutes. You weren't talking about your stats homework."

"Oh, that. He just asked me to be his girlfriend."

There are no follow-up questions, not right away at least.

There's just screaming. My friends swarm me on the far side of the Fords' island, shaking my shoulders and hyping me up. I feel a little guilty not telling them the whole truth, but the truth at the heart of it all is still pretty embarrassing. I'll be keeping that to myself.

"Please tell me you kissed him?" Tatum squeals.

"And don't lie," Saylor says. "I will walk across the street and get my neighbor's porch camera footage right now. That lady sees everything."

"Kissing may have happened," I reply. There's more screaming. Saylor shakes me so hard I almost drop my phone. Mr. Ford walks through the kitchen, cringing at all the noise we're making. I'm sure he pictured his life going differently.

"Sorry I didn't say something to you first," I tell Saylor. "I got kinda swept up." Which I did. She doesn't need to know about the plan, but I could have said something earlier.

"Oh, it's fine. I just—" She looks over at Glory. "I don't know. I think maybe I said something about this earlier in the week. Maybe I already knew that you and Jacob would make a good couple. Maybe you should have listened to your friend."

I let out a deep sigh and let my eyes roll into next week. "You were right."

Saylor gives me a big hug. "You're welcome. And you just let me know if I need to put any other boys through a screening process for you. I'll do it happily. Free of charge."

"Let's actually hope we don't have to do that part again."

"Deal." Saylor laughs.

Later, when only Glory and I are still awake, watching *The Great British Bake Off*, I finally text Jacob.

> I told my friends.
> They approve.
> Saylor is taking credit.

I don't know if he's still awake, but my heart flutters the second he texts me back.

> I told Axel and Heaven too.
> Heaven wanted me to send
> you this. 🤮

> Tell Heaven I said . . .

I send over a clip of two Real Housewives of New York City trying to beat the crap out of each other in a fancy restaurant.

> She says you win.

> Talk tomorrow?

> Yeah. Good night.

> Night.

He sends over a picture he took of our pictures from our trip to the photo booth. I'm even happier that we actually had a good time. I look at my phone wallpaper for a few seconds, strawberries and cherries and little pink hearts. I change my phone background to the picture that Jacob took of the picture of us in the photo booth. We look cute as hell.

"Hey," I whisper.

Glory rolls toward the end of the couch she's sharing with a sleeping Saylor. "What's up?"

I hold up my phone and show her my new lock screen. "Is this too much?"

She smiles at me and shakes her head. And then she shows me her phone. An image of Glory sitting on Landon's lap with her lips pressed against his smiling cheek looks back at me. I've seen it before, but it's a good reminder that Jacob and I probably won't get to their level before we pull the plug next month.

"You two better get married," I tease her.

"Oh, we will."

19
JACOB
(is finding his focus)

tell Bethany about our Sunday skate day, and at first I'm relieved she doesn't ask to come along. Saylor and Poppy asked. I had to tell them no. Valentina seemed to get it right away. Turns out she has church with her family and then they spend the day at her grandma's. The skate park is our church. Axel's dad has to work his ER shifts sometimes, like today. Ink & Pearl is open, but Dad doesn't take clients on Sundays. Dr. Campbell, Heaven's dad, is a food scientist. He sometimes has to do scientist stuff on the weekends, but today he makes sure his afternoon is clear too.

This park is where they taught us how to skate and where I learned to use my Steadicam, and how to fall with my Steadicam. Esther's a pain in my ass, but it's been cool to watch her get better and better, and braver and braver. It's the one day a week she actually asks for my help, the only time she really tries to show off for our dad. And me sometimes.

Our Sundays are sacred, but we've only been here for like an hour and part of me is wondering what Bethany is doing right now. She told me she and her mom were going down to the arena to watch the Lakers play the Rockets, but I don't know if she's courtside or doing National Sports Network VIP stuff.

I take my turn on the wave ramps and then get out of the way for this small kid who is finally ready to give it a try. I ride over to one of the benches and pull out my phone. I go straight for my camera roll. I have some good stuff on my phone of the dance. Some good pictures of Bethany with her friends and a few with the two of us together. I actually look relaxed. I look happy.

I have thirty-six days to figure this all out. Thirty-six days to figure out how to just be myself around a girl who isn't Heaven. It sounds kinda pathetic when I think about it too much. And yeah, it's kind of a ridiculous plan. I'm taking the details of it to the grave for sure, but it's a good thing Bethany and I are seeing eye to eye on this. And now I have to figure out how to do my part, for more than just one night.

Basketball tryouts start tomorrow. She hasn't said much about it, but I know she'll be there and I know Coach Miller. It's gonna be a hard practice. I'll be making the rounds for yearbook all week. Maybe I should do something to hype her up before tryouts or see if she wants me around after. I've seen enough *30 for 30* docs to know that athletes have their rituals. She might think it's bad luck to look another person in the eye for twenty-seven minutes after each practice and game, or something else weirdly specific.

"Your phone holding you hostage again?" I look up at Dr.

Campbell. He does this little shimmy shake with his shoulders, then turns on his neon-green roller skates. Heaven picked them out. He glides backward with ease, then turns and rolls backward again.

I'm trying to figure out what kind of boyfriend I want to be, I almost say. "Oh, nah. I was just checking something."

I slip my phone into my back pocket just as Heaven skates over and I know she's about to blow this completely chill conversation for me.

"He tell you about his eighth girlfriend of the year?" she says.

Her dad stops his backward gliding and looks back and forth between me and Heaven like a shocked cartoon. "Eighth?"

"No. Not eighth," I reply, and of course my dad picks that exact moment to skate over. Esther is right behind him. I've made the mistake of looking at my phone during our sacred Sunday. I also made the mistake of telling Heaven anything, ever.

"Everything okay?" Dad asks.

Then Axel comes flying over. He narrowly misses taking out my sister. My dad gives him a look and then turns back to me.

"Sorry, E," Axel says. "Does Jacob need medical assistance? Are you dehydrated?"

"I just sat down on a bench to look at my phone for a second. Everyone can go about their day," I tell them.

"I gotta say, Jacob. I'm still concerned about the eight girlfriends," Dr. Campbell says.

"Eight?" Dad says.

"Ugh, yuck," Esther says, then she skates away. That's one down.

"I've never had eight girlfriends. Let's all go back to skating. How about that?" I reply.

"No, but, like, eight?" Dad asks again. I can see it in his eyes. He has these moments where you can tell he's questioning his parenting style in real time.

"Fine, just one. At a time. He has a new one," Heaven says. "But he is technically on his third girlfriend this school year and it's not even Thanksgiving break yet."

I sigh and try using telepathy to let her know that she's on my shit list. "Yeah, I have a new girlfriend."

"Wait, Betty?" Dad says.

"Bethany."

"She's cute," Heaven says with an annoyed shrug. I give up and pull up one of the selfies I took of us in front of the Fords' house.

"Jake got himself a sista." Dr. Campbell looks impressed as he takes my phone. He looks at the picture for a second, then hands my dad the phone. "She's a little cutie. I like the matching tie-dress situation."

My dad squints and holds the phone away from his face. He left his glasses at the shop again. "This is the homecoming date?"

"Yup."

"Okay, yeah. Your mom showed me pictures she took last

night. She said she's a real sweet girl. What's the problem?"
Dad asks.

"There is no problem. I'm just sitting on a bench."

"I like Bethany," Axel announces. I think that pretty
much sums it up. I look at my dad and Dr. Campbell. They
look at each other. Heaven acts like this isn't all her fault
and just skates away. Dad turns his board around with the
toe of his sneaker.

"Five minutes of young-love texting, then come back out
here and join us."

"Got it."

Dr. Campbell nods like he agrees with my dad's *dad* decision. "Come on, kid. I'll race you," he says to Axel.

"And you lose," Axe replies, dropping his board to the
ground. Dr. Campbell gives him a light shove and takes off
across the park. Dad takes his time following. I wasn't even
going to text Bethany, but since I've been given an official
green light from the dad committee, I go back to our text
thread and message her.

> Hope the game is real life inspiration
> for tryouts tomorrow.

I'm second-guessing the text as soon as I hit send. I
should have said something more romantic. Or something
not about school or sports.

> I'll FaceTime you tonight.
> The truth is too much for text.

I can just imagine the long explanation she's gonna have for me. I can't wait to hear it.

○ ○ ○

I'm almost done with my Spanish homework when Bethany calls. I grab my phone and try to act like I haven't been waiting for her to call all night. I hit the accept button and totally fail at playing it cool.

"Hey!"

"Hey." She giggles. A little voice in the back of my head is really focused on how good it feels just to see her face. I tell him to chill.

"How was the game?"

"Good, Lakers won."

"Are you in your closet?" I ask her. It looks like there are clothes dangling next to her head.

"Yeah, it's the only truly soundproof place in my house."

"Are you gonna cut an album in there or . . . ?"

"No, but it would be a great place to start a podcast."

"Do it. I'll help you record video for your social media. It'll really drive traffic."

"Thanks." She smiles.

"So you were gonna tell me some long, complicated thing about how you get ready for basketball?"

"Yeah," she says with this deep, pained sigh. I hope she's not doping or involved in some underground high school sports-betting ring. Though that would make a really cool movie. "Since you are now my boyfriend and I should be, like, vulnerable and open with you or whatever, I guess I should tell you. But no one else knows this. I mean, I think Saylor has an idea, but she doesn't know how deep it is. You have to keep this between us."

"Okay. Please don't tell me something crazy illegal. I won't tell anyone, but I'll feel really bad."

"I think it's only illegal to my moms. Okay." I watch her as she closes her eyes and lets out a deep breath. "I hate basketball."

"What?"

"Actually, I don't hate that basketball exists. I personally hate playing basketball, like on a team. I hate playing basketball with the intention of playing it in college. A fun, no-stakes game of one-on-one in the driveway? Sure. I'm all for it. But I would rather roll through glass and jump in a kiddie pool of salt and lemon juice before I play an official game with any kind of stakes."

"That's very vivid imagery," I say. "Huh."

"I know, and I know it doesn't make sense considering my family and pretty much my entire life up to this point, but it's true. I hate playing basketball competitively and I have a little less than twenty-four hours to enjoy my life until basketball consumes it for the next five months."

"Damn. That's a lot."

"I know!"

"So how do you usually cope with it? I mean, if you've always hated it and it's about to be your third season on varsity, you gotta have a system."

"Well, unfortunately for me, I'm a bit of a perfectionist.

If I'm doing something I have to do it well. You should see me make a sandwich."

"Saylor told me about your sandwiches." I laugh. "She said you wouldn't ever let people buy them off you."

"'Cause they are my masterpieces. Also, why would I go to the trouble of making something I really want to eat and then just give it away? Where's the logic there?"

"No, you have a point. So wait, your moms don't know? Your sisters?"

She sighs again, shaking her head. "No. I mean, it's kinda the family joke that I hate doing any of the workouts that don't involve shooting drills, but they just think that's me being stubborn or quirky or something. I don't know. It really doesn't help that I'm actually good. I wish I sucked and then my moms would just have to admit some sort of defeat and let me do something else."

"Is there something else you want to do?" I ask her. My parents have been pretty awesome about letting Esther and I sort out what we like. I can't draw, but I have my film thing. Esther's a great artist. My parents aren't pressuring her to become a tattoo artist, though.

"It's silly, but I kinda want to take classes at LA Cooking School. They have a kids' program for elementary schoolers but I emailed them last year to ask what their age limit was, and they said for some of the adult classes they can accommodate ages sixteen and up, with permission from a parent or guardian."

"And you didn't ask your moms?"

"No, because the day after they responded to my email, I

hit that half-court shot. The one you so wonderfully helped go viral."

"Shit," I say, wincing. "I'm sorry." That video was everywhere.

"It's okay. I had a scout come up to me at the next game and say that if I lose some weight, I'll have real D1 potential. It was a real uplifting moment."

"What the hell?"

"Yeah, sports are really fun for me."

"I'm guessing your moms won't take any of this well if they find out?"

"Did I mention I'm in my soundproof closet? No, my moms are . . . I love my moms, but basketball is their whole lives. I don't think they would look at me the same way if I told them I didn't want to play anymore."

"Yeah, I get that. That's a lot of pressure."

"So I'll suck it up and do my best not to hit any more half-court buzzer-beaters this season. Knowing my luck, I'll nail one every game and the Sparks will make me an offer on the spot."

"Anything I can do to help?"

"Nah, just be you, I guess. Like, don't suddenly become the world's biggest basketball fan. That is not what I want."

"I can do that."

This sad smile creeps across her face. I'm not sure what else I can do, but by tomorrow I'll figure something out.

20
BETHANY
(puts on her game face)

Jacob lives much closer to school than I do and he skates to school every morning with his sister, Esther. It seems silly to change our morning routine for a lot of reasons, so we agree to meet at my locker before first period. I come in the side entrance with Saylor and let out a few measured breaths as we walk down the hall. She's mid-Rhys-story, when I spot Jacob coming from the direction of the main office. I'm fuzzy on the exact science of it, but the second he turns his head and spots me, I feel like there's a tiny magnet inside of me and it's drawn straight to Jacob's magnet. I also know that my whole magnet theory is not something I should mention out loud.

Jacob smiles at me and lifts his hand in this little wave. It's really cute. He moves to the side of the hallway and leans against the wall. He's waiting for me. My little magnet sprouts tiny butterfly wings and they start flapping like crazy.

"I think I need to slow down this time," Saylor says. "Like, get to know him more before we make it official."

"Do you think Jacob and I moved too fast?" I ask her. The plan was kinda sudden.

"Um, no. Because I think you two are perfect for each other. Look at him," she says.

"Oh, I'm looking. Definitely take things slow with Rhys if that's what you're thinking. He seems nice enough. Though I never saw you with a tuba player."

"He played for me last night. It was kinda funny and sweet. I'm definitely going to make out with him today after practice," she says as we reach Jacob. "Well, look who it is. My ex-husband meeting up with my best friend. Can you imagine the betrayal? Disgusting," she teases.

"Not funny," I say.

"I'm messing with you guys. Well, my Bethy Boo, I'll catch you at lunch. I'll give you two lovebirds your alone-in-a-crowded-hallway time."

"Yeah, thanks."

"Bye-bye." Saylor glides off down the hall and I look up at Jacob.

"Hey." My voice sounds a little breathy, but it's not like I can take it back.

"Hey." His voice cracks so maybe we're even. He clears his throat and tries again, the bass returning to its proper place. "Hey."

I think I missed him, which doesn't make any sense. It's only been like a day and he's only my experimental boyfriend, but still, it's really nice when he nods toward my gym bag.

"You want me to carry that for you?" he offers, even though he has his skateboard and his camera bag strapped across his body.

"No, I got it."

"Cool. Is this okay?" he asks before he takes my hand.

"Yup. So what's going on with you today? I feel like we talked about me and my emotional problems all night." I was up pretty late talking to him in my shame closet. Mama T finally came in and broke up the whole situation.

"Not much. Just have to have another conversation with Mr. Wei about my grade in film lab," he says. We reach his locker first and he sticks his skateboard inside. I chuckle at the screaming skull surrounded by rose petals painted on the back. "What?"

"Nothing. I was just thinking about poor Skull Face screaming in your dark locker all day," I tell him.

"Should I leave him some water?" He laughs.

"That would be the humane thing to do. You were saying about Mr. Wei?"

"Oh yeah. I'm not doing all that great in his class."

"That's shocking. You're, like, a natural filmmaker. I figure he'd let you teach half of the class by now."

"Thanks, but it turns out that I'm just really good at one aspect of the whole filmmaking thing. I can't write a coherent script to save my life. I'll probably come out of this semester with a B, but that's not good enough for the film schools I'm looking at. I gotta figure the writing part out and try to get my grade up." We stop at my locker, and I very carefully tuck my lunch box onto my top shelf. "What's for lunch today?"

"Okay, don't laugh, but I made my go-to comfort sandwich. What some might think is an excessive amount of

thinly sliced honey ham and some Swiss cheese with butter lettuce, sliced tomato, and honey mustard on a toasted
croissant. The key to a sandwich surviving until lunch is a
perfectly toasted bread. It soaks things up but doesn't get
all mushy. I brought some sour cream and onion chips and
some strawberries too," I say. And I am really glad for our
little arrangement because I can't imagine a single boy on
earth wanting to listen to me talk about sandwiches like
this on purpose.

"Wow, that sounds really good. I just brought a leftover
burrito from Cerveteca."

"I mean, their burritos are really good. But yeah, my
grandpa used to make ham-and-cheese sandwiches for us
when we were little and I loved them. Turns out it was the
only thing he knew how to cook. That and spaghetti. Those
are my two comfort foods."

"Let me know when you bring spaghetti for lunch," he
says with this cute hint of a smile. If we weren't in school,
I would definitely kiss him. Note to self, hand holding in
the hall: yes. Smooching: no. We continue down toward my
homeroom and that's when it happens.

"Is this a new-couple alert?!" Madlyn Lowell literally
yells in the middle of the hall, pointing at our clasped hands.

"Jesus, chill." I cringe.

"I'm just saying, Jake moves fast."

"Madlyn, what the hell?" Jacob says.

"Yeah, great. Excuse us." I pull Jacob around her and
keep walking down the hall. "How long do you think that's
gonna be happening?" I ask him.

"Uh, at least two days."

"Great." We get to my homeroom and I'm glad to see Oliver is already sitting at his desk. The last thing we needed was to run into him and Poppy in the hallway. "Well, I'm pretty dramatic, if you can't tell. If you need someone to bounce your script ideas off, I'll try my best."

"Thanks, I appreciate that," Jacob says, and then we just sort of stand there, looking at each other. I wanna kiss him, so badly, but yeah, not now. "I'll kiss you later," he says.

"Okay," I snort.

"Bye."

I squeeze his hand and then go sit down. Of course, Oliver wants to chat.

"Hey, Greene," he loud whispers. If he asks me about Jacob, I'm throwing my desk at him.

I turn around and plaster on a strained smile. "Hey, Oliver. What's up?" Am I still a little bitter he turned me down for the dance? Yes, maybe I am. Do I still think he's extremely cute? Yes. And yes, I hate myself for it, but I'm only human and I like what I like.

"You ready for tryouts today? I saw you on TV with your mom last night. You get any pointers from Obie Rose?"

"Yeah, after the game, we ran some passing drills," I say.

"You did?"

"No. I imagine he went home to his family."

"You know him though, right?"

"Yeah, I guess." Yes, I know the Lakers' power forward. We've been to cookouts at his house, but more importantly I want to know what I did to deserve this human interaction.

I almost text Tatum to see where they are. Thank god they pick that exact moment to walk into the room, saving me from this conversation.

o o o

It's a rough morning. I really underestimated how annoying people would be about this whole me-and-Jacob-getting-together thing. At least eight different people ask me if we are really a couple. Madlyn's older sister asks me if it's true that Jacob cheated on Saylor with me. Someone else tells me that Jacob is bad luck and I should watch out for him. I almost ask her to explain further, because that's a really interesting theory, but I decide to be on time for chem instead.

"So, how's it going with Jacob?" Tatum asks as we sit down at our lunch table. He was right. We will be the hot topic for at least a couple days.

"Good. Having a boyfriend at school is weird," I declare.

"Why?" Emily laughs.

"I don't know. It's just weird I have to do stupid stuff like go to class. By law I should be able to just hang out with him all day. Why do I need to learn about covalent bonds? I'm not joining NASA."

"It sucks," Glory announces. "I just had to go and be good at math. It screwed up my whole Landon-focused schedule. But don't worry. Absence makes the heart grow fonder and all that. You'll see. But I did find out something interesting today."

"What's that?" I ask as I watch her pull out a Trader Joe's salad and half a sandwich.

"I was in English and Genna Ames told me she thought you weren't allowed to date. Like the moms have you in some weird women's Olympic basketball super-training camp and they don't want you distracted by boys."

"What??"

"Then, Tyler Alvarez, who was definitely not minding his own business, said he heard the same thing. Not the part about the training, but he said he thought you weren't allowed to date."

"B, this might not have been a *you* problem," Saylor says. "Oliver might have been telling the truth, kinda. Your single situation might have been a people-are-scared-of-the-moms problem."

"This information is truly blowing my mind."

"You want me to ask Landon if he's heard anything about this?" Glory offers.

"No, 'cause I guess it doesn't matter now, but between that and Crybaby Bethany, things are starting to add up." I unwrap my sandwich, thinking about how these new bits of information might actually keep me up all night. Could that have been part of the reason not a single boy has ever looked in my direction? I picture Mama T sending out a parents' newsletter telling people to keep their sons away from me. She wouldn't do that, but she'd think about it for a second. This is good though. It helps with the plan and might change my perspective moving forward. I'll talk to Jacob about it later.

We move on to some more hot goss that Tatum picked
up during French class. Some real juicy stuff about Kallie
Reynolds trying to do a little date switch of her own with
Matt Limb and Matt Kim. It did not work out for her.

My sandwich hits the spot and I'm only mostly dreading
the rest of the day.

I make my way to art class and get ready to butcher another watercolor when my phone vibrates in my pocket. I
have two minutes to look at it before Ms. Bennefield asks
us to focus our energies forward. My sisters are blowing up
our sister chat.

> Jocelyn: Do you have a boyfriend?!
> Also Momlissa sent me some
> homecoming pics.
> You looked so cute!

> Trinity: WHAT!

I hold in a groan and text my sisters back.

> Thanks.

> Trinity: Not thanks! I want details!
> Who is this boyfriend, young lady??

> Sorry I can't hear you.
> You're breaking up.

God, my family. I haven't mentioned this new development to my moms. I was going to wait until it was absolutely necessary, but there are apparently narcs lurking the halls of CCHS and I have about six minutes before one or both my sisters text the moms and ask them if they know anything about this. Tonight is going to be interesting. I'll have to survive tryouts first.

21
JACOB
(needs to pause and trust his gut)

Mr. Wei stops our viewing of *The Birds* and turns on the lights. I've seen it twice before because it's one of my mom's favorite movies, but it's cool to watch it in class. I pack up my things and do the mental math on how fast I'll have to walk to catch Bethany before she heads into tryouts.

"Jacob Yeun," Mr. Wei says. "Please come see me."

"Ooh you in trouble," Ashley Simmons says to me. She's getting an A and probably a full ride to USC, so I don't think it's really cool for her to make fun of us less fortunate people who aren't nailing this class. I ignore her though and make my way over to Mr. Wei's desk. I already know I screwed up. I got a B plus on our paper about the use of various frame techniques, but now I'm not so confident about the last short script I handed in.

He pulls up my grade on his computer. "So we're about at the midterm. Talk to me."

Mr. Wei offered to help me and for some reason I thought it would be smarter to just strike out on my own and try again. Not the move. Another C minus stares back at me. Apparently my short about getting lost at a Star Trek con wasn't as thrilling as I thought it could be.

"I don't know. When I'm writing, it seems fine, and then it feels like the second I hand my scripts in I know I've screwed something up."

"So maybe this isn't so much an issue of skill, but you getting in your own way. And maybe a time-management issue. Are you rereading through your stuff before you send it in?"

"Yeah," I say. I do, but more for spelling. Usually by the time I finish, I'm panicking about getting it right. He reaches back to his printer and then staples a few pages together before he hands them to me. "I know digital is the best, but sometimes it's more helpful to put pen to paper. When you get home tonight, take thirty minutes and read through that. Write down the differences you see."

I flip through the papers and it's two copies of the same short. I look a little closer and one is actually an updated and revised version.

"Look at what's different, the big and small changes, and then we'll talk about it. You have good ideas, but I need you to see them all the way through. Okay?"

"Okay. Thanks, Mr. Wei."

"No problem. I'll see you tomorrow."

I missed my window to catch Bethany, but I do feel better now that I actually talked to Mr. Wei. Hopefully pulling someone else's short apart will help. I head down to the yearbook office and walk by Madlyn and go right to my desk.

"What gives, man?" Troy says behind me.

I really don't want to hear what he has to say next. I turn

around to face him as Birk makes his way over. "I will pay you if the next thing you say to me is about yearbook and yearbook only."

"No. It's about Bethany Greene."

"No." I spin back around and log in to my computer. Noah and I actually have a lot of work to do this week and I have to get down to the gym to check out tryouts. We haven't gone through the homecoming footage either.

"I just wanna know when you became such a slutty slut," Madlyn jokes. I don't really laugh though.

"Yeah, agreed," Troy says. I spin around in my chair and look at them both like they've grown a bunch of extra heads.

"You're serious?" I ask.

"Three girls inside a month and two of them are best friends. That's ho behavior if you ask me," Madlyn says.

"How does my getting dumped twice make me a slut?"

"I don't know. Maybe all of these girls are realizing you truly belong to the streets." She shrugs.

"Whatever." I spin back around and start transferring the time-lapse footage of the dance. I don't have time to think about how anything Troy or Madlyn are saying right now makes any sense. Especially since Poppy dumped me because I wouldn't have sex with her. I don't get people. I don't understand any of this dating logic.

"Little Jakey Yeun, slutting it up," Birk says.

Two more days, I tell myself. And they'll be talking about someone else's business.

○ ○ ○

Noah wants to record something at the pool, so he takes water polo tryouts while I head out to the soccer field. I don't know if I'm uninspired or just lying to myself about wanting to watch Bethany on the court, but I bail sooner than I meant to and head into the gym, stopping to get a few pictures of Tatum at cheerleading practice on the way. One side of the bleachers are pushed and the practice hoops are down from the rafters. The boys' team is trying out on one end of the gym and the girls' team is on the other. Coach Miller is in the middle of the girls' court using Bethany and Dylan Smith to demonstrate some play. I have no idea what's going on, but I go to the corner of the court and wait with my camera at the ready. He hands Dylan the ball and they walk through the motions of the play one step at a time, and then he tells them to go full speed.

Dylan is quick on her feet, but so is Bethany. She reaches in and steals the ball. Coach Miller blows the whistle.

"See what Greene did there? You are focusing on two things: where the ball is and where the ball is going, and where your teammates are and where your teammates can be. Again." He hands the ball back to Dylan. This time she trips Bethany up and manages to make a basket.

"And that's a foul because Greene forced the pressure. Okay, Jung and Hollis. Let's go." Bethany and Dylan low-five each other and go back to the sidelines. Bethany doesn't look at me, but she drops her hand by her side and does a little wave in my direction. I'm a professional, so I try to keep my smile to myself.

I stick around until the end of practice, moving to the other side of the gym to get some footage of the boys' team. Landon is really good and so is Dylan's brother Kayden. When it's over, I get out of the way and hope Bethany gives me some sort of signal if she wants me to stick around or not. She comes right over to me and Saylor follows.

"Hey," Bethany says with a smile.

"Get anything good?" Saylor asks, nodding toward my camera.

"I think so." I pull up my display and scroll back through.

"Ooooh," Saylor says when I stop at a picture of Kayden Smith. I look between them as Saylor nudges Bethany's elbow.

"What?" I ask.

"Nothing. That's Bethany's celebrity crush."

"Saylor!" Bethany jabs her in the side. Not hard though 'cause Saylor just laughs.

"What! It's the same way I feel about Marcus Scribner. I'm not about to run off with him and neither are you. Anyway, I'm gonna go find Rhys. Byeeeee." Saylor skips off to the locker room, leaving Bethany and me alone on the corner of the court.

"Another crush I have to worry about?" I joke, kinda.

"No, absolutely not. He's— No. I'm gonna grab my stuff and then go home and shower. You wanna come—to my house! Not to the shower. Just to my house to do homework or something."

"Yeah, sure. I'll meet you in the parking lot."

"Sounds good."

I head back down to the yearbook office and get my stuff and then go wait by Bethany's car. Looking back at the school, people leaving practice, teachers leaving for the day, I think about all the times I met up with Poppy and the times I met up with Saylor almost in this exact same spot. Just standing here, thinking I should have left school to go meet up with Axel and Heaven. Or even my sister. I want this time to be different.

When I see Bethany coming out of the gym doors, I know I won't be dealing with any doubts or what-ifs a week or a month from now. This is exactly where I want to be.

o o o

When I get to her house, Bethany gives me another tour of her kitchen, then runs upstairs to shower. I sit down at the kitchen island and try to read through the script Mr. Wei gave me, but I can't focus. I pick up my phone instead and bounce back and forth between TikTok and the school's IG account. I'm still scrolling when Bethany comes back into the kitchen. She's changed into this pink sweat suit she looks pretty comfortable in. And cute. She looks really cute.

"There we go. Fresh, clean, and baby soft," she says as she comes over to the side of the island.

I try to give a casual nod in agreement. "You smell nice too." It's an understatement. She smells amazing. Like mangoes and spring rain or something. It's good.

"Thanks. My whole bathroom is just skincare products and smell goods. It's one of my happy places."

She looks over my shoulder at the script pages I'm supposed to be reading. "For film lab?"

"Yeah, just some sample scripts Mr. Wei gave me. Two different drafts of the same thing. I gotta find that emotion I'm missing."

"I bet you're getting lost in the technical side while you're writing, huh?"

I sit back and look at her, shocked. "Yeah, I think that's it. I can see that story in frames and shots, but that's kinda it. Getting it on paper is hard."

"Reverse engineer it. I mean, do whatever Mr. Wei suggested, but when I get stuck on something I don't understand, I work it backwards. If you can visualize how you would film something on the technical side, why not think of what kind of emotions you want to come through at the end and then work backwards?"

I blink and then look down at the pages like a whole new world has been opened up to me. "I think I'm gonna try that. Thanks."

"Sure. It's the least I can do as your supercool girlfriend," she says with a smile.

I laugh and fiddle with the edge of the script pages. "So, day one. Or is it day two of our supersmart plan?"

"Right. Serious relationship business. It's day two," she says. "And thanks for coming over. Today was really eye-opening. We needed to talk somewhere where the hallways don't have ears."

"Yeah, I got called a *slutty slut*." I tell her about the weird conversation I had in the yearbook office. I was glad Troy and Madlyn were already gone when I came back to get my stuff.

"I don't think Troy or Madlyn know what a slut is, but yeah, I learned some pretty interesting and crucial information for my own files." She tells me about the stuff Glory and Saylor told her, the rumors about her not being allowed to date. "I see how that's gotten me to this point, but I still need this practice. That's why I wanted you to come over. We should make out."

"Oh. What?" I feel like I heard her wrong.

"We should make out. Seems like the after-school activity of choice for the average high school couple. And I need to get comfortable with it. Let's get to kissing. Come on." She turns and grabs her backpack.

I stand up too quickly and almost knock over the stool. "No," I blurt out without thinking.

Bethany slowly turns around. "Okay. We can do something else."

Okay, so the blurting was too forceful, but I stand by my decision. But now I feel bad because I definitely hurt her feelings. She swallows hard and hikes her backpack higher on her shoulder. I walk around the island and go right to her side. "I didn't mean it like that. I do want to kiss you. Remember I said I was gonna kiss you later?"

"You did mention that," she says with a little smile.

"It's just before, with other people, it was like this every day. Leave school. Make out. Leave school. Make out. And don't get me wrong, I like the making out." That makes her laugh. "I was just doing the making out and then I got dumped 'cause I wasn't doing more than making out fast enough. And then I did the making out and I got dumped because I didn't actually say anything."

Her lips twist to the side in this really adorable way and she lets out a little sigh. "No, I get that."

I step closer and put my hand on her shoulder. "I just don't want to be used for my sexy body. My slutty days are behind me."

"No, you're right. And I'm sorry for being so pushy about it. Sometimes I get so in my head I think if I don't just say something, I'll never say it. I spent my whole shower thinking of how to tell you that I'm really nervous about being a bad kisser and I think I need practice, and instead I just came down here and disrespected your person."

"See, that actually makes sense. Let me just grab my stuff and then we'll go make out."

"What do you need your stuff for?" she asks. I shove the scripts and my notebook back into my bag.

"We gotta at least pretend we're doing our homework and then we make out. Also, if your moms come home, everything will already be out and in place."

"Oh, one mom is back on the road and the other mom has to do TV things until ten o'clock. We can do whatever until I have to kick you out at nine. One mom knows you're here. She will check the driveway cameras."

"That's plenty of time to work up to the making out." I take Bethany's hand. "Lead the way."

22
BETHANY
(is pleasantly surprised)

We head to the living room and we put on *Stranger Things* from the beginning. Good background noise since we've both watched every episode twice. We sit on the floor between the couch and the coffee table Momlissa spent a week agonizing over before buying. We spread out our books, I pull out my laptop, and we do get some work done. I try not to bother him while he's reading through this sample script Mr. Wei gave him. I get part way through my English reading.

It's hard because I'm so aware of him, which seems so weird because a week ago he felt like just another person who would ignore me if it wasn't for my friends. I've hung out with Landon and Oliver and their friends plenty of times, but it's never just been me and a boy. Me and my complicated boyfriend, for the next thirty-five days.

I catch myself looking at him. The side of his head really. His long hair is back in a loose ponytail and a few strands are trying to escape. I think about Glory and how easily and *constantly* she touches Landon. How Tatum and Emily have this cute thing they do where they touch fingertips when they think no one is looking. I want that, I realize. Not those same exact things, but I want it to feel easy to be around someone like that.

Thirty-five days and maybe I'll be brave enough to go looking for it. And maybe now that people know my moms haven't banned me from the dating pool, someone special and really cute will want to be that easy and constant with me.

Jacob catches me staring. He doesn't say anything though. He just scoots closer and puts his hand on my knee, then goes back to making notes on his script. I focus back on the TV where Joyce is absolutely losing it looking for Will, trying to ignore Jacob's fingers on my leg. His long, slender fingers. I can feel the warmth through the fabric of my sweatpants. The focusing is not working, but thank god, he turns around and looks at me again.

He scoots even closer. And then he kisses me.

And then we make out. We make out. So much.

23
BETHANY
(is full of thoughts—specific thoughts)

I can't stop touching my lips. They don't feel as puffy as they did when Jacob finally went home at nine fifteen, but they feel smooth in this new way, like we kissed so much I feel so nasty. In a good way.

I didn't ask Jacob if he thinks I'm a good kisser. He kept kissing me, so I think that's the answer to my question. I have nothing to compare it to, but I liked kissing him a lot.

I skim my fingers over my lips again as I look at the TikTok of two huskies screaming in this poor golden retriever's face. The group chat is lively as ever. Rhys told Saylor she was the most beautiful girl in the world, which is very sweet. Tatum has a hot tip about a pregnancy test someone left in the bathroom. It was negative, but that's a great way to get halls talking. Landon's birthday is coming up and Glory isn't sure what to get him. His parents get him whatever he wants. It makes it hard to shop for him.

I switch over to my conversation with Jacob.

> When's your birthday?

Aug 12. When's yours?

Feb 17. Same as Michael Jordan.

Oh man, basketball is your destiny.

Noooooo.

Not that it's important, because all of this ends in a little over thirty-five days, but I skip over to google his zodiac sign and then I look to see if Leo and Aquarius are compatible. Not that it matters, but it seems like we could have our ups and downs but definitely have what it takes to go the distance. Not that it matters.

"Bets!" Momlissa's home. I lock my phone and head out into the hallway just as she makes her way up the stairs.

"Heylo," I say. It's weird being the only one to greet her now. Our house used to be so loud and full and now it's just me. It sucks when sisters do things like grow up and go to college. I walk right into Momlissa's arms in the middle of the hall and she kisses my forehead. I want to be like her one day. Not working at NSN, but she used to be kinda *scrappy*. That's what my grandpa used to say, and now she's so glamorous and fancy. She's on camera talking in coherent sentences every day. Meanwhile, the idea of public speaking makes me nauseous. I'm hoping at some point her confidence will rub off on me the way it rubbed off on Trinity. She's not afraid of anything.

"Hey, sweetie! Did you catch the game?"

"I watched a little bit of it. Jacob and I were mostly studying," I say. I follow her to her bedroom and plop down at the foot of her bed. "I saw Trace foul out."

"Yeah, they coulda used him. Winning by one is still winning." I glance at my phone while she walks into her closet. There's a new notification from Tatum but nothing from Jacob. My mom comes back a second later and tosses some neatly folded pajamas on the bed next to me. "So when were you gonna tell me that Saylor's boyfriend is now your boyfriend? And is there a reason you're ignoring your sisters' texts? Joc told me you've been mysteriously busy all day."

"I mean, I had a very full day," I tell her. "And really the situation between me and Jacob is no big deal. We're just hanging out."

"That's not what Cris said." What I wouldn't pay for Saylor's mom to stay out of our business for like an hour.

"Mom. I mean this in the most respectful way, I swear."

"Oh, this is gonna be good," she says, rolling her eyes. "Go ahead."

"We gotta get you and Cris a new hobby. The two of you just texting each other back and forth and back and forth about the lives of teenagers? I mean, come on, Mom. Let's do better."

"Uh, no. See, if you ever decide to get married or have a family, you'll realize the only way for that situation to be a safe and healthy place is to walk away from the mess, from the drama. In order to make up for it, I get to invest in the mess that belongs to the teenagers who live in my house. I get to be a little nosy." She stops next to her dresser and takes off her earrings. "Do we need to have the talk again?" she says all light and breezy, because she's a cool mom.

"No," I say, shaking my head. The moms sat my sisters and me down, more than once, and gave us the most comprehensive sex talks. Honestly that might be a part of what scared me off boys. Mama T presented the whole thing with the same professional intensity she applies to coaching. There were diagrams, there were videos, and of course, Jocelyn had questions and the moms had answers. It was all good information, and I do know I can ask my moms anything, but geez it was a lot. "I don't think I'm ready for any of that," I tell her truthfully.

The making out is A plus material, but I'm glad that's where we stopped. I can see why Jacob didn't like being pressured to go faster and further before he was ready.

"Okay, well. I'm gonna leave things in your bathroom just in case. And you let me know if you need a refresher course on anything. Safe is best, yeah?"

"Yeah." I stand up to head back to my room when Momlissa's phone starts ringing.

"It's Mama." She tosses the phone to me and heads into the bathroom. I hit accept. Mama T smiles as soon as she sees me.

"Bethany. Hey, baby."

"Hey, Mom. How's Vegas?"

"Meh. It'll be nice to be home. How were tryouts today?"

"Oh yeah." Momlissa pokes her head out of the bathroom. She's mid-makeup-removal. "I was so focused on your situationship, I forgot to ask you about practice."

"What situationship?" Mama T asks. Clearly, she wasn't looped into my business today.

"Jacob and I are just hanging out. Tryouts were great. I did great. I'm pretty sure I will make varsity again. There's this freshman Tikah Hollis who is really good, so hopefully we get her on the team. Everything's great. I can smell another winning season."

"Good. Did you finish that ham that's in the fridge?"

"No," I say confused. "I think I have enough for two more lunches. Why?"

"Okay, you should switch it out for something with less sodium now that the season's started." I'm not sure what stings more, that she only wants to talk to me about basketball or that she thinks the one thing that brings me a unique kind of joy is the thing that is gonna tank my basketball career.

"Teresa," Momlissa says. I try not to think about how much they talk about my weight and supporting my body positivity or whatever when I'm not around, but Mama T is still in coaching mode. Not am-I-giving-my-daughter-a-complex-that-will-take-years-of-therapy-to-fix mode.

"I'm just saying. You'll feel better on the court if you're eating more balanced foods. Excessive salt can really do a number on you."

"This weekend I will roast a whole chicken," I say.

"You don't have to do that."

I kinda want to, I almost say. Chef Evie has this lemon chicken recipe I really want to try.

"You can eat whatever you want, Bets," Momlissa says, before she raises her voice so Mama T can hear her clearly. "Your mom seems to have forgotten the Crunchwrap Supreme eating contests she had with a few girls on our team right in the middle of March Madness. Everyone survived."

"Yeah, I won't be doing that, but I hear you. I'm gonna go get in bed. Deli meats or not, I need plenty of sleep. I'm a growing girl."

"I'll see you soon. Love you," Mama T says.

"Love you too," I reply, with maybe a little less enthusiasm. I kiss Momlissa on her makeup-free cheek and hand her back her phone. It's quiet as I walk back to my room and I'm sure she's waiting for my door to close before they start talking about me. I guess I got off easy because Mama T didn't grill me about Jacob, but the rest wasn't so fun.

I wash my face and brush my teeth, then apply moisturizer and this fancy, sponsored cream sleep mask Cris let me have. I apply some fresh lip balm too and remind myself to stop touching my lips. I climb into bed and finally text my sisters back.

> Yes, I have a boyfriend.
> And yes we are super cute.

I send them the picture Jacob took of the pictures of us from the photo booth. I think Trin's asleep. UConn's season has already started, but Joc is still in our time zone. She texts back right away.

> Oh the yearbook kid!
> Nice work, Bets.
> You two are adorable.
> He got CUTE.

And for the next thirty-five days, he's all mine. And so far, he doesn't care what kind of deli meats I choose for my sandwiches.

24
BETHANY
(makes the roster)

Thursday at four-thirty p.m. PST, I make the Culver City High School Minotaurs Varsity Basketball team. We get our jerseys tomorrow right before our first scrimmage with Hamilton, and we have team pictures on Monday. Coach Miller assures me that I'll get my number thirty-four back. I pretend to be excited, especially when he yells Bethany "the Beast" Greene is back. Saylor and Emily snicker at the face I make when he says it. They make the team too. It's all jokes in theory, but I'm still trying to think about how far I can get in my car before my moms know I'm gone. If I leave right away, I could get to Mexico before curfew. Might not even have to stop for gas.

I'd miss my friends though.

I'm not sure I'm to the missing-you phase of things with Jacob, but I'd think about him a lot. Maybe I'd write him a few letters.

He's waiting for me when I come off the court, camera in hand. Like he's been every day this week. I know it's just for yearbook. He told me the schedule. He and Noah trade off checking out the soccer teams, and Jacob has basketball while Noah has water polo. It's all very professional, but it's good to have an example of what it would be like to have a boyfriend waiting for me after practice. I don't hate it. I've decided to ignore the glitter butterflies that spark up in my stomach every time I see him walking into the gym. Or when I'm running back up the court and he's just there. He keeps it cool. No dramatic waving or anything. But I know he knows I saw him. It's a whole dance, but I'm learning a lot.

I'm also learning a lot about the attention span of my fellow students. Jacob was right. It took about two days for people to get over the shock of us being together, mostly because yesterday morning during second period Chris Porter thought it would be a good idea to take a Viagra pill he stole from his dad. By the time lunch came around, he was in the office crying because he couldn't sit down right and his mom had to come pick him up and take him to the doctor. Or so I heard. I also heard it was a dare. I'm mostly glad I didn't have to witness any part of it. Still, Chris's very bad life choices have taken the heat off us.

I stand in the middle of the court listening to Coach Miller and the JV Coach, Mr. McGuinn, saying what they have to say about work ethic and drive. I won't lie. I tune out. I'm waiting to steal a few seconds with Jacob before I have to go home. We huddle up, hands in, *"Go Minotaurs!"* and all that, then practice is finally over. I very, very calmly stroll on over to my boyfriend.

"Fancy meeting you here," I say.

"Yeah, I just happened to be in the neighborhood."

"You get anything good?" I ask him, nodding toward his camera. "I mean, I know you did, but I wanna see."

"Here." He tilts the display in my direction, showing me the picture he got of me while I was getting into position to guard Tikah Hollis, the new freshman who also made the team. Sweat is pouring down my face. I'm bent at the waist, one arm out in Tikah's direction, and my eyes are on Coach. I've been in the local paper three times and each time I looked like a cased sausage in a jersey, looking for the easiest escape. This picture makes me look kinda cool.

"Don't show this to anyone," I tell him.

"Why?" He laughs.

"Because I look like I'm enjoying this whole sports thing," I whisper. I'm joking, but when I look up, Jacob's frowning.

"Are you okay?" he asks. "Noah and I went over the winter schedules. It's a lot of games."

"Yeah," I say, wiping my forehead again. "I don't really have a choice. At least my moms will be happy and I can help the seniors look good in front of any potential scouts. It's a win-win."

He doesn't say anything, but the look on his face tells me he's not buying it. I do appreciate that he keeps his thoughts about this to himself, because there is nothing I can do about it. I'm a Greene. Basketball is what I'm supposed to do. On the court is where I belong.

"Jacob, can we borrow your girlfriend for a few minutes?" Dylan asks. She's gonna be named captain for sure. "We gotta huddle up in the locker room."

"Yeah, sure," he says with a smile before he tells me he'll text me later. Mama T's home tonight, so I have to get in some quality time with her before she's back on her own court. It's a shame really. I like hanging out with him. Even if it is just as friends. He's easy to be around and he actually listens to me when I talk. And then there's the kissing. We've gotten a lot of practice with the kissing this week. I'm sad we have to put it on pause since I barely see him during school, but hopefully we can make up for it this weekend. For research purposes.

I let Dylan tug me to the locker room and only look back once to see Jacob showing Landon, Oliver, and Kayden the pictures I'm guessing he took of their practice. It would be weird if I asked him to send me the pictures of Oliver and Kayden, but I do think about it for a split second.

25
JACOB
(creates a distraction)

"Hey, you all right?"

I blink and look over at my dad standing in my doorway. "Hey, yeah. I was just thinking." I look up at my monitor, at the script I was trying to fix before I zoned out. I was able to point out the differences in the scripts Mr. Wei gave me and I thought I'd try to reverse engineer the last script I handed in, just like Bethany suggested, but I can't stop thinking about her and this whole basketball thing.

Maybe it's none of my business, but it sucks to see her put her all into something she hates so much. I wouldn't know how to tell her moms I hate the thing they built their whole life around either. I just wish there was some way I could help make all this easier for her. Show her how much the team appreciates her. Or maybe convince her to talk to her parents.

"You looked like you were focusing pretty hard there," Dad says. He comes into my room and sits on my bed. Maybe I was thinking so hard I forgot I screwed something up. He only comes in and sits down when he's about to launch into a dad talk. I don't get them very often. Esther gets them all the time 'cause she can't stop being a smart-ass at school.

"I was just thinking about this weekend."

"Yeah, about that," he says before he winces, rubbing the tattoos on his knuckles. This is gonna be bad. We-have-reason-to-believe-you've-been-doing-something-illegal bad. I start searching my memory. Did I not lock Mom's car and it got stolen? Did I run a red-light cam? There's a gnarly one not too far away. "I know you and Bethany have been hanging out a lot this week—I still want to meet her, by the way."

"Uh, sure. We've been going over to her house, but I'll bring her here sometime. Or we'll swing by the shop."

"Cool. So yeah. I don't know if you have plans this weekend, but I need you to stay home with Esther."

"Ugh. Dad," I whine. Esther is old enough to be home alone and old enough not to burn the place down. "Why?"

Dad sighs and I know it's bad. "She helped a kid cheat. That kid is in bigger trouble with the teacher, but your sister is in big trouble with us. She was supposed to spend the weekend with one of her friends, but your mom said no."

"So I'm grounded too?" Now we both have to pay the price for her being a smart-ass.

"No, you're not grounded. I just can't have her at the shop. We're busy this weekend. And I don't trust her not to mess with the security system and sneak out a window."

"So Friday and Saturday night it's me and Esther?"

"No, that's the good part. You can have your friends over! And Bethany! Esther just needs to stay in the house. No TV, no devices. She can rediscover the magic of reading. A paperback. She can't use your mom's Kindle either."

"Yeah, okay." I sigh. "I'll stay home with her."

"Thanks, man. What were you doing when I came in here?"

"Thinking of what I wanted to do with Bethany this weekend."

"Oh, my bad. Sorry."

"It's okay. Nothing a new custom deck with some Sector 9 components won't fix." My current skateboard is fine, but there's never a bad time for bribery. Maybe Esther and I have more in common than I realize.

"Uhhh, I'll think about it."

"You know what you could help me with? Can you draw something for me?"

"Yeah, sure. Let's go down to the Thunderdome."

I grab my phone and follow him down the hall to the art studio/office he shares with Mom off their bedroom. I don't think I can fix all of Bethany's problems, but I can give her something handmade. From my dad.

o o o

Dad is almost finished with his masterpiece when Bethany texts me to let me know she's done with moms time. She tells me to FaceTime her whenever I'm free, if I want to. I do. Dad and I finish up our art project, then I head back to my room and call Bethany. She's back in her closet again, but this time she has on one of those pink clay face masks. Her braids are pushed back with this headband thing that has cat ears.

"Did I catch you at a bad time?" I laugh.

"I think you deserve to see the true me," she says. "Night-time is the right time for skincare. It helps me relax."

"I dig it. How was it with your moms?"

"Good and awful. I love my moms. I love spending time with them. I don't love talking about basketball right after I get out of practice and during dinner. You know what we did after dinner?"

"What?" I ask her.

"We watched basketball."

I choke on laughter. "Okay. You weren't joking. It's really basketball, all the time."

"And it's like this every year. I'm in hell, Jacob."

"I can't shut down the NBA—"

"I don't want that. Mama T loves her job. I just need some sort of, like, laser ray or a magic box that makes it so I don't have to participate."

"I'll get right in the lab first thing in the morning."

"Thanks. 'Preciate it." She lets out this cute sigh and I wish I was there in her room with her. I want to kiss her, even with her clay mask. "How was your night?"

"I got some pretty devastating news. I have to watch my sister tomorrow after school and all day and night Saturday, until the shop closes." I tell her how Esther's mega-grounded and I'm officially her jailer. Tell her about the silver lining, that she can come over and hang out. If she wants to.

"Oh, sure. You've been at my house all week. Only seems fair that we sit on your couch every once in a while."

"You don't have a little sister lurking around, so going to your house seems like the right move."

"Hey! I'm a little sister. It's not as easy as it looks."

"Right. Sorry."

"It's okay. I forgive you," she says. I watch her as she goes to tuck her fist under her chin, but she remembers she has that mask on and drops her hand. "Unrelated. Or maybe kinda related. I had to make an executive decision."

"Yeah, about what?"

"Us. I've decided I have to think about you as two different people. Jacob who is, you know, you, and the other you who is the Boyfriend with a capital *B*."

"Yeah, you might have to explain," I say, 'cause I'm kinda confused and so is the other me with a capital *M*.

"Well, 'cause I like you. As a person. Not just a certified hottie with great hair," Bethany says.

"Thanks. I like you too. I like your hot face and your hair too."

"Thanks. But we're still working on a plan here, for the next thirty-two days. When the time comes, I have to let go of Boyfriend. But I still want to be friends with Jacob and still hang out. If you want to."

"I do. I was thinking about that too. Like, when it's over, do we just stop talking?" I tell her. I leave out the part where I'm worried she won't want to talk to me anymore. That someone like Oliver will finally say yes to her and then it's like none of this ever happened. I don't want that. "We weren't that tight before. Though it was my idea, I thought this was gonna be weird, but it's not."

"Right?!"

"I like hanging out with you. And Saylor and your other friends aren't treating me any different. Glory said hey to me in the hall this morning."

"Good." She smiles. "I don't want it to be weird, even if it did start off that way. But that's not the only part."

"Hit me with the rest of your plan." I move to my sack chair and get comfortable.

"I was thinking some more after I tried to bully you into making out and here's where I've landed. If I have a thought, about us, I can stop and see if this is a Boyfriend thought or a Jacob thought. And then I can have some clarity before I open my mouth. If that makes sense."

"No, it does. That's really smart."

"Like I wanna hang out with Jacob this weekend and I'm nervous about what it's like to be around a boyfriend's sister in a real way."

"I heard her tell my mom you seem pretty cool, so I think you've already won her over."

"Oh, thank god. A little sister can really make or break a situation."

"But I like what you said," I say, mostly because it will help when I'm struggling between thinking about Bethany as a friend and my girlfriend partner-in-plan. Which I can see happening a lot. Maybe I need to hang up a picture of Oliver Gutierrez in my room so I don't forget who she's doing this all for. And then I realize that would be weird and would maybe lead to another awkward, yet supportive, dad talk. "I'm gonna have to use that."

"Thanks. My gut reactions get me in trouble sometimes," Bethany replies.

"Yeah, you and my sister will get along fine." I laugh.

26
BETHANY
(tries to put on her game face)

've only seen Jacob a couple times today. If this were a true long-term thing, we'd have to coordinate our schedules next semester because not seeing each other after stats, except for maybe once or twice a week, is BS. Anyway, we have like no time to grab our stuff and get on the bus to Hamilton, and I just wanna say bye to him real quick before we go. He said he had to give me something before we left. We agreed to meet outside the locker rooms. I'm here and he isn't.

The boys have home court today for their scrimmage. I'm not worried about the game itself. I'll do what I have to and hate every second of it, and I'll have the bright spot of seeing Hamilton's team discover the secret weapon we have in Tikah Hollis. It'll be pretty dope. Part of me wants to have a terrible game, on a personal level, but I know that won't happen. I'm incapable of not trying my best. We'll just have to win, I guess, and my sports-related suffering will continue.

I'm about to text Jacob when I see Tatum coming right for me. "You Hamilton ready?" they ask.

"Yeah, sure, whatever. I'm waiting for Jacob. We're supposed to meet before we go."

"Oh." They laugh. "He was right behind me when I came out of art." Just then I see him at the end of the hall. "There he goes."

I don't think he's spotted me yet, but he picks that exact moment to do this entirely erotic hair flip. He usually keeps it up, but maybe he lost his hair tie during the day.

"Okay, that was hot," Tatum says.

"Yeah, I'm in trouble." I let out a deep breath and pray to all the gods that he just wanted to tell me good luck or give me street parking tips for when I get to his house later. We're gonna watch a movie and make sure his sister has absolutely no fun.

He says hey to Tatum and me when he reaches us and then he hands me this giant handmade black envelope with the word GIRLFRIEND written in gold pen.

"Holy hell. That's cute. I'll give you guys a minute," Tatum says before they head off to get ready to cheer at the boys' scrimmage. I mutter a thanks. I can't take my eyes off the envelope.

"What's this?" I look up just as he pulls his hair band out of his pocket and ties his tresses back. I don't know why, but the act of it is so hot.

"Open it."

I open it. Inside there's this big, square card. On it, there's this really cute illustration with a jar of peanut butter and a jar of strawberry jam standing on top of a sandwich. The sandwich is on top of a skateboard. There are little hearts hovering over both the jars' heads. Underneath it says JUST CALL ME PEANUT BUTTER BECAUSE YOU'RE MY JAM.

"Are you kidding me?" I whisper, and then I start tearing up.

"Don't cry!" Jacob laughs.

"What did I tell you? I cry at anything and everything." I try to keep it together, but my own laugh shakes a few tears loose. I wipe them away quickly.

"Happy tears this time. Right?"

"Uh, yeah. This is so cute. I love it."

He steps a bit closer and lowers his voice. "I know you can't get out of the scrimmage or the season. But Jacob to Bethany, I just want you to know that you're pretty cool with or without your skills on the court."

And, of course, a few more tears jump out. "Okay, so your girlfriend and your friend really want to hug you right now."

He doesn't say anything. He just closes the small space between us and wraps his arms around me. He sort of held me during the dance, but that was more in a formal way. Considering all the kissing we've been doing, it's kind of wild we haven't hugged yet, but this feels like a real first. No boy has ever hugged me like this before. I've gotten a lot of weird one-armed side hugs and those loose, no-contact air hugs.

I'll never, ever tell him this. But sometimes people don't want to touch you when you're fat. Like they're afraid your fat is gonna rub off on them. Or worse, if they touch your skin, you'll turn into some old-school movie blob and just inhale them into your body. Even if I could do that, I wouldn't, because gross. I don't know where you've been. You could have crud on your shoes or never wash your hands.

Too bad they don't know how much they're missing out. I give great hugs and I'm really soft. Soft with the highest rebound average in Lady Minotaurs history. I'm really the whole package. In the back of my mind, I know this is actually why Saylor and I clicked. She hugs me all the time. She let me know, back when my baby fat was cute and not what some people consider to be a problem, that she loved me for me.

And now Jacob hugs me for real. He gives me the perfect squeeze and I just sort of melt into how warm he is. He's wearing an Ink & Pearl hoodie. The zipper scratches my cheek and I cannot bring myself to care. Still, I have to force myself to step back. It's gonna be hard to pass or dribble with my arms around him. I look at the drawing again.

"You really made this for me?"

"Okay, I gotta come clean there. My dad drew it for me. But the concept was my idea."

"It's really cute your dad helped. Can you hold on to it for me and I'll get it from your house tonight? I don't want it to get messed up in my bag."

"Yeah, sure." He takes it and carefully slips it back into the envelope. And then he kisses me on my cheek. I don't walk out to the bus. I float.

o o o

We win the scrimmage. Yeah, sweet, whatever. We hype
Tikah up for her game-winning basket on the bus, but after the driver politely tells us to do our celebrating sitting
down, I do the kinda desperate thing and text Jacob. I have
to thank him. I was on such a high from that super sweet
card and that hug, my team thought I was actually excited
to play. Maybe if I just have Jacob hug me before every
game for the rest of my life, I can make it through this whole
basketball thing.

> On our way back.
> Just gonna shower
> And then I'll come over.

I'm psyched.
We're gonna order pizza.

> You need me to bring snacks?

Nah. My dad stocked the
kitchen to bribe me.
Just need you.

> Boyfriend or Jacob?

I'm playing with fire. I know it, but I send the text anyway. My heart camps out in my throat while he's texting

back. I wait for the worst. The premature friend-zoning, but that's not what happens.

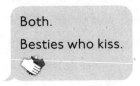

Both.

Besties who kiss.

My teammates are screaming the words to some TikTok sound, so they don't hear me snort. I text him back.

So romantic.
I'll text you when I'm on my way.

And then I take a real big gamble and send a few hearts. He sends a heart back and the little sandwich emoji. I have to remind myself that in thirty-whatever days, when this is over, I want my next boyfriend to send me perfectly appropriate emojis too.

Emily and Saylor have their own romantic plans for the night. Tatum is waiting for Emily in the parking lot the second we get back. Say hasn't made things official with old Tuba Lips, but she and Rhys seem pretty into each other. I don't feel bad about the way I power walk straight to my car and drive as fast—and safely—as humanly possible back to my house. I text the moms to let them know I'll be at Jacob's. It's a working night for them both.

I make the rookie mistake of taking a hot shower and am sweating anew by the time I get out. The AC is on, but the duct in my room gives more of a light breeze than the gust I need to cool off. I grab the fan from Jocelyn's room and put it on high, trying to cool off as I lotion up. I tell myself to breathe and slow down. To help with the sweating and so I don't run out of the house in mismatched socks. The outfit selection is crucial. Jeans and a white crop tee that shows the perfect sliver of my belly and an Ivy Park hoodie Trinity got me for my birthday a few years back. A little TLC for my edges, and I grab my stuff and go. I have to make one stop on the way.

I don't know if he was waiting by the door, but he steps out onto the porch and closes the door behind him just as I walk up the side of the driveway.

"Hey," I say, trying to sound completely normal.

"Hey." Jacob smiles and I'm cool. I swear everything is cool. He comes down the steps and he kisses me. It's quick, but perfect. And then he reaches for the Ralphs bag in my hand, like a true gentleman. "You want me to grab that?"

I hand it to him. "I might be trying to bribe Esther in my own way."

"Oh yeah?" He laughs.

I nod toward the bag and then hold up my Caboodles in my other hand. "Cookie sundaes and makeup."

"Genius. That's why I came out here. Esther is gonna try and be cool about you being here, but she asked me seventeen times when you were coming over. She really wants to hang out with you."

"As long as I get to hang out with you too."

"Actually, I was gonna leave. Good luck."

"Funny. Let's go." I follow Jacob inside and he leads me into the kitchen.

"Can I ask how the game was?" he says. I watch him put the ice cream and the cookie dough in the fridge.

"Fine. I mean, good. Tikah and Dylan and I work really well together, so of course that's terrible. We're looking at another winning season," I reply. Just then Esther comes strolling into the room. She has a big picture frame in her hands. This is the first time I've seen her since Halloween. No white wig, but her hair is bleached blonde with pink streaks. The hair of a true middle school outlaw. She sets the frame on the counter. It's the card, with the envelope tucked behind it, nicely mounted inside.

"I told him he should frame it for you," Esther says, her tone telling me she knows she made the right call.

"We stopped at Target on the way home," Jacob explains. He steps beside me and puts his arm on my shoulder. It feels natural to put my arm around his waist.

"I heard you're banned from all forms of visual entertainment?" I tell Esther.

"Just because I tried to help my fellow students. I did it for free too! I could have made him pay me."

I try not to laugh because I'm supposed to be the mature one here, setting a good example and all that.

"Well, I thought I could do your makeup."

"Hmm, I don't hate that plan, but I have a better idea. Let's do Jacob's makeup." The devious look on her face finally breaks me.

"Great. Let's do it." I slap the edge of the counter and look up at him. "Come on. You're gonna look gorgeous."

"I don't get a vote?" Jacob asks.

"You can do my makeup after."

"Hmm, okay, deal."

"Yessss," Esther whispers. She runs to get her own small makeup collection. The pizza arrives while I'm showing her my eyeliners. We eat and then Esther and I make cookies in the air fryer and have our sundaes. Esther details the totality of her crimes. And then it's time to transform Jacob's true beauty.

In the end, Jacob looks glamorous. I look like I was attacked by a four-year-old with crayons. It's the best time I've had in a long time.

27
JACOB
(hatches one heck of a plan)

don't know if I'm doing too much asking Bethany if she wants to come over again on Saturday, but she says yes. She has to eat brunch with her moms first, but then she'll be over. She's cool with Axel, Valentina, and Heaven coming over too. I won't lie, I am nervous about throwing them all together, but both Boyfriend Jacob and Jacob Jacob need to give this a try. My friends didn't vibe with Poppy or Saylor and I think I was too stressed out to really try a little harder to see if there was some common ground there. I didn't try at all, actually. I thought if I just followed Saylor and Poppy around, things would just work out. Everyone would just be happy. I know now that makes no sense.

I think my friends will get along with Bethany, but I need to be ready for this all to blow up in my face. At least I feel like I can talk to Bethany about it if it goes south. She talks a lot, but she really does listen. She let Esther talk her face off all night and talked Esther's face off just as much. They get along great. But I know that she'll hear me out if something goes down with my friends. Still, I'm praying it all goes well.

I have a bunch of notifications on my phone when I get

out of the shower. A text from Axel to our chat with Heaven, saying he and Valentina aren't coming. He sends a link to some information about how menstrual cramps can really take you out.

> Gonna chill with my lady on the couch til she's ready to kick some ass again.

I'm bummed they aren't coming, but I get it.

> I can respect that.
> Catch up at the park tomorrow.

> Fo sho.

There's a text from Bethany too.

> Running a little late.
> Be there soon-ish.

> It's all good.
> We'll be here.
> ♥
> 🔷
> 🦇
> ⛵

I finish getting dressed just as Heaven shows up. Pull my shirt on and go let her in.

"My girl Kelly leave already?" Heaven asks, stepping out of her sneakers. Heaven loves my mom. My mom loves Heaven.

"She had three appointments today. Dad left with her. He's got some big eight-hour back piece to work on."

"That's too long to have someone drilling your back."

"Says the dentist's kid," I joke.

"My mom never has anyone in her chair for eight hours." I shrug. "Eh. Not my back. Did you see Axel's text?"

"No, why?" She pulls her phone out of her back pocket and looks at the screen. "Oh, man, come on!"

"What?"

"It's just gonna be me and you and her. At least when Axel's around, he keeps things interesting."

"Bethany is interesting and she wants to hang out with you," I argue, because both things are true.

"Yeah, yeah. Whatever. I'll hang with Esther, I guess."

"Did someone say my name!" Esther says, barging into the hallway. Heaven high-fives her and I realize my sister is wearing the purple eye shadow Bethany gave to her last night.

"Hey, E. You hung out with her? What do you think?"

"Who? Bethany? She's cool." Esther shrugs like she's not thinking about putting together a We Love Bethany channel on YouTube.

The doorbell rings and I point to both of them. "Be cool." Heaven just rolls her eyes. I glare at her, then turn to open the door. It's Bethany. She smiles at me. Or at least she tries. Something's wrong.

"Hey. You okay?"

"Yeah." She is not okay. "Hey, Heaven. Hey, Esther. Nice to see you." This kind of hilarious laugh sputters out of her and then she starts crying. I pull her inside and even though she's almost sobbing she remembers to take off her sneakers. I hug her then and she hugs me back, hiccupping against my chest.

"Oh hell," I hear Heaven say before she steps behind Bethany and hugs us both. It's a stretch 'cause Bethany has her backpack on, but she makes it work.

"Hey, let me in," Esther says before putting her arms into the mix. Bethany starts laughing harder through her sniffles.

"Okay, this is amazing. I feel really supported, but I can't breathe." We all disengage, but I take her hand and lead her into the TV room. I direct her to our big armchair and sit down on the ottoman in front of her.

"What's going on?" I ask.

She looks behind me, where Heaven and Esther have flopped down onto the couch. "It's about that thing I told you about that I haven't told anyone else."

"Do we need to call the FBI tip line?" Heaven asks.

"No." Bethany laughs. "We don't need to get the Feds involved. It's just some stuff with my moms and my extra-curriculars."

"Before you go on, is what you're about to say going to change my opinion on thee Melissa Greene, because she is my gay idol. And I can't handle any more disappointments."

Bethany chuckles again. "No. It's an issue with my other mom. Well, both of them, but no, I don't think this will challenge your love for her. I'll even get you her autograph."

"Ah, you're the best. Go on."

Bethany focuses back on me. "The tears are hard to turn off."

"It's fine. Flood the house. What happened?" I say as Esther shoves a box of tissues onto my lap.

"Nothing. We went to get brunch and my mom was, like, giving me crap for ordering waffles. I love waffles." She laughs and more tears run down her face. I shouldn't be laughing, but I do. Then I hand her a tissue. She wipes her cheeks. "I don't think she cares that I'm fat, but she cares if my diet doesn't support optimal performance on the court and it's, like, lady, I had hella rebounds yesterday and you're upset because of a waffle. And some bacon. The waffle came with a side of bacon. It was good."

"My mom does that too except she uses my teeth as an excuse. And then my dad starts talking about food acidity and I just know if I was skinny they wouldn't bother me about it," Heaven says.

Heaven and Bethany have different body types, but I guess Heaven is plus size too. She's been the same size she is now since the sixth grade—same height, everything. Her mom thought skating would magically make her skinny, but that didn't happen. It doesn't change how good of a skater she is, though.

"What does your dad do?" Bethany asks.

"He's a food scientist." Heaven shrugs. "I mean, they're both cool, but a scientist and a dentist really know how to harsh your vibe when you just wanna know what SKITTLES mixed with Mountain Dew tastes like."

"Oh my god. That's neat and awful. I do love your mom though," Bethany confesses. "If you can believe it, I cry at the dentist. She's always so sweet about it."

"Yeah. She's good at her job."

"What happened after the waffles?" I ask Bethany.

"We went home and I was getting ready to come over and Mom Teresa was like, *You should get in a workout before you go.* Mom Melissa said I could leave, but they had, like, a mini argument about it right in front of me about how I need to take basketball more seriously, as if I'm skipping practices or something. I just—I don't want to do this for two more years."

"So don't," Heaven says.

"Yeah, not that easy." Bethany sniffles.

"Yes, it is." I almost tell Heaven to back off, but I agree with her in a way. "Legit what's the worst thing that could happen? I get disappointing your parents isn't fun and all that. I'm pretty sure my mom wishes she could give me back, but your moms aren't gonna kick you out if you stop playing a sport. You're not dealing to small school children. They'll be mad, but they'll get over it."

"Yeah, no. I don't think you understand what basketball means in our house. And they won't understand that I could possibly just be a normal human being without it."

"I think you should tell them about the cooking school,"

I say. Bethany just shakes her head, her shoulders slumping even more. Maybe I said the wrong thing.

"What cooking school?" Esther asks.

"It's nothing," Bethany says.

"I don't think it's nothing," I admit. I don't say it out loud, but I think if she took the time to email LA Cooking School, it means something.

"I have an idea," Heaven says.

Bethany sniffles again before she responds. "What's that?"

"If you wanna sell an idea, you have to come up with a good pitch," Heaven says. I glance back at her and try not to laugh at the big smile on her face. "Or you can do like me and bulldoze your way through life."

"Heaven might be onto something. I pitched a whole plan about film school to my parents," I tell Bethany.

"And you used your skate reel to get into that film class," Esther says.

"Right. And it worked, even if I'm stinking up his class big time. If you're cool with it, I can help you make a video pitch to your moms. You can tell them what's been bothering you about sports. Tell them about the cooking school, all that. They can watch it with or without you there. That way you don't get stage fright having to tell them straight out."

"Sounds like a good idea to me," Heaven adds.

"If they say no, then at least you tried," I say.

"Can I think about it?" Bethany asks.

"Yeah. It's just an idea. Or you can try something else, but just keeping it a secret doesn't look like it's working."

"You can cook something for them too!" Esther chimes in. "Like we did with the sundaes last night, but something fancier."

I look at Bethany and give her a *what do you think* tilt of my head.

"I made Momlissa a fancy sandwich once, and she did like it. I could try something more complicated." She looks down at the tissue and her hand, like she's actually considering it.

"We can shoot it here," I tell her.

"Hey, I'm happy to be a taste tester," Heaven offers.

"Me too," Esther says.

"I'm a punk, so I still need time to think about it. Anyway, I didn't mean to ruin your day with my sobbing. Just give me a minute and we can set off the fireworks I have in my backpack."

"You brought fireworks?!" Esther says, her whole face lighting up.

"I'm kidding, you little psycho. I did bring some nail polish though. And my homework because we do have a stats test on Monday."

"We can study, but we might have to sneak and let E watch a movie or something."

"Yesss. Let's break the law," my sister says.

"Can I get a glass of water first?" Bethany asks.

"Sure, come on."

She gives Esther a big ziplock bag of nail polish and then follows me into the kitchen. I lean against the counter while she chugs some water.

"I do not mean to spend the rest of this time between us crying. I promise," she says.

"Is this who you are?"

"Yeah. I'm one sobbing bitch." She laughs and fresh tears spring to her eyes.

"I know you think I'm annoyed, but the laughing and the crying together thing is cute. And seriously, I don't think repressing your emotions is a good idea. I saw Tagger Evans punch a locker the other day. I bet he'd handle things a little better if he just cried every once in a while."

"That is a very good point. I hung up your card in my room," she says, and I can feel myself turning a little red.

"Oh, cool. Esther made a good call with the frame."

"I do like that your whole family pitched in with the project. We still have to go on a first date."

"I know. I'll talk to my parents about it. Esther could be grounded forever. She's cool, but I'd rather be outdoors with you."

"Same." She chuckles. "Can I put in a formal request for a hug from my peanut butter boyfriend?"

"Come here, my little jar of jam." I laugh. I step closer and Bethany wraps her arms around me. I think about how Poppy used to say I was too skinny, but Bethany doesn't seem to mind. I hug her back and I think I'd be totally fine just holding her on the couch all day too, until she's ready to kick some ass again.

28
BETHANY

(has made mistakes, but this one feels like it really messed her up something good)

"Is LP okay?" Tatum asks before they look at me across our lunch table and nod at the orange slices I'm carefully peeling apart.

"Yeah, she's fine," Glory goes on. "But it was so scary and kind of hilarious. Like she busted her shit wide open and was still yelling at Tim the whole time. Holding her shin." Leigh-Payton Albright fell off the stage during *Little Shop* practice, which is horrible, but kind of funny, 'cause it happened while she was going off on her costar, Tim Wesley, in a way that was honestly the definition of doing too much. I only know because Ruby Allan recorded play rehearsal and posted the whole blowup on TikTok. I watched it twice to make sure Leigh-Payton didn't die and then I went back to focusing on my own problems.

I think I like Jacob. I think. I don't know. This stupid plan. It's working. We walk down the hall now holding hands and it feels right. Most of my weird fears about boys have been washed away. Not like my thoughts about the general evils of mankind. Stranger danger is still very real, but I now see that my crying about Glory and Lucas was pretty over the top and unnecessary. Not that Jacob and I are even close to doing it. But the other day, his hand accidentally brushed my boob and I didn't hate it.

We spent most of the weekend babysitting his sister, but I had fun. And even though Heaven was there, we spent most of Saturday on his couch, cuddled up watching movies. We let Esther sneak in and watch with us. Heaven did all of our nails. She's very skilled and precise. And then Heaven and I both quickly skimmed half of some novel about this little girl befriending a dragon and saving a whole fantasy world so Esther could report back to her dad about her reading progress.

I went home and texted Jacob until I fell asleep. We did our own thing on Sunday. Saylor came over and we studied while the moms did their courtside thing. The second Saylor left, I texted Jacob until the moms got home. And then we fell asleep talking to each other on FaceTime. Is this what it's like when you really like someone? You just want to talk to them all the time? You want to be around them whenever you can? And it's not just about the kissing, even though the kissing is good. I didn't get the full make out I wanted this weekend, for research purposes, but I did steal a few kisses here and there. They were worth it.

Everything is going great. Excellent, even. I'm learning so much, but thinking about Jacob nonstop is really harshing my whole situation. Getting all heart fluttery when I see him in the hall, almost being late for school because I'm standing half-dressed in my bedroom looking at the little peanut butter and jam hanging on my wall. Wondering if

he likes what I'm wearing. *Barf!* I am not supposed to care
about this at all, but he did tell me that he liked the way I co-
ordinated my shirt and my sweater jacket with my Jordans
this morning and it definitely made me blush. This feelings
crap is for the birds. Especially since I'm not supposed to
have warm and mushy feelings for Jacob at all. I kinda don't
want to acknowledge that I have to let Boyfriend Jacob go,
and the more I think about how hot he looks when he lets
his hair down and how good his hugs are, the more screwed
I know I am.

And the worst part! I can't tell my friends. This situation
is something I would absolutely run by the homies, and here
I am sitting on a big secret and big feelings. I'm in hell. The
best thing to do is remember the actual reality of our little
arrangement, no matter how depressing it is. Jacob doesn't
actually like me as more than a friend. And yes, I think the
friendship we're developing is good, but the kissing practice
and the hand-holding—all that is for Crybaby Bethany, not
him. And it seems like he's already better at asserting what
he actually wants when it comes to being around a girl. So
yeah, I'm down bad and I just have to deal with it.

"B," Saylor says, lightly elbowing me in the side. I snap
out of a daydream that involves Jacob and I kissing in his
driveway.

"Hmm yes?"

"Welcome back. I almost took a bite of your sandwich to
get your attention." She laughs. I look down at the chicken
caprese sandwich I made, now that there's an official
season-long ban on ham in our house. I overtoasted the

bread, but I'm not telling anyone that. I can part with some of my orange and my chips. But this girl cannot be parted from her sandwich.

"Sorry, I was just thinking about taking a bite out of you." I glare at her until she starts laughing.

"We just wanted a Jacob update," Glory says.

"Yeah, I didn't see you all weekend. How are things with our new little lovebirds?" Tatum asks.

Yes, please. Let me talk about my pathetic growing feelings out loud. Man, when this brilliant plan of ours ends, and I'm weeping, it's gonna be so embarrassing. "Good," I say, because I know how this works. Just part of having a boyfriend. You don't have to get all nasty with the kiss and tell, but you gotta say something. "He's a good hugger and I like that."

"Have you hugged him with your mouth yet?" Glory teases. For her troubles, she almost gets an orange segment between the eyes. Too bad I don't like wasting food.

○ ○ ○

Of course Glory gave me another thing to worry about. I don't think Jacob wants me to do anything to him with my mouth, but what if that changes? What if he wants to do more than the kissing? Of course I'm thinking about it, and that means I'm anxious about it, and I know what I told him about talking to Boyfriend or Jacob or both, but I don't know if this is a conversation I even need to bring up. For once I think basketball will be my savior, but I forget we have team pictures before practice and Jacob is there.

We line up for our individual shots with the professional photographer and then our team picture. And we have to shoot photos with the boys' team. Jacob got Coach's approval to make a TikTok with both teams before we actually start practicing. I get my picture taken and then casually slide my way over to Jacob.

"I have to talk to you about something later," he says with this little smirk and then he laughs at the look on my face. Why does he have to be so cute?

"Should I be nervous?" I ask him.

"Nah, the opposite. Heaven said I must really like you because I was holding back on Saturday."

"Holding back what?"

"When we watched *The Lost Kingdom*. Usually when I watch a movie with anyone, I just start breaking the whole thing down. Well, all the shots at least and the lighting and the editing. It really drives Heaven nuts. My mom hates it too. My dad thinks it's funny 'cause it's the only time I publicly nerd out."

"Oh, and Heaven noticed you were so captivated by my beauty, you couldn't focus on pulling the movie apart?" I tease.

"Yeah, something like that."

"I don't care if you get all clinical with me. But maybe the first time we do it with something I've already seen so I can listen to your expertise and not miss any of the plot."

"Genius. After practice? E's still grounded, so I have to go get her from the shop, but I'll tell her to go hang out in her room this time."

"Sounds good." I smile a little more than I mean to and of course he raises his camera and snaps a picture.

"Hey, Yeun, you glad you linked up with the best rebounder in the county?" Oliver says as he makes his way over to us for some reason. We're not *not* speaking anymore, but he's been talking to me less now that he and Poppy are a thing.

"Yeah, I find it helps me a lot in the real world. Stealing fruit from my neighbor's trees and stuff," Jacob says. I bite my lips so I won't laugh.

Oliver lets out this weird ha-like chuckle and then starts trying to low-five me. I low-five him back, kinda confused. "We gonna crush this season, Greene?"

"Yes?"

"Nice," he says. Then he high-fives Jacob and walks back over to where Landon is standing on the edge of the court.

"I don't know what that was about."

Jacob just shrugs and then gets a picture of Grace Jung fixing Emily's ponytail a few feet away. I'm still thinking about the weird interaction with Oliver when we head back into the locker room to change for practice.

"Guess what Lan just told me?" Saylor hisses. I let her tug me into the corner by the gym teacher's office.

"What??"

"Poppy dumped Oliver. She told him his breath stank."

"Jesus!" I gasp, covering my mouth on reflex.

"I know."

"Damn, Poppy. That's brutal." I've never noticed anything about his breath, but Poppy has been shoving her
tongue down his throat for the last two weeks, so she'd have
firsthand knowledge.

"For real. I don't know if Jacob mentioned this to you, but
I heard she said some really mean stuff to him about him
being so skinny. Valentina told me when Jacob and I were
together."

And that really pisses me off. "Why can't people just not
talk about people's bodies? It's really easy."

"Yeah, I don't think Poppy's that nice. I do think it's
really interesting that Oliver picked like five minutes ago
to get all in your face in front of Jacob," Saylor says as we
walk over to our stuff.

I cringe, even though a bunch of mixed feelings are ris-
ing to the surface. My lusty feelings for Oliver aren't exactly
gone, but I don't like the way this smells, no pun intended.
I shake off all the icky emotions and try to fix my face. "He
could have just said yes when I asked him to the dance and
he wouldn't be quoting my stats to Jacob on picture day."

"Well, it looks like you won this round. How embarrassing for him?"

I think I need to carry a picture of Oliver around for good measure. And maybe a picture of Kayden Smith too. I need a reminder that Bethany does not like me, Jacob. I know she likes me as a friend, but she's been so upfront about how anxious everything about dating makes her. She's been super blunt about it in fact, so I cannot sit here for a half a second and forget that Oliver Gutierrez is the reason she was ready with her own terms and stipulations for our deal in the first place. I can't forget that Kayden Smith is her ideal man.

I know how this plan kicked off—it's my fault, and at the time I was definitely still looking at Bethany as Saylor's friend and my hostage-situation homecoming date. I thought she was cute, but I had perspective when I proposed this brilliant idea. That perspective is long gone. I like Bethany. Plain and simple. I like her a lot. Asking my dad to draw that illustration should have been my big clue. But sometime when we were on my couch, watching movies, it clicked.

I didn't say anything about some of the editing choices because she was so upset after what happened with her mom and so drained, she kept dozing off. I didn't want to bother her. She's really cute when she's sleeping too and I'll have to see if scientists have developed a foolproof memory wipe sometime in the next thirty days because I can't go on like this.

The way Oliver blatantly flirted with Bethany right in front of me made me realize our plan might be working for Bethany's intended purpose already. Madlyn couldn't wait to tell me as soon as I got back to the yearbook office that Poppy dumped him. And then everything started to make sense. Oliver is back on the market and maybe has his eyes set on Bethany.

Or maybe that's just how they are together. Jokes about basketball stats and low fives. Sports things. I think about asking her if she wants to end things early, so she can maybe give Oliver another try, but then I remember this is Bethany. If she wants something, she's gonna tell me. I might as well enjoy this while it lasts, but still pin a photo of Oliver above the desk in my room so I'm not surprised when this all ends and it's the two of them deciding what to get each other for Christmas.

By the time I pick up my delinquent sister from the shop and make it back to the house, Bethany is already on her way over. I break the news that this is a me-and-Bethany type hang to Esther.

"Bethany and I are gonna watch a movie in my room. Please don't burn down the house."

"Yeah, whatever, don't make a baby in there or I'll tell Mom," she replies.

"Yeah, we'll try not to." I let Bethany in and we go straight to my room.

"You have a whole production studio in here," she says, checking out my editing bay setup on my desk.

"I have to make all those TikToks look good."

"Yeah, I get it now." I watch her as she looks at the abstract mural my mom did on one wall and my autographed skate decks and mounted Star Trek Funkos. "I have to pretend to do my history homework, but I'm excited to get your expert opinion on the technical stuff."

"I wouldn't say expert. I still have a lot to learn."

"How'd you get so interested in all of this?" she asks.

"When I was little, we used to go over to my dad's best friend's house and he would have movies on in their playroom all the time. I would sit like two inches from the screen and watch whatever was on."

"That's so cute." She smiles.

"Once, his other friend, who was a camera operator, came by when I was watching a movie he worked on. He sat down next to me and told me all this cool stuff about how they did different shots and editing tricks, and I was hooked. I feel like that guy was my fairy godfather or something 'cause I only saw him that one time. Never saw him again.

"But yeah, I kept asking my parents about working in movies and they encouraged me and didn't freak out when I broke my dad's phone trying to make my first movie with Axel."

"What was it about?" she asks.

"It was a horror movie called *Eat Your Vegetables*."

"Love it." She laughs. "It must just be amazing to have a hobby you love that you're allowed to turn into more. You know I used to draw, like a lot?"

"You did?"

"Yeah. I stopped a long time ago, but I was actually pretty decent and I could have been an artist, but Mama T didn't want me sitting around the house. She'd always make me go out and play with my sisters. Which was her code word for exercise."

"You can still pick that up, you know? My mom didn't paint for a few years because my grandparents wanted her to get a real job."

"And then she ran away from home and became a tattoo artist?"

"Basically. My dad got really bad grades in school, so his parents were just glad he was good at something. And it all worked out."

"So you're saying I should run away?"

"Or we could make your moms a really well-produced pitch on why you deserve to be LA Cooking School's brightest young star?"

That sad smile is back as her gaze drops to the center of my chest. "Let's just watch a movie, yeah?"

"Okay, but first I have a confession," I tell her. I have a flash of a fever dream where I confess my feelings for her and she tells me she likes me too. But this thing between us is definitely not a movie, so I have to give her one of my other truths.

"Are you dumping me? Because a verbal agreement counts, we still have twenty-eight-and-a-few-hours couple of days until we call this off," she says.

"A-few-hours couple of days?" I laugh.

"Yeah, it's a perfectly normal unit of measurement."

"No, I'm not dumping you. We've barely scratched the surface of how much of a loser I am and I need to get comfortable showing girls just how bad it gets."

"Okay, good. What were you going to tell me?"

I ignore the way my chest is suddenly tight and warm. She doesn't want me to get out of the way so she can be with Oliver. Not yet at least. Thank god. "You know the picture I gave you?"

"Yeah, I freaking love it."

"I didn't have the courage to tell you before. But my favorite sandwich is peanut butter and jelly. I hope that's not too embarrassing for you."

"How could that be embarrassing? My comfort sandwich is ham and cheese. You wanna know what's the best way to do peanut butter and jelly though?"

"Of course you have a PB&J recipe," I say. "Let's hear it."

She steps closer and wraps her arms around my waist, and that warmth in my chest turns into heat.

"You get your bread of choice, but it should be a thick bread. I've actually used an everything bagel once and it was so good. You toast it, get your choice of jam or preserves, because jelly is just not that girl, and then here's the key. Chunky peanut butter. Smooth can turn into a runny mess, but the chunky really holds it all together."

"Wait, what's the difference between jam and preserves?" I ask.

"I'll send you a link. You do not want my passionate take on preserves."

"Okay." And then we're both quiet for a second. I want to kiss her, but I also want to do more than kiss her. Not take things as far as they can go, but more. I know she likes honesty, but I don't know how to explain what I'm thinking because it's more like a feeling than a concrete action. And while I'm thinking, she kisses me. I know I can't, but I want to make a short film about how soft her lips are.

o o o

I pull down my projector screen, thanking Bethany again for not making fun of me for having a full movie-theater experience in my bedroom, complete with hidden surround sound speakers. We put on *Skyfall* and both of us manage to fit on my sack chair. Bethany's seen this Bond movie a long time ago, and doesn't remember it, but also isn't emotionally invested enough to be bothered by me talking over it. Which is good because Roger Deakins is one of my idols and I need to be able to share that fact with any future girlfriends. She seems really into it and everything I have to say about the light tricks and the panning shots, but then there's a scene where we're both quiet and focused.

And the next thing I know we're kissing again. I wish I could just tell her what I want to happen next, but every time I put it into words in my head it sounds real creepy. But maybe she's thinking the same thing because after we've been kissing for a while, she takes my hand and slowly puts it up her shirt. Those words that were in my head completely disappear and I just feel like a live wire. I'm just touching her bra, but that's enough to bring me to a new place of understanding with my own body.

Deep in the back of my mind I remember the sex ed class Axel and I had in eighth grade and how Mr. Mendoza talked about the moment of *enlivenment* and how Axel and I laughed about that for weeks. The *enlivening* of our boners. The *enlivening* is happening now. I don't stop the kissing, or move my hand, or tell Bethany to move her hand from where she has it on my leg, but if I can figure out how, later I'll tell her about the *more* I was thinking about and how this is what I meant.

I hear my door fly open two seconds before Bethany and I pull apart. That two seconds is not enough time for me to get my hand out of her shirt.

Esther stands there making a grossed-out face. "Jacob— Oh eww."

"E, get out!" I say as I finally get my hand down.

"Check your phone, dickhead. Dad and Aunt Patty are on their way back. Now."

"Oh shit." I grab my phone off the floor and there's definitely a text from five minutes ago. We only live seven minutes from the shop if there's traffic.

> On the way with Aunt P.
> She has gimbap!

Bethany jumps up and starts to fix her shirt, but I can't really get up.

"Uh, give me a second," I tell her.

"Oh crap. Yeah, I'll—just. Esther, wait up." She dashes out of my room after my sister. I hop up and close my door. It takes a few minutes, but I get myself under control. I owe Esther like ten favors because my dad and my Aunt Patty come walking through the front door right as I pass through the kitchen. I meet them in the front hall.

"Hey," I say. Wishing I'd checked to see how red my face is in the mirror.

"Hey, kiddo," Aunt Patty says.

Dad doesn't say hi as he steps out of his Vans. He looks suspiciously around me like he knows I'm up to something. "Where's your sister?"

"We're in here!" Esther yells.

"Who's we?" Dad asks.

I swallow, happy I'm not sweating. "Oh, um, Bethany's here."

"Oh, is this the girlfriend?" Aunt Patty whispers, and I don't think there is a worse time for them to meet.

"Yeah."

I follow my aunt into the living room, and I don't know how, but Bethany is sitting in the armchair with both of our stats homework spread out on the coffee table. There's even a pencil that doesn't belong to me on top of my papers. Bethany stands up and smiles at me and then my aunt, just as my dad walks into the room.

"Is this the famous Bethany, mystery-date-turned-girlfriend?" Dad says.

"That's me. Very nice to meet you, Mr. Yeun, and thank you for having me in your home." She lays it on extra thick, but I can tell my aunt is impressed.

"Oh, sure. Anytime. You're Esther's new favorite person and I think Jake's."

"Dad," Esther groans.

Aunt Patty introduces herself and then holds up the big bag in her hand. "Well, Bethany, I hope you like Korean food. I went to this bridal shower and all of us bridesmaids were sent home with enough food to feed ten people."

"That sounds great," Bethany replies.

"Come on." We all follow Aunt Patty into the kitchen and dig into the leftovers. I don't think I exhale for a good twelve hours.

30
BETHANY
(needs a new game face)

t's game day. The first official game of the season. We play right after school, while the boys get that coveted prime-time spot and the max effort from the marching band, which definitely uses our game for practices even though we've had a better record for the last ten years in a row. But this isn't about the band; it's about putting all of my emotions aside and playing my heart out.

Jacob's been doing his best all week to cheer me up. He knows I'll never get up the nerve to tell my moms that I'd rather support their passion from the sidelines, so he's resorted to making me laugh and smile and kissing me a lot.

I close my eyes and let out a deep breath, then I follow our team captains out onto the court. The stands are pretty full, but all the faces are a blur. The cheerleading squad and the band are hyped and ready, but I don't see Tatum or Rhys and his tuba; I just hear their noise as it rises to the rafters. The nerves in my stomach immediately fade away when I see the Beverly Hills squad gathered around their bench. 'Til that final buzzer, my only job is to help my team win. There are announcements, the anthem, and then I and the rest of our starting five take the floor. I walk to the center of the court and I allow myself one glance into the stands.

I see Jacob on the corner of the bleachers, camera in hand. I see Momlissa and Cris and Mr. Ford and Saylor's demonic twin sisters sitting beside them. Mama T is in town but the Lakers are home against Boston tonight. She'll ask me about the game later. I catch a glimpse of Oliver and Landon and the handful of members from the boys' squad who bothered to show up. Kayden's right behind Landon. Not that that's important, but he is there. And still very hot. And then I see Heaven, Axel, and Valentina at the top of the stands. I see the signs they are holding.

BETHANY IS BEAUTIFUL! SAYLOR IS KIND! EMILY IS SMART!

I try not to look back at Jacob, but I have a feeling he put them up to this.

I hide my smile as I focus back on the ref and remember the defense we've been running all week.

There's the whistle. The ball in the air. Dylan's fingertips bat it right in my direction.

We win by eight.

o o o

After our final huddle I leave the court and say hi to my mom and the Fords. They are all very proud of me and my mom just loved the signs. She tells me to see if I can get mine from Heaven. I'm sure I will. She reminds me of my curfew and then splits for the arena so she can catch the rest of Mama T's game. Driving all over Los Angeles on a Friday night, the woman truly loves her family.

As a team we decided to stay and watch the boys' game, so I brave our school's showers, then head back out to the stands. Jacob is still in full-yearbook action, but at halftime he waves me down.

"I'll be right back," I tell Saylor.

"'Kay." She smiles at me and gives my knee a little pinch.

As I make my way down the stands, saying thanks to the handful of people who want to congratulate me on our win and laughing it off when a random parent asks me if I'm gonna hit another half-court shot, I wish I could trade places with Saylor. She loves basketball. Tonight was actually fun for her.

Jacob and I slip out into the hallway and walk down toward the library, away from the band's halftime show so we can actually hear each other.

"I wanna try your idea," I tell Jacob immediately.

"About the pitch to your moms?"

I nod. I feel like I should be happy now that I finally know what I want. I finally made a decision, but I know what happens if this goes all the way left. I know what Mama T is like and how Momlissa will be slightly more chill, but they always back each other. I know how my sisters will react too, how they'll take sides. Jocelyn for and Trinity against. I hate it, but I have to do this. I don't say all that though because I will definitely cry and even though it is after hours, I am still at school.

I refuse to bring Crybaby Bethany back after all the hard work I've put into looking sexy and desirable on the arm of my boyfriend.

Jacob does the right thing and hugs me. "We can start tomorrow, if you want, and then I still need to take you on a real date."

"Please. Where do you want to go?"

"The Lakers museum," he teases.

"Oh, you mean my house?"

He kisses the top of my head and squeezes me tighter. "We can go where you want."

I know Glory would give me a lecture on how it's his responsibility to plan the date, but I have the perfect plans in mind.

31
BETHANY

*(sits down for her first
exclusive one-on-one interview)*

The next morning, I tell the moms that I'm heading out to show Esther the basics of dribbling. It's truly excellent news to both their ears. Mentoring the youth and practicing on the weekend. The way an ideal daughter should spend her Saturday. I'll be back later to change and shower because I, Bethany Greene, no longer a crybaby, have a date. Mama T wants to finally meet Jacob too.

I try to tell myself to breathe as I drive over to his house. This will work, and even if it doesn't, at least I tried. That's the new me, right? The Bethany who at least tries. After all, you miss 100 percent of the shots you don't take. I roll my eyes as the thought crosses my mind. Why does everything have to come back to that dang sport?

I pull up to Jacob's and park on the street. His mom's car is still in the driveway, but he assured me both his parents were heading to the shop today. Another deep breath and I grab my things and head to the front door.

I ring the doorbell and Mrs. Yeun welcomes me in. "There's our movie star," she says.

"Oh yeah." I smile nervously as I head inside, step out of my sneakers, and push them into the corner.

"Jacob told me you guys are making a short project for class today."

We definitely should have gotten on the same page about alibis before I came over. "Yeah. It should be fun."

"I'm sure it will be, and I told his sister to leave you guys alone if she can't find it inside herself to be helpful."

"No, she's been awesome." I laugh.

"Yeah, she has her good moments. Come on. I think Jacob's in the backyard." I follow her through the house and, sure enough, Jacob is in the backyard, getting his tripod set up on the back porch. His laptop and mic stand are also set up. I don't know what I expected, but of course Jacob is in full-production mode.

"Wow, you should intern for my mom at NSN," I tell him.

He shakes his head, cringing a little. "People have been trying to get me into sports photojournalism since my first skate video. It's fun, but it's not the ultimate goal."

"I told him he should focus less on filming sports," his mom says.

"It's how I get out of gym."

"It is?" I ask, shocked.

"Yeah, Noah and I get our gym requirement waived because we go to almost every school sporting event. Mr. Wolfson rigged it up for us."

"That's genius."

"You hear that, Mom? I'm a genius."

"Uh-huh. Your dad has a long day, but I'll be back at four. We're all behaving ourselves, yeah?"

"Yes, Mom."

"Yes, ma'am," I add, so she knows I heard her loud and clear, which reminds me that Jacob and I still haven't talked about the hand-on-boob situation. I'm not sure if I have the guts to bring it up or if I should act like it never happened. Either way, just as Mrs. Yeun goes back inside to finish getting ready for work, Heaven comes strolling out onto the porch. She's offered to help.

"Okay. I'm here. Let's do this," she announces.

"What exactly are we doing?" I ask. I'm working on my nerves. I have no real plan formulated in my head.

"I think we should do an interview portion. The sky's clear, so we can use the natural light in the backyard. We shoot that today and then when you decide what you want to cook, we can shoot footage of you in action another day. We'll get a few people over here to taste samples so you don't have to cook enough food for a bunch of people, but we can get a handful of feedback. And we can even do secret taste tests where you're not in the room."

"Oh god. What if people hate my cooking?"

"That's fine too. That's what editing is for. If your food is gross, then that's all the more reason your moms should let you work on getting better. If they see this is something you really care about."

"Damn, that's good," I admit.

"I mean, I think we should take the low road here and

play on their actual love for you. Even if they don't like it or understand, making them feel bad is also worth something," Heaven says with a shrug.

"Heaven, are you our one-woman crew today?" I ask as I set down my bag on an open deck chair.

"No, I'm gonna be the one interviewing you," she says, gathering her big curls back into a ponytail, like she's about to do some heavy lifting.

"Oh?"

"I figure your moms will know I made it," Jacob says. "But it feels less like your new boyfriend is a bad influence on you if you're talking to someone else. I'm gonna set up the shot so it's just you. You won't see Heaven."

"I definitely don't want them to think I started dating and then suddenly lost interest in sports. That will not help my case."

"Well, I'm all set up if you wanna start. The light back here is pretty good."

I look around the yard, taking in the sunlight. It is pretty great, but that also means I should probably go through with this. "Just let me make sure I don't have anything in my teeth."

I go inside and duck into their powder room. I look completely fine and there's nothing in my teeth. My hair is holding it together and generally I just look cute. I can do this. And if it blows up in my face, maybe I can call Omari up and see if he wants to adopt me for Christmas.

I head back outside and Heaven and I get comfortable in the deck chairs. Jacob adjusts the tripod until he's happy with the way things look. We test the mics and then it's go-time. I laugh as soon as Heaven looks at me.

"It's okay. If you laugh, you laugh. You're not acting. You're just being yourself," Jacob says.

I take a deep breath and focus on just talking to Heaven. I tell her everything. About my family, my sisters, my grandpa and how much I miss him. I'm honest about how playing basketball makes me feel and how I don't see a future for myself in it. She asks if I want to play in college. I tell her the truth. I don't even want to play next season. I explain how I know how my moms will react to this news, but then Jacob reminds me of the email I sent to the cooking school. I show it to Heaven and the response they sent back. I'm not giving up on basketball. I want to embrace something new.

I talk about my love for Chef Evie and this new TikTok account I've been following, Chef Jeff Chen, who talks to his pug, Thadeus, before he starts making every meal. I'm honest about how I like making things with my hands, delicious things that I actually get to eat and enjoy. How even the simple act of putting a fancy sandwich together relaxes me. I tell her how I love discovering different flavors and the thrill of finding a new chef's recipes. I admit that I'm afraid to cook anything more complex at the house because I know how Mama T will react. And I explain that I know how it looks to people when you're a fat person who enjoys food.

We laugh about that together, the contradiction of how we definitely need food to live and how people who know how to cook are so well respected and loved, but don't be a fatty who isn't rich off cooking yet. We laugh about that some more and vow to go snag some SKITTLES and Mountain Dew as soon as we're done filming.

I only cry once, just a little, but Heaven makes me laugh my way through it. In the end, whatever my moms say, I told the truth about myself, what I want and how I feel. And in the end, I feel pretty good.

32
JACOB
(in awe and much deeper trouble)

Hours later, I'm still impressed by how much Bethany just let it all out. But not surprised. That's just how she is. Heaven and Axel have that honest way about them, but they use their honesty and weirdness to scare people. Bethany just wants people to understand her. She wants her moms to see her. I don't think I've been that honest and open about anything. We still have the other half to film and I have a ton of editing to do, but if her moms don't at least give her the chance to take one class after they see this, then they must really love basketball.

Bethany goes home for a couple hours after we finish, and I skate with Esther at the park up the street for an hour. Then I come back and get ready for our date. I want tonight to be good. It's not my first date, but it's Bethany's. She told me she'll lay her whole plan out when I go pick her up. That's part of her plan too, that I drive. I can't wait to see what is on the schedule.

I shower and blow-dry my hair so it's not dripping everywhere. I grab a fresh Ink & Pearl T-shirt from the Thunderdome and ignore my sister when she tells me I'm forgetting something.

"If you like her, you'll give her a hoodie. The boyfriend hoodie, but not one you wear a lot 'cause all of yours smell," she says.

I pause for a second to consider the smell bit and then play it off with the foolproof solution of telling my sister to shut up.

I do like Bethany a lot, but Ink & Pearl apparel is a big commitment. As I get behind the wheel of my mom's car, all I can think about is six months from now, Oliver being over at her house and borrowing the sweatshirt. After, Bethany forgets to ask for it back and then next thing I know I'm photographing baseball practice and here comes Oliver Gutierrez walking out on the field in the boyfriend hoodie I gave her.

It probably wouldn't go down that way, but the vision of it is brutal enough for me to stop myself from texting Bethany to ask what her ideal comfort size is. I think it's best if I keep really personal symbols of affection to myself. I'll just ignore the whole peanut butter and jam situation that's still hanging up on the wall of her bedroom.

I drive over to the Greenes' and text Bethany to let her know I'm outside. Their gate buzzes and I walk up to the door. It swings open and I get a waft of Bethany's lotion or body wash or whatever it is she's wearing. We smile at each other.

"I just want to apologize in advance. Both moms are here and you might get grilled," she whispers.

"Okay. I'm ready." I follow her inside and step out of my

sneakers, the 1s we both bought for the dance, and then head to the kitchen. Both of her moms are standing by the island. Her mom Melissa looks like she's on the phone with someone.

"Jocie, hold on," she says. "Hi, Jacob."

"Hello, Mrs. Greene. Mrs. Greene." I nod to them both.

"Do you prefer Jake or Jacob?" her mom Teresa says. She's peeling an orange. Not hard to miss the tattoos that cover both of her arms. I'm not sure which one my mom did, but it's at least one sign she'd get along with my parents. Outside of the shop.

"Either is fine. Thank you."

"Wait, turn the phone around!" I hear from the phone that her mom Melissa has in her hand. She flips the phone around and I see Bethany's sister Jocelyn.

"Oh, hey, Jacob! I remember you. Yearbook kid," she says.

"That's me. Still on the yearbook."

"Mommy, he posted that video of Bethany's half-court shot," Jocelyn adds, and I try not to cringe. Not basketball again, but Bethany saves it.

"Yes, he's a very talented photographer. And I'm sure he's parked on the street somewhere Mr. Gordon would love to complain about, so we gotta go," Bethany says. She starts backing toward the door.

"Hold on, Jocelyn. I'll call you back," her mom says.

"You kids have fun tonight!" Jocelyn yells out before her mom ends the call. I swallow as both moms focus their attention on me.

"So, what are you getting into tonight?" her mom Teresa asks.

"Um, I'm not sure," I say, glancing between Bethany's parents. "I was told there was a plan."

"You didn't even tell the boy what you wanted to do tonight?" her mom Teresa laughs.

"No! It's kind of a surprise, but since you want me to ruin it—"

"I just want to know where in Los Angeles County my sixteen-year-old and her boyfriend are going to be on Saturday night."

I try not to smile as Bethany fakes a dramatic sigh. "Fine. But I did actually want this to be a super romantic surprise. There's this pizza place I wanted to try by 3rd Street Promenade and then I got us tickets to go on the Pacific Wheel."

"Wow, that is romantic," her mom Melissa says, before she lightly taps Mom Teresa's arm. "How come you've never taken me on the Pacific Wheel? Living in LA twenty-three years. Tuh!"

"As soon as the season is over, it's me, you, and the wheel. Anyway, I just wanted to make sure your stories line up." Mom Teresa smiles so I think she's just giving both of us a hard time. "All right, well. Bethany's curfew on Saturday nights is eleven."

"We'll be back at ten fifty-five," I say with a nod.

"Love to hear it. Off you go. Have fun. *Stay together.* Don't take any drugs from strangers. If anything happens, call us or Jacob's parents."

"We will— Oh wait!" Bethany turns to me, her eyes lighting up. "I wanna show Jacob the package we got today first."

"Oh god," Mom Melissa groans before she snorts. It's the same snort Bethany does. "Okay, but be quick. You don't wanna miss the wheel."

"Come on, I have something to show you." Bethany takes my hand and tugs me through the house to her mom's office. I haven't been in this room before. It's nothing like the Thunderdome. It's all white with light furniture. The walls and shelves are covered with her moms' NBA and WNBA things. Trophies, framed jerseys. It's like seeing all the pressure she's under in one room. She ignores it all though and grabs a big envelope off the desk. "This came while I was at your house."

"What—"

Bethany opens the envelope and pulls out a huge—probably eleven-by-fourteen—photo of us from homecoming. We're in front of Mrs. Ford's step and repeat. I have my arms around Bethany's waist and she's looking down at the ground. I look up at her, cringing, then look back at the photo.

"Right?!" She laughs. "It's fucking weird."

"It looks like—"

"An engagement photo?"

"Yeah!"

She pulls out some smaller prints that look more normal, where we're both looking at the camera, both smiling, both in the moment. Those pictures are good. I pick up a four by six where Bethany is posing with her lips pursed, chin and deuces up. I'm squatting in front of her with my tongue out. That one's definitely frameable.

"Were we supposed to order prints?" I ask.

"Oh, an eight-by-ten and a few smaller sizes will be sent to your mom whether she likes it or not. I figured Saylor would have told you. You've seen the photos around their house. Her Instagram? The TikToks? The Halloween costumes? The woman is intense."

"We're not her kids?!" I laugh.

"Well, for one shining evening you were. My mom threatened to order a life-size cutout of us as a joke."

"If there's a cutout option, I want it," I joke. Kinda. My brain starts thinking of all the cool camera tricks I could do with a cutout. I pull out my phone then and show her a still I grabbed from what we filmed this morning. Bethany was laughing at something Heaven was saying about her mom's prized dogs, Fergie and Di. Over the last few weeks, she's filled up my phone, but I think this is my favorite picture of her.

Bethany scrunches up one side of her nose and it makes the dimple in her cheek really pop. "I'm really pretty."

"Yeah," I tell her. "You are." There's a lot more I could say about knowing how to find the perfect shot and beauty of the subject, but I picture Oliver high-fiving Kayden and that stops me from getting too sappy. The clock is ticking.

"Can you send that to me?" she asks, handing my phone back to me.

"Of course." I send her the picture right then and there. We say bye to her moms, then drive down to Santa Monica for our date.

o o o

TWO HOURS LATER . . .

"Oh my god!" Bethany groans as we burst from the pizza
place.

"We should have gone somewhere else." I laugh, taking
her hand.

"There should be some sort of law against playing music
that loud. That was *trash*."

I found a spot in one of the parking garages pretty
quickly, but dinner was not good. We had to wait forever for
a table and we couldn't really ditch the wait and go somewhere else, because it's Saturday night and the Promenade
is packed. We were so glad to finally sit down, at first we
didn't notice the pizza place had the music up so loud, the
active Mars rover could probably pick up the signal. But
then we tried talking to each other. The food was pretty
good, but we had our whole conversation over text.

"Anyway, I was trying to ask you if you'll ever get a tattoo when you're older?" Bethany says. We start walking toward Ocean Avenue so we can make our way down to the
Santa Monica Pier, perfect for all your sport fishing and
boating needs.

"I have one," I tell her.

"Where?" The look on her face is pretty funny, like she
doesn't believe me and is scared to find out the answer.

"Here." I pull the side of my hoodie off my shoulder and
lift up the sleeve of my T-shirt.

She takes my hand and pulls me closer so we're not

blocking the sidewalk. "That little line right there?"

"Yu—yeah," I mutter. She touches the line and goose bumps break out over my skin. "I asked my dad like fifty times to tell me what it felt like, so he gave me one little line. I had to do the whole aftercare process too to make sure it didn't get infected."

"How was it?"

"It hurt like hell, but it was worth it."

"Yeah, my mom always complains when hers are healing and then every off-season she goes back for like three more."

"Apparently it's addicting. I mean, you've seen both of my parents. My mom is more tatted than my dad."

"That's 'cause your mom is really cool. Come on." We join the crowds of people walking around the Pier and push our way past the vendors selling stuff under the arch. We get past the concrete barrier that separates the walkway from where it looks like cars can drive down to the boardwalk, but there are no cars. It's still crowded, but there's less people going up and down to the Pier.

"Okay, we gotta chill a bit walking down this hill," Bethany says. "I have a different center of gravity than you. I will roll boobs first all the way."

I almost choke on my laugh, then grip her hand tighter. The hill is pretty steep and I know if I tripped I'd eat it and fall all the way down too. "I won't let you roll anywhere."

There are more vendors and some street musicians. We head right for the little amusement park. I look up at the kids screaming on the roller coaster, but it looks like the entrance is blocked off. There's a security guard and a sign: CLOSED FOR PRIVATE EVENT.

"Excuse me," Bethany says to the security guard. "We have tickets for the Wheel."

"Yeah, they are still good, but just not tonight. This whole park is closed for a party. You can come back anytime."

"But just not tonight?" Bethany asks.

"Sorry," the guy says with a shrug.

"Thanks," she grumbles.

"We can still walk around," I tell her. I look down at the rest of the Pier. There are more cart vendors and another street musician getting ready to fire up his electric violin. And a bunch of old dudes fishing. It's all kinda underwhelming if you can't go on the Wheel. "Let's walk down toward Venice."

"Yeah, okay." I know she's trying to hide how bummed she is, but her whole mood has completely dropped. She doesn't say anything else until we get down to the walking path on the beach. I usually only skate down here. It's different with her though.

"We can come back another time," I say.

"I know." She lets out this little laugh and then shakes herself before she smiles over at me. "I don't know why I expected this to go well."

"What do you mean?"

"I had this whole super romantic plan. I know it sounds silly and I know this is, like, a super corny, touristy place.

But I've only been to the Promenade and the Pier with my moms and my friends. I always wanted to have my first date down here, and it all kinda fell apart."

I didn't forget that this was Bethany's first date, but maybe I didn't really understand what it means that it's not mine. I never thought I'd have a bunch of first dates to compare. Still, so far, this one is my favorite. "Are you having a bad time?"

"No. No. But we have to come back. I need my movie moment, Jacob. We are gonna kiss on that wheel. And it's gonna be romantic as hell."

"How about this?" We step onto the sand and I tug her over to these two massive palm trees. "Why don't we kiss right here? We got the ocean waves, two majestic trees, the lights of Santa Monica and Venice Beach meeting in the middle. I think that's a waxing moon. Why not? And we have the most important thing of all."

"What's that?" she asks, one of her eyebrows arching up.

"We have each other."

Bethany rolls her eyes. And then she kisses me. The Pacific Wheel seemed like a fun idea, but somehow this is so much better.

33
BETHANY

(still gazing at the waxing moon:
it's waxing—he was right)

We walk the beach. We run into this guy Jacob knows from skating named Dog. He's a total weirdo, but he's sweet and he tells Jacob I'm cute. Dog is a-okay in my book. We walk back up to Ocean Avenue and make our way back to the car, agreeing to come back as many times as we can until we do everything on my ideal romantic trip to the seaside.

We stop and get ice cream and then Jacob drives me home. We're early so we sit in the car on my street and he tells me about the time Axel broke his arm skating at the beach and how he and Heaven learned they were both very cool under pressure. I tell him how Jocelyn broke her arm jumping off the back of the couch. I almost tell him I want him to hang out with my sisters when they come back for Christmas, but our deal will be over then. Maybe he can still come over sometimes, as a friend.

There's a Boyfriend/Girlfriend thing I almost mention, something I've been meaning to talk to him about since Esther walked in on us. I'm a little embarrassed by the whole hand-on-the-boob thing and maybe more embarrassed that

I would have let more happen. Not 'cause I think what we did was bad, but because I know it has everything to do with my real feelings that I can't share with him.

I almost ask him how he wants to lose his virginity. Not where and when, but if he wants to just get it over with one day or if he wants it to be with someone special. *I know we can't do more*, I think as I bite my tongue, *because the truth is, I don't think it would be a bad thing if Jacob was my first.* And that is information I *definitely* need to keep to myself. Instead, I grab my phone and see what phase of the moon it really is. A waxing crescent. Jacob smiles at me with a little up nod of his head, his subtle way of gloating even though we both know it was a lucky guess. I almost feel bad Saylor didn't get to see this side of him. Almost.

When the clock hits ten fifty, I tell him he should kiss me because I don't want to have to rush our good night. I need to walk through the door right on time so the moms know how responsible we both are when we're together. We kiss and kiss and I manage to come back to my senses to make it inside right on time. I check in with the moms and head upstairs to wash my face. I respond to texts from my friends, vowing to tell them everything in person on Monday.

I'm still smiling when I get into bed.

Sure, everything I'd envisioned for my first date hadn't gone as planned, but it was easily one of the best nights of my life. I will never, ever say this out loud, but I kinda hope my next boyfriend—my first real boyfriend, since it can't be Jacob—is just like Jacob.

34
BETHANY
(is ready for the kitchen and its heat)

Thanksgiving break sneaks up on us, but it works out perfectly because we get out of school early that Tuesday. Heaven, Axel, Esther, and Valentina have volunteered to be my taste testers, and Jacob lets me know his mom will be home too and she's happy to help. I have plenty of time to hit the Ralphs between my and Jacob's houses to get the stuff we need for my cooking debut. Cook and then get back home before Momlissa gets back from the studio.

When I get to Jacob's house, he answers the door and lets me in. He helps me with the bags and the pan I casually snuck out of my house. We kiss, but something is off.

"You okay?" I ask as we walk into the kitchen. We set the stuff on the counters and then I take his hand.

"Yeah. I just checked my grade for Mr. Wei's class and I think I'm gonna end the semester with a B. I really needed that A. Your tips did help though. He asked us to write a short about a holiday gone wrong and I wrote about a dog eating a Thanksgiving turkey right before it's supposed to be served."

"I like that." I laugh.

"Yeah, I still only got a B minus on it, which is better, but not the A I wanted. I'll try that reverse engineering again."

"Is there any way you can do some extra credit?"

"I'll ask him. It just sucks. I wanted to crush it in that class and it turns out I'm just slightly above average."

"I think you're way above average, but I get it. I'm sorry." I lean up and kiss him on his cheek.

"It's okay. I just got too in my head with the writing portion."

"Oh, if anyone understands getting in their head, it's me."

"I know. Thanks. So I'm guessing you figured out what you're going to make?" he asks. I feel bad, taking the focus off of him, but I am really excited.

"Yes. I thought I'd make Chef Evie's braised ribs, but we don't have a million hours and for some reason the lady at Ralphs didn't want to sell me red wine. So I decided to make my take on my grandpa's spaghetti."

"Oh, nice," he says, smiling back at me.

"I'm a little nervous, but I think I got this."

"Of course you do. Heaven said they'll all be here in a few minutes. I'm gonna edit out the sound in this part, so let us know if you want anyone in here with you or if you want to be left alone."

"Oh, um. I think it's fine if you guys hang out, but, like, don't distract me, if that makes sense. I don't want to burn anything."

"Sounds good."

We hear the doorbell ring and a second later Esther runs through the house. "Got it!"

I step close to Jacob and kiss him again. When I step back, he's blushing a bit. It's cute. "Everything will be okay with Mr. Wei's class. I know it."

"Thanks."

"'Sup, hos." Heaven walks into the kitchen, Axel and Valentina right behind her. And Saylor. She brought Saylor with her. I almost choke on my tongue when she walks around the counter and drapes her arm over my shoulder.

"Can I have a minute to speak to my bestie, please?" Saylor says.

"Ah, yeah," Jacob says, looking back at me with wide-eyed terror. This is not how I planned to tell Saylor my true feelings about basketball. "We'll be in the living room."

Jacob herds everyone out and I secretly wish I had the ability to teleport. Saylor turns to face me, her hand going right to her hip, her eyebrow arching up. I thought she was busy hanging out with Rhys today.

"When were you gonna tell me about all of this, young lady?"

"How much do you know, exactly?" I ask her, wondering how much trouble I'm really in. My friends just think I'm spending my free time with my boyfriend. They have no idea about any of this.

"Heaven told me everything. I had to hear about this from Heaven, Bets. I didn't know you hated playing like that. I just thought you were sick of Mama T being so intense about it. And the running. We all hate running."

"Uh, yeah. It's not my favorite thing. I didn't want to tell

you guys if this sales pitch doesn't work. I wanted to celebrate the victory together but wallow in secret pain with
my defeat, if that's the way it goes."

"Okay, first off, this is gonna work. Jacob's idea for this
whole confessional sales pitch documentary is genius. If
your moms understand anything, it's the behind-the-scenes
struggles of the student athlete."

"That's true," I say.

"Well, then I want to help. Jacob's video idea is great, but
you know it never hurts to have a Ford on your side. I mean,
we shoulda told Cris about this and she would have called in
some megacelebrity endorsement to back this whole thing."

"I don't need her influencer power just yet." I laugh. "I
appreciate it. But—how will you feel if this all works?"

"Like if you quit the team? Great. I mean, I don't want
you to quit. It'll cut my Bethy Boo quality time in half, but
I don't want you to do anything that makes you unhappy.
That's wild." She steps closer to me and then whispers,
"Um, later, I think we will talk about how this boy is in
love with you."

"What? No."

"Bethany. Things are going swell with Rhys. Fantastic,
even, but please look around. He would never do this sort of
thing for me. Shoot, Glory and Landon are, like, the perfect
couple and he would never do something like this for *her*."

I glance around the kitchen and notice he's pulled almost every spice the Yeuns own out of the cabinet and set
them next to the stove. He already has one camera set up in
the corner and his phone mounted on a minitripod on the

counter. I know part of this is his film-nerd side that just can't be helped, but the rest of it is for me. I open my mouth and almost tell Saylor everything, about the deal and its ticking clock. How at the heart of it all, Jacob and I are just really good friends now. Friends who can't stop kissing each other and holding hands. A friend I want to keep as more than a friend.

But looking up at those big hazel eyes of hers is the re- minder I need, why Jacob proposed this deal in the first place, to understand what went wrong with Saylor.

Thank god Jacob's mom comes strolling into the kitchen and that gives me the second I need to tuck my feelings back away into my secret-feelings pockets.

"Hi, girls," Mrs. Yeun says. She opens the fridge and takes out some sparkling water.

"Hi," we both say in high-pitched unison.

"Bethany, I am excited to try your dish. I'll be in my of- fice if you need anything."

"I'll let you know for sure. Thank you," I reply.

Saylor gives me the look as soon as Mrs. Yeun leaves. "Even his mom loves you," she hisses.

"I cannot talk about love right now. I must cook."

"Ugh, fine. I'll go get Jacob. You start setting up. You can do this, Bets. And even if you burn all of this and it tastes terrible, tell your moms anyway. Even though you never share your sandwiches with me."

"I will make you a sandwich, Say."

"Thank you." She beams at me before she goes to grab the rest of the crew.

Once I'm alone, I take a deep breath and look around the kitchen. I can do this. I can do this. Jacob comes back with Saylor. She helps me pull everything together while Jacob makes his framing adjustments. And then it's go-time.

I'm nervous, I won't lie, but by the time I'm done chopping my onions, I feel like I'm not exactly in my groove, but pretty obviously at the point of no return. Mrs. Yeun comes back into the kitchen and even though I'm supposed to be doing this on my own, I appreciate the way she adjusts the heat under my pan for me and then shows me an easy trick for smashing garlic. She also grabs the can opener for me so I can open my tomato paste. She leaves again with a wink that I think will fortify my confidence for another month.

It takes me about a half hour to get my two-meat sauce to where I want it to be, and then I leave that to simmer. My grandpa would have added a little sugar, but I like mine more on the spicy side. I know he'd understand.

My water boils and I add the rigatoni 'cause while we all stan a classic spaghetti noodle, there's something about a rigatoni or a penne that's perfect for maximum sauce distribution. I look up at Saylor as I pull my garlic bread out of the oven and my heart thumps a little at her thumbs-up. I'm glad Heaven told her.

I drain my pasta and combine with my sauce because that's how I like it. Jacob hands me the small party plates I grabbed from Ralphs with pink unicorns on them, and Saylor helps me plate everything. She goes to grab everyone else and I sneak a quick bite. It's perfect, to me. I hope they like it.

"I'm gonna go hide," I tell Jacob.

"Okay. I'll come grab you when we're ready."

I go to hide in the bathroom. I realize how fast my heart is beating. I could never be on *Chopped*. I'd pass out. I don't want a life in front of the camera like my mom. I just want to learn how to make good food and then feed people I love. And people who just need a good meal, even if they're kind of jerks.

I get too anxious to wait anymore and sneak back into the kitchen. Heaven and Saylor are eating more of the pasta out of the pot. "God this is good," Heaven groans.

"Yeah, I don't think my mom can actually cook." Saylor laughs.

"So?" I ask, stepping into the room, and then I step back a bit as Axel jumps up from his stool and gives me a fierce and proper military salute.

"Well done, Greene," he says.

"Yeah, Bethany. It's really good," Valentina adds. I get a thumbs-up from Esther, who is cleaning her plate with her second or third piece of garlic bread, and another from Heaven, who makes a show of moving Saylor's hand so she can get another bite.

I look over at Jacob, who is sitting in the corner still recording on his phone. "Did you get any?" I ask him. He doesn't say anything, but he looks up at me and nods, this devastating smile touching the corners of his lips.

"I'm gonna have to get this recipe from you," Mrs. Yeun says. "That spicy bite? Perfect."

I glance over at Saylor, who is shoveling more pasta into

her mouth. "Just carb loading for the tourney," she mumbles. I groan. I almost forgot about the LA Turkey Day classic. Whatever. I'll go play my heart out and then hopefully Jacob can put all this footage together quickly. And if everything works out, I'll never have to touch a basketball again.

I grab the last piece of garlic bread and help myself. I think my grandpa would be proud. We all hang out in the kitchen together, just talking and laughing. Everyone helps me clean up and I'm a little bummed I didn't make more so I could have some leftovers for myself.

Jacob and I go out to the back porch and he sets up his camera and mic again. I don't talk to Heaven this time. I just talk to him. I focus on the food and how good it feels to cook, which seems like the right move. Otherwise I'll go on and on about how glad I am that he has my back. And how cute I think he is, my little peanut butter boyfriend.

35
JACOB
(actually didn't see that coming)

Thanksgiving break goes by too fast. My parents do a really messed-up thing and actually make me spend time with my family. I mean, I should spend time with my baby cousins, Hazel and Zoe, but I also feel like I should be able to make out with my girlfriend or at least hide in a corner and text her all night. Bethany's sisters aren't back from school, but she still has to spend the week with her moms. The Lakers have one game and Bethany has to go. I get it, but we are running out of time and I want to spend as much time with her as possible before we have to end things.

I feel like I am cursing myself because time just seems to go by faster between school, yearbook, and life—I feel like I blink and another week goes by like that.

It's another Friday night with two more basketball home games. The boys win by four, but the girls' game is an absolute blowout. Bethany scores the three that puts them in the lead. And then it's like Saylor, Dylan Smith, and Tikah Hollis spend the rest of the game running up the scoreboard. They are having a great season, undefeated so far. The Turkey Day tourney didn't even count toward their school record, but they swept that too. I'm there for it all, recording every minute for the yearbook. I still have to finish editing the video for Bethany's moms, but something in my gut tells me it's going to work.

She's focused when she's on the court, but she was happy when she was chopping and mixing. I don't think her moms can look past that.

It only makes sense to celebrate another double win, so Kayden and Dylan Smith decide to throw a party at their house. I don't really wanna go. Bethany and I only have ten days left in our deal. I'd rather go back to my house and watch movies, but a win is a win, so when she asks me if I want to go, I say yes. I do what I do best as soon as we get there and start getting some great stuff for a few TikToks. I record the tense final moments of Landon kicking Oliver's butt at beer pong. I'll send that to Landon and he can decide if he wants to post it on his own account. And then Tatum has a specific request.

"I need proof of this." They laugh as they drag Saylor into the middle of the living room. "Jacob, please record this. Okay, Say, in one, two—" Tatum goes on, reciting the lyrics to this Beyoncé song while they're trying to show Saylor the dance moves.

"I'm doing it right!" Saylor says.

"No, you aren't." Tatum laughs.

"It's not my fault my mom's white!" Saylor cries.

"Here." Bethany grabs Saylor's other hand and starts walking her through it again. "One, two, hip, hip, ass, front, ass, front."

"That's not it at all." Tatum falls onto the couch laughing.

Emily joins the fray and they only need Glory to make the picture complete. I glance up from my phone and spot her in the kitchen talking to Kayden. He says something in her ear and I feel like that's my cue to look away. It's weird to just watch people when you're not recording them and I now realize how creepy that thought is too. Also, get permission before you record people. Whatever they are talking about is none of my business either way. I stop the recording and start again. Then stop it again when Glory comes power walking into the frame.

I look up as she grabs Bethany's arm. "Excuse us for a second. I need to borrow your girlfriend."

"Whoops. Be right back, I guess," Bethany says, scrunching her nose at me before they slip by.

"Here, Jacob, come here," Tatum says, waving me forward. "I bet I can teach him faster."

"No way." I back up. "You think Saylor is bad, try getting me to dance."

"He's right. He's terrible," Saylor says with a smile. I'm glad we're on the same page. I keep recording Tatum's attempt to get Saylor on the beat, which I have to admit is pretty funny. This will make a good TikTok.

"What!" I hear Bethany screech from the other room. I turn around and I can only see Glory in the doorway, but she's clearly bent over telling Bethany something. Probably just a game of telephone from Dylan to Kayden and back to the girls on the team. Not my business, and if it is, Bethany will tell me later. I turn back around and hit the record button on my phone screen.

"Here, Tatum, you do it the right way. Without her," I say.

"Gee thanks, Jacob." Saylor laughs.

"Listen, I have a vision here. Trust me."

Tatum puts the song on her phone and starts doing the dance. She's partway through it when Tikah comes flying into the room and starts doing it with her. They do it all the way through, laughing and high-fiving when they finish.

"And that's how you do that, biiiitch." Tikah laughs, pointing in Saylor's face as she struts back into the kitchen. I capture that too.

"Damn, freshman," Saylor groans.

"I'm just saying. Do what you will with that information," I hear Glory say behind me. I turn around as she and Bethany come back into the room.

"Yeah, thanks," Bethany says, letting out a wide-eyed breath. Her face completely changes when she looks back at me.

"Everything cool?" I ask when she comes back to my side.

"Yeah," she says, but then she starts chewing her lip like maybe that's not true. I almost start recording Glory trying to walk Saylor through the moves again, but then Bethany turns to me. "Uh, yeah. Well—I—I guess I should tell you. Let's go outside." I follow her through the house and out the front door, onto the Smiths' driveway. It's a perfect night out, clear and not cold, but I have the worst feeling in the pit of my stomach. No one with that look on their face wants to go out to the quiet, deserted driveway for a good talk.

"I don't want to say it's nothing 'cause, all things considered, it is something, and I think it would be pretty weird if I acted like it wasn't something," Bethany tells me.

"Sure," I say slowly. "What happened?"

"Um, the gist of it, Kayden asked Glory how serious we were. 'Cause he was thinking about asking me out."

I think I might pass out. My ears are suddenly hot and my head is swimming, but I force myself to focus on exactly what she's saying. "That's what you wanted, right? Well, I mean, you wanted Oliver, but what did Saylor say? Kayden was your celebrity crush. This is good, right?"

"Yeah. It's good, I think. I'm still kinda processing it."

"It sounds like we did what we set out to do. I'm not afraid to have a real conversation with a girl who isn't Heaven, and I'll make sure my next girlfriend is prepared for my eighteen-part presentation on the importance of light sources. And you can go out with Kayden." I'm rambling. I know it.

"Jacob—"

"We decided it would be mutual, yeah? I can dump you if that'll make things easier." She swallows because she feels bad for me and then I feel like a huge asshole because I know she's going to cry. That makes two of us. I take her hand and pull her close, wrapping my arms around her. "It's all good. Don't worry about me," I tell her. "This is the best outcome, right?"

"I guess," she hiccups and then the floodgates open. I hold her a few seconds longer and then I have to step back. Part of my brain is already packing its bags. There's no point in hanging around or begging. She has it bad for Kayden. I knew this the whole time. Of course she's psyched he wants to go out with her. Hell, the part of me who is her friend is happy for her too. The part of me that's falling . . .

"I think I'm gonna go," I say.

"But wait, I drove. Your stuff is in my car," she says, dabbing her face with the sleeve of her Lady Minotaurs hoodie.

"Right, can I grab it?"

She swallows hard, then walks past me toward the street. I follow her to the car, glad she has her keys on her, and grab my backpack and my skateboard out of her trunk.

"We're still friends," I tell her. "I'm not moving away or anything."

"Yeah, but who am I gonna make out with for research now?" she says, doing that hilarious laugh-crying thing she does. A snort bubbles out of me.

"Kayden. Duh."

"Yeah, I guess," she says.

"So we stick with the plan. You go back in there and say we decided we'd be better as friends? That way no one is the bad guy and we can still just be friends?"

She doesn't say anything at first. But then her lip twitches and she lets out another breath through her nose. "Yeah, okay."

"Or you can tell your friends *whenever* you want. I'll tell Madlyn on Monday and she'll tell the whole school."

That makes Bethany do that laugh-cry thing again and I know I have to leave before I hug her. No such luck though. She steps closer and wraps her arms around me. "Okay, but don't actually move. I do want to be friends."

I put my hands on her shoulders and step back for my

own sake. Then I grip my board with both hands in front of me so I won't be tempted to hug her one more time. "I should be done with the pitch for your moms by the end of next week. I'll let you know and then when you're ready to show them, I'll get it all set up."

"Okay," she says.

I give her a weak smile and then turn to leave, and then turn back again. "Hey, say no if it's too much, but do you think I can show it to Mr. Wei? I won't show it to the whole class, but maybe I can get a few points for effort or something, and maybe see if he has any editing tips that will really wow the moms."

"I think that's a good idea." She tries to smile back, but it doesn't really work. "I mean, you did the hard part."

"Uh, I definitely didn't. I just observed and documented your genius."

"Whatever you say. Yeah, show it to him. He'll be crazy not to bump you up to an A minus at least."

"That won't be happening, but I'm gonna try."

We're both stalling. She feels bad and I feel like I just got knocked off my board by a speeding car. I pull in a deep breath and smile. Then I point at her as I start backing down the street. "You still my jam, B."

"Shut up." She laughs through her tears.

I walk all the way home. I've skated plenty at night, but it's hard to look out for cracks and dips and cars when you can't stop crying.

36
BETHANY
(is convinced that escalated a little too quickly)

I lean against my car, still crying after Jacob is long gone. We only had ten days left in our deal, but this is not how I wanted it to end at all. But I guess I should be glad he pulled the plug first, because if it had been up to me, we wouldn't have broken up at all. That's the problem though, us staying together was definitely not a part of the plan. I have no clue what he's going to do next. If there's some other girl he secretly has his eye on. Someone like Madlyn or more like Heaven, but, you know, not gay.

I never thought liking someone could hurt like this. I cover my mouth with my sleeve so I don't sob out loud. Maybe I need to stay single. A boy who doesn't even like me ends our relationship agreement a few days early because the boy of my dreams steps into the picture, and I'm crying like a widow in a period drama. I can't help it though. This isn't what I wanted. I wanted Jacob.

He didn't like you *like you though*, my brain decides to gently remind me. And I know it's important for me to remember that even though he was a good friend to me, that doesn't mean he caught feelings the way I did. So that's it, I guess. The plan is over and it worked, I think.

And now I just have to deal with feeling like this.

There is no way in hell Crybaby Bethany is making a re-appearance tonight. I text Saylor and ask her to come out-side. Of course, she doesn't come alone. Tatum, Glory, and Emily are right behind her.

"Bets. What happened?" Saylor asks. My friends swarm me on all sides and I start crying harder.

"Jacob and I broke up."

"What?" Tatum gasps. "You guys were so cute together."

"Was this over Kayden?!" Glory asks.

Saylor looks between us, confused. "What happened with Kayden?"

"He came up to me and asked how serious Bethany and Jacob were 'cause he's been meaning to ask her out since *last year.*" Yeah, that was the little tidbit I left out of my conversation with Jacob. I was still processing the informa-tion. I kinda wish Glory had waited to tell me.

"Wow," Emily whispers.

"But like some other people, he thought she wasn't al-lowed to date. I just told you so you'd know. I didn't think you'd break up with the boy."

"I didn't, ugh. That's not what happened," I say. I hate this so much.

"Well, what happened?" Tatum asks softly. They step closer and link their arm with mine.

"Nothing, we were just talking and he said something and then it just sort of happened."

"What did he say?" Saylor says. If she could breathe fire, I know smoke would be coming out of her nose right now.

Jesus, Jacob and I really should have thought this through a little better.

"I just asked him if he was having a good time 'cause he's had his phone in his hand all night and he finally admitted it wasn't really his scene. So we decided to just be friends. Neither of us wanted to force any part of this," I say. I hate how easily the lie rolls off my tongue. "But. We're good. It was good. Just hard."

Saylor relaxes a bit. "I mean, he hung in there for a while, but it wasn't really his scene when we were together either."

"That's true," Glory adds. "I like his friends, but it's not like we're all a big, happy family now."

"I guess it doesn't matter now, but don't be mad at Jacob," I say. "We had a good honest talk. I'm just sad, that's all."

"Hey. You can lead the skater to a team party, but you can't make him ball," Saylor says, her lips quivering, trying not to laugh at her own joke.

"I'm calling the police," I say.

"Um, not to be that person," Emily says, "but what are you gonna do about Kayden?"

"I don't know. Marry him, I guess." I snort and more tears run down my face.

"You don't have to make that call right this second," Glory says.

I'm not done crying and it's getting late, so we decide to pack it in and start our sleepover at Saylor's. Tatum stays with me while the girls run inside to get their stuff and so Saylor can make sure Rhys is cool without her and so Glory can say goodbye to Landon with her tongue. We head back to Saylor's house, and she must have texted Cris because she's waiting for us in the kitchen with snacks and a big hug just for me. The woman is too much, but I do appreciate the mom love.

We get ready for bed and pile into the Fords' den and Glory thinks it's a good idea for us to sneak and watch her favorite parts of those *365 Days* movies on Netflix. I don't think horny old white people will help, but she keeps pausing it and giving her dramatic notes on hand and tongue placement. I can't help but laugh through my drying tears.

I hold out as long as I can before I text Jacob.

> The homies know.
> I just told them we agreed as this wasn't really your scene.
> But we're still on good terms.

I watch my phone screen as he stops and starts typing three different times. I almost say something again, just to put myself out of this misery of waiting. Finally, he responds.

> Cool.
> My mom asked cause we got home at the same time.
> She's bummed. She loves you.
> Esther's asleep.
> I'll tell her next year sometime.

> Probably for the best.
> I'll see you around?

For sure.

I almost say good night, but I think it's best if I just leave it. If I text him again, I'm going to want him to text me back, and then the next thing you know I'll be showing up at the skate park tomorrow with a sign begging him to take me back. *Pull it together, Greene,* I tell myself. *You got what you wanted and you learned your lesson.*

"Texting Jake?" Saylor whispers.

"No." I shake my head and lock my phone. "Just texting Jocelyn back. She had a question about the moms' Christmas presents."

"You're lying, but that's okay." She sinks into the couch and focuses back on the TV where these two naked white people are doing a little bit too much on the dude's boat. I look at my phone again; the picture that Jacob took of the picture of the two of us in the photo booth at homecoming is still my background. I don't want to change it and that's exactly why I have to. I dig through my camera roll, which is clearly a mistake because I have to scroll by all of these pictures and videos of me and Jacob, pictures Jacob took of me.

It's tragic he didn't fall in love with me. I'm so hot.

I pull my borrowed blanket over my chin to cover my sniffles and change my background to this cute pink-cloud wallpaper I saved over the summer. I think Saylor is getting up to go to the bathroom or something, but she shuffles down to my end of the couch and cuddles the hell out of me. Thank goodness for friends.

37
JACOB
(a man truly struggling for his art)

My parents give me the weekend to sit in my misery. Esther feels bad for me and makes me Eggos with cream cheese and cinnamon. Something new she's trying. She doesn't say who inspired her to take risks in the kitchen, but we both know. I spend hours wondering whether or not I should text Bethany and tell her how I feel, that I know the plan was my idea, but things changed. I still like her, a lot. And then I think about that squealing noise she made when Glory told her about Kayden. We had a good thing. We had fun, but I can't compete with Kayden Smith.

And then I spend hours just missing her and wondering how bad Monday is going to be. I guess it's good we only have one class together. It's too late in the semester for me to transfer to a different math class, but it's gonna suck not sitting next to her or holding her hand as we walk to our next class.

Saturday night, Axel and Heaven try to stop by, but I tell them it's not a good idea. I love my friends, but I've never felt this bad before, and I don't know that I need to share that with anyone who doesn't live in my house. They understand though, and after Heaven offers to beat up Bethany and Saylor for good measure, they reassure me they'll be around when I'm ready to emerge from my cave of sorrow.

I'm kinda shocked my dad doesn't say anything when I say I'm not up for the skate park on Sunday morning. It's the first time I've skipped it in a while. I just can't do it. My whole body feels like it's being weighed down by every rock on earth and taking that energy and hopping on a skateboard doesn't seem like a great idea.

Finally, late Sunday afternoon, I pull myself out of bed and get back to editing the video for Bethany's moms. The sooner I finish it, the better. The sooner I finish, the sooner I can stop looking at each frame, thinking just how cute Bethany is. I'm getting close to finishing the first cut without music when there's a knock on my door.

"Come in."

"You okay?" Dad asks. He walks across the room and flips my blanket back over my bed before he sits down. I spin around in my desk chair to face him.

"No."

"It's pretty wild. I feel like just yesterday—"

"Oh, Dad, don't do it," I groan.

"Oh no, I'm doing it. This is part of my midlife crisis. I get to look at you and think about how I'm old now. And how I have no clue where the time went and how the hell you got so tall because I don't think it's genetics. I'm also just bummed I can't just zap my wisdom into your brain to make things easier for you."

"Okay," I sigh. "What were you gonna say?"

"Thanks. I was gonna say that it's just wild to think about the years you were even smaller than Esther is now and taking you and Axe and Heaven to the park. Now you have this whole life of your own and girlfriends and breakups. When I was your age, I was dating this girl, Angelica Garza—"

"And then she dumped you, but it all worked out because you eventually met Mom and now you have one perfect kid and an Esther."

"I didn't say all that and that's not what happened." My dad laughs. "I was gonna say that I'm glad I can look at you now and not downplay what's going on with you and Bethany because when Angelica dumped me, I felt like my world ended. And I didn't just get over it. That's not how heartbreak works, no matter how old you are. Your mom and I used to joke that if we ever saw some of our exes, we wouldn't even be cool about it. We would jump behind a parked car and hide. What you're feeling is some real shit. Getting your heart broken sucks."

"It does. What happened with Angelica?"

"Oh, I was a little punk back then and her parents didn't think we were good together, so she broke up with me. I didn't get over it for a long time, but I dated other people and then, yeah, I met your mom, and that's my best friend," he says with a shrug, like he's trying to stop himself from getting all mushy. I can't deny that my parents love each other. That's one thing I've never doubted. Which makes what I'm feeling hurt even more.

"I think Bethany was starting to become my best friend," I admit, feeling really pathetic about it.

Dad leans forward and pats my knee. "Just give yourself time. It'll get easier."

"I think I might shave my head," I say. I reach back and pull down the bun I shoved my hair into two days ago. It needs help.

"Don't," Dad says, shaking his own shaved head, the left side tatted with a dagger and rose. "I had a really slick style going when you were like three. Shaved my head and never grew back the same."

"Maybe just the sides."

My dad considers it for a moment, then shrugs. "Hmm, growing it back out will be a pain in the ass, but I guess it's part of the heartbreak process. Come on. I'll grab my clippers and then after you can take that shower you've been avoiding."

"Yeah, good call."

I make sure my editing progress is saved and then follow my dad into the bathroom. Of course, Esther has to come see what we're doing. My mom usually trims my hair, so she has come in to consult on the whole process. We finish the left side and I realize I've made a mistake, but it's too late to go back. My dad finishes and my mom cleans up the back and, in the end, I don't look half-bad. I take that much-needed shower and then Esther decides we need to go out to dinner, her choice of course. We end up at Lucille's in the mall and I realize I haven't eaten much since Esther's apology Eggos.

I don't say much during dinner, but that's fine. Esther has a lot to share about school and her own friends. She seems happy to have the spotlight on herself for a little while. I'm still sad as hell when we get home, but I give Esther a big hug before I go back to my wallowing.

○ ○ ○

I stay up all night editing, another bad idea, but I convince myself that being a zombie at school will be easier than trying to act like I'm okay. Heaven and Axel do me a solid and just sort of orbit around me most of the day, brushing off all the random people who ask me if it's true that Bethany and I broke up. I get asked at least six times before I make it to second period.

I sit in the back and try to make myself invisible, but of course Bethany looks at me when she walks in the room. She gives me a little wave and an even smaller smile. I wave back, but I can't smile. She sits near the front and doesn't turn around once. We only have a few more weeks until the semester is over and maybe the universe will help me out and make it so we have no classes together next semester. I know I'm being dramatic, but this really sucks.

I make it to the end of the day without crying. Making it through this conversation with Mr. Wei might break me though. "I don't know how many points this is worth," I say when the class finally clears out. "But I put something together for my friend to show her moms and she said I could show it to you. For extra credit."

"I haven't officially offered extra credit to the whole class, but let's see what you got," he says. Not exactly what I wanted to hear, but on-brand with the last few days. Why not pile on a little more disappointment? I bring everything up on my laptop and press play. I keep my eyes on the floor while it plays, trying to focus on my end goal with the final edit and nothing else. When it finally ends, Mr. Wei closes the laptop and turns back to me.

"Jake, this seems like it was a lot of work," he says.

"It was."

He frowns, leaning back in his chair. "Your friend, huh? I thought this was your girlfriend. That's what the walls tell me."

"We broke up," I say.

"Hmm. Has she seen this?"

"Not yet. I thought you might have some notes for me. And maybe some extra credit, bring my B up to an A minus or at least a B plus."

"You know a B is okay, right?" he asks.

"I mean I guess, but not for USC."

"Who says that?" he asks.

I just shrug. I had a whole argument here, but I'm too tired.

"Look, I don't know what tips I can give you about your love life because I don't want you kids to think I actually care about you, but a B this semester is not going to ruin your chances of going to USC. And I'll be honest—and if you tell anyone I said this, I will deny it—but if you keep making stuff like this, you're gonna make an excellent filmmaker. That natural light during the confessional? That's excellent."

"Thanks. I've heard you dropped kids from the next class for less though."

"Yeah, I don't know who is spreading that rumor. I've only dropped people who were failing. This class has a limited capacity. I want there to be room for the students who take it seriously. I have one student who is dropping next semester to get into the robotics clinic."

"Yeah, but my writing kinda sucks."

"Yeah, and you're sixteen and I'm your teacher. My job is to tell you your writing sucks and to help make it better. And any teacher you have at film school, it's their job to do the same thing. And if you decide to become a screenwriter one day—"

"No. I just want to be behind the camera."

"Cool." He chuckles. "I'm just saying, you are gonna be getting notes for the rest of your life. From studio execs, directors, your own crew. Critics and awards associations, since you want that Oscar so bad."

That does make me smile. I do want that Oscar.

"It's not to knock you down. You'll hate those notes sometimes and sometimes they'll be really bad notes, but you'll have those moments where you get good notes and you end up making something good with a lot of input from a lot of people. That make sense?"

"Yeah," I say.

"I appreciate the effort though. I gotta think about if there's time to level the playing field with this for the rest of the class. I don't think everyone else has a near-Emmy-worthy documentary just hanging out in the cloud. But yeah, keep this up, I will write you a glowing recommendation to any film school you want."

"Thanks, Mr. Wei."

"Not that I care, but why did you guys break up? Looks like you're pretty in love with this girl."

"I didn't tell her how I felt when I had the chance," I admit, which is really the whole truth. She might have still been pretty pumped about Kayden, but at least I would know I tried.

"Tough break, man. Well, just don't do anything creepy with all of your emotions and you'll be all right. As for your culinary project here, I would adjust the audio levels when you come to the taste-testing part, but other than that, I think it's pretty good. I hope her moms let her quit. Make Coach Miller sweat a little. Don't tell anyone I said that either."

"I won't."

"Also, nice haircut," he adds, nodding in my direction. "I frosted my tips after a breakup once. I looked ridiculous. There's nothing worse than a depressed Asian guy with patchy blond hair."

That makes me laugh. "I'll keep that in mind." I pack up my things and head down to the yearbook office. The room gets weirdly quiet when I walk in and the tiny bit of hope I got from my talk with Mr. Wei goes right out the window. I ignore the way people are looking at me and go right for my desk.

"Madlyn announced your breakup during the huddle," Noah whispers.

"Great."

"Guessing you're not gonna head down to basketball practice today?" Noah asks me.

"Nope. I still have to go through the footage from Friday anyway."

"I'm cool switching water polo with you from here on out if you want."

I think for a second, what it'll be like watching Bethany and Kayden before and after practice, or games. I know Mr. Wei and Mr. Wolfson would tell me I shouldn't let my personal stuff get in the way of my professional duties, but as Mr. Wei also pointed out, I'm only sixteen. I won't do anything weird like standing outside Bethany's house asking her to choose me, but petty is an emotion I'm gonna hold on to for a second. I want her to be happy, even if it is with Kayden, but I don't want to be there to document it.

"Yeah, I'd appreciate that, thanks."

"Cool."

o o o

When I get home, I see a big envelope on the counter and my stomach tries to leave the room without me. It's addressed to me and Mom. I know exactly what it is. I don't want to get rid of it, but I'm gonna have to tell my mom that whatever is inside is not for display. I almost make it to my room, but I turn around instead and go back for the envelope. I rip it open and see those pictures from homecoming. Cris Ford has slapped a sticky note to the largest print just over my and Bethany's heads.

Kelly and Rick,
Big apologies for the delay. Mix-up with the
printers, but please enjoy these absolutely

adorable prints of Bethany and Jake from
homecoming, compliments of the Fords! They do
make the cutest couple.

XO—Cristine

We did make the cutest couple and I'm guessing Mrs. Ford mailed these out sometime last week. She probably didn't think we were gonna break up over the weekend. I put the pictures back into the envelope and take it down to the Thunderdome and leave it on Mom's desk. I go right back to my room and collapse onto my bed, burying my face in my pillow. I glance at my phone as it vibrates with a text from Axel. Behind the text preview is a picture of Bethany and me from our first date at the beach. I should probably change that.

> Wanna pick up that Next
> Generation rewatch?
> My dad is refusing to let me
> start Picard until we finish.

> Yeah. Just give me a few.

In all the movies I've seen, this part of the hero's journey, where he's down and out, only lasts a few minutes. There's always a light at the end of the tunnel, love saved, reunited, rekindled. I know *my* misery will never fade. I can't believe movies have betrayed me this way.

38
BETHANY
*(hopes it gets better soon because
it has definitely gotten worse)*

I didn't think it was possible, but I finally stopped crying. I hold it together at school, but at night my eyes are just leaking. Jocelyn comes through when I text her and Trin asking them how to get over this. Cold compresses under my eyes should help, and they do. I make it to Wednesday and realize Jacob and I aren't going to magically get back together. We're civil in stats and I'm not saying he looks happy about it, but when I do see him around school, he says hi like everything is normal and goes about his business. And I'm just sitting here trying to act like I don't love his new haircut. I'm so glad he didn't chop it all off, but the shaved sides are working for me. Sob.

He did stop me this morning to tell me Mr. Wei liked his director's cut of our presentation for the moms. He just has a few more things to fix and he'll get it to me this weekend.

I spend the rest of the morning trying to pay attention in class, but really focusing on the fact that I have to present this to the moms alone now. I guess I figured Jacob would be there, if not as Boyfriend then at least as Jacob, my friend, but I know that seems awkward now. Mostly because every time I see him, I want to cry. But I refuse. Not at school. Crybaby Bethany is banished forever.

I grab my lunch. Mama T is back on the road, so I'm having ham and cheese today. I make my way down to the quad. It's cool and cloudy out, but luckily it's not supposed to rain. I huddle next to Saylor on the bench of our table and pull out my sandwich.

"Okay. I've waited as long as I possibly can," Glory announces. I look up and she's staring dead at me.

"Waited for what?"

"Bethany, my little Bethy Boo, you know I love you and I want to be very sensitive to Jake being your first boyfriend and all that, but Kayden Smith is interested in you. He asked Landon about you again this morning."

"He did ask me yesterday if you guys really broke up," Saylor adds with a wince.

This is not news I need to hear. It is too soon. Maybe. I don't know. But either way, it's Kayden Smith. Being with Jacob opened my mind to a lot of things, but I don't know if I'm Kayden Smith's level yet.

"How do I just go out with Kayden Smith?" I ask.

"Easy," Saylor says. "You let me go up to him after practice. I get the temperature of the situation one more time to be sure and then I slip him your info. He slides into your DMs. You go out with him and smooch him like crazy."

"And then you're like this untouchable basketball power couple," Tatum says. I swallow as Saylor nudges me under the table. My friends don't know about my plan yet. The moms cooking plan. The possibly-quitting-basketball plan.

I have too many secret plans. I need to stop lying so much.

"Am I power-couple ready yet?" I cringe. "It's Kayden Smith!"

Glory shoots me that look. "Do you really want to look back on this and think: Oh wow, I really had a chance with Kayden Smith and I said no just 'cause?"

"No," I groan, shuffling in my seat. I know my friends are right. This is exactly what I wanted. Exactly why I jumped right into shenanigans with Jacob. I'm not over him, not by a long shot. But my friends have a point. If I don't say something to Kayden soon, he'll think I'm not interested at all and he will move on. You do not keep someone like Kayden Smith on ice for too long. My heart isn't in it, not yet, but my head will never forgive me if I screw this up. I let out another groany whine.

"Listen, Jake is out here with his cute little haircut," Glory goes on. "I'm sure he'll be getting his groove back any day now."

"Fine. I'll make sweet, sweet love to Kayden," I say.

"Don't sound *so* excited." Glory sighs.

"I'm just scared."

"It'll be fine. Kayden's nice," Saylor says.

I look over as Tatum nods in agreement. They wouldn't be pushing me toward this if they thought he was a jerk. "Okay. I'll do it."

Saylor gives me another nudge of encouragement. I have to look at this as a good thing, right? Sure, I'm not entirely convinced I won't puke on Kayden if he does actually try to talk to me. I was at his house barely a week ago and I didn't

even say hi to him. *But this is what I wanted*, I remind myself. It's more than what I wanted. I wanted Oliver to notice me in moderately horny and romantic ways. Kayden
wasn't even an option. Well, now he is, and if I was willing
to dash my own heart into a million pieces by falling for
Jacob when I knew good and well he wasn't into me, I might
as well go for a guy who is interested, even if he is the hottest boy in this hemisphere.

Saylor and Glory work their magic. After practice, Kayden
Smith walks right up to me and I've never been happier for
the fact that Jacob stopped coming to watch us play.

"Hey," Kayden says.

Somehow, I don't faint. "Hey."

"I'm gonna go grab my stuff, but you wanna meet out in
the parking lot? We can talk for a sec. Off the court."

"Sure," I say. I am sweating, so much.

"Okay." He flashes me this million-dollar model smile
and I swear I forget my name. I power walk into the locker
room and tell Saylor she has to come with me, just in case
this is part of some elaborate prank. She laughs at me, but
she grabs her stuff and comes with me. Thank god there's
no prank. Kayden walks out with Dylan and a few other
guys from the team but comes right to me.

"Message me later, Bets," Saylor says, all subtle as she
backs toward her car.

"I will." And then it's just me and Kayden standing near
my SUV. It's starting to get dark, but there's still enough
light for me to look up at him and his perfect face. *It's now
or never, Greene*, I tell myself. *You got this.* "So." Of course

my voice comes out all weird. But Kayden just smiles.

"I just wanted to see what you were up to this weekend. I thought we could go to the movies or something." The movies. Jacob loves movies. "Or you could teach me how you somehow nail every single three."

"Just watch Steph Curry. Learned everything from him."

"Really? You watch tape like that?"

"You know who my mom is, right?" I try to laugh.

"True. I'm sure she coaches the hell out of you in the offseason."

"She tries."

"But you're just naturally that good?"

I try to be cute and shrug. It does not feel natural. Still, I roll with it. "What can I say?"

"Kayden! Let's go!" Dylan yells across the parking lot.

"That's not about you. She has something to do later and she wants to get home and shower."

"Don't we all." I smile.

"Let me see your phone right quick."

"Oh, sure." I unlock my phone. So, so glad I already changed my background.

"You can DM me on IG, but here's my number." He hands me my phone back and I don't really know how to process the fact that Kayden Smith just gave me his number on purpose.

"Thanks. Well, you should go. Everyone needs a shower."

"Definitely." He smiles at me again and then heads back to his car. He turns and looks at me again and I know this whole situation should be making me swoon, but I'm just

not there. I'm just in shock at this point. I get back home
and climb into the shower and then text the homies and
let them know contact has officially been made. The whole
group chat is very excited.

o o o

Okay, so I'm a little relieved that Kayden isn't even in my
grade, but I spend the next few days an absolute mess. We
text some and he walks with me the couple of times we see
each other in the hall. And we talk for a few minutes before and after practice. He's treating me the same, I guess
you could say, but now he's talking to me. He's not all up
on me trying to hold my hand or anything, but he is nice
and chatty. Word gets around that we're going on a date on
Saturday, thanks to his sister, but I just ignore it because
it's just one date. He hasn't asked me to be his girlfriend.
And in the back of my mind, I'm still thinking about Jacob.

I've seen a few girls flirting with him in the halls and it
just reminds me I need to get over him, like now.

Friday, both our teams have night games. We're away at
Hollywood High. Dylan invites everyone back to her house
for another party because both teams won again. Thank
god I have to take my braids down. Our braider Tiffany
is coming first thing in the morning to put in some fresh
twists. I text Kayden and tell him I won't be there. And he
says some cute thing about getting my hair done for our
date, which is more of a coincidence than anything, but it is
a nice thought.

After Tiffany is done with my hair the next day, I look amazing. I feel nervous as hell and the moms don't help the situation. I finished getting ready early. Too antsy to sit in my room, I head back downstairs and join the moms in the living room, watching the Nets game already in progress on the East Coast.

"You all set?" Momlissa asks.

"Yeah, I still have time though."

"Well, you look cute."

I look down at my crop hoodie and my jeans. "Thanks. The booty's poppin' and the titties is sittin'."

Momlissa swats me with a pillow, laughing. "Stop it."

Mama T tries to hide her own smile, shaking her head. But then a second later her expression drops. "I still don't know the full story about the Jacob situation." The game goes to commercial and she finally looks over at me.

"We just decided to be friends," I say. It takes a lot to swallow the lump that just lodged itself in my throat.

"That's a shame. Well, I'm glad you guys are still friends. I liked that kid. He seemed really sweet."

"You'll like Kayden even more. He's looking at a full ride to Auburn." I know Alabama is really far away, but I need Kayden and me to make it through one date before I think about a long-distance relationship a year from now.

"Really?"

"Yeah. He's Dylan Smith's brother. Our captain? We're not the only family of basketball stars in town."

"Oh!" Mama T says. "Okay, good to know."

Kayden shows up right on time. He comes inside and

mixes it up with the moms for a bit. They. Love. Him. He and Momlissa are having this really intense talk about LeBron's legacy and I have to remind him the movie will start without us. My moms remind us both of my curfew. We say goodbye and head out to the car. Kayden is a perfect gentleman, opening the door for me, making sure I can see where the seat belt clip is, and then he starts talking.

"Man, your moms are so cool. It must be awesome going to Lakers games all the time."

"I actually only go to a handful a season."

"Really? I'd be courtside every game," he says as he pulls his car out to the street.

"It's actually a pretty demanding schedule. Going to every home game would be like a part-time job and I have to, like, study and hang out with my friends."

"True, but those family seats must be nice."

"They are. So—" I realize then I know absolutely nothing about Kayden Smith.

"It's gonna be pretty tight when both our teams go undefeated this season, huh?" He smiles at me as we hit the first light on Overland and I realize that Kayden thinks I absolutely love being good at basketball. I've made a serious mistake.

39
JACOB
(puts on his bravest face)

I finish editing Bethany's video on Thursday. But then Friday she has her game, and thanks to several people who can't just mind their own business, I hear that she has a date with Kayden on Saturday. It's good, I realize. The firm proof I need to try to move on. Not to anyone in particular, but just move on from how I feel about her. I still have to see her at school though, and I need to close the door on our last chunk of unfinished business. Then I can start my true lone man's journey to healing. I guess it's good it's pouring outside or I'd use our Sunday trip to the park as an excuse to put this off for at least another day.

I give myself my other pep talk of the day and finally text her.

> Hey, finished the doc.
> Would love to show it to you.
> See if you have any notes.

I stare at my phone and wonder what happens if she never responds. Maybe she woke up early and went on a second date with Kayden. Maybe she changed her mind about the whole thing because she's finally dating another basketball player and they stayed up all night talking about stats and the draft, and the importance of endorsement deals. I'm about to toss my phone onto my bed when she texts me back.

> Hey. I can't wait to see it.
> When's good?

>> Today.
>> My parents took Esther out for the day.

> K cool.
> I'll come by in a bit.
> You want anything from Taco Bell?

I force myself not to smile. She's just being polite. Friends can buy each other Taco Bell sometimes. I want to say yes. I could destroy at least two Crunchwrap Supremes right now, but I need to stay focused. Show her in and get her out. If she stays too long, I might fall in love with her all over again. I've moved on from petty to dramatic.

>> I'm good, but thank you.

> NP.

I tidy up my room and wait and wait a little longer. It only takes her fifteen minutes to get to my house, but it feels like forever. The doorbell sounds louder for some reason when she finally rings it. I let out a deep breath and go answer the door. *Just show her the video and then you can let this all go.* When I open the door, I realize how screwed I am. I realize just how much I missed her.

"You changed your hair," I say without thinking. She had braids before, but now her hair is in these long twists.

"So did you!"

I rub my hand along the shaved side of my head and almost ask if she likes it, but I really need to keep it together here. Saying nothing makes this awkward silence between us though. She inhales shakily and plasters a smile on her face. "No skate park today?" she asks as she steps inside, gripping her Taco Bell and her Baja Blast in her hands.

"It's not that much fun when it's raining."

"Right. A little dangerous, I bet."

"Yeah, it can be a little dicey."

"Here," she says. I follow her through the house into the kitchen where she sets down her food. "I was starving, so I ate in the car, but I got you a Crunchwrap. Drink's yours too."

"Thanks," I say. I can feel my face going red, but she doesn't say anything when she looks up at me. "You wanna come see what I got? I'll eat after."

"Yeah, let's do it."

I lead the way to my room, glad I made it look presentable. I pull out my desk chair for her and she takes a seat. "You just tell me if there's anything you don't like or want to take out?"

"What did Mr. Wei say about it? You showed him, right? Is he gonna give you the points?"

"He really liked it and we had a good talk. He's still thinking over the points because he didn't give the rest of the class a chance to do extra credit. But he did tell me he was impressed." I leave out the other details of that conversation.

"Oh, fair, but good, right?"

"Yeah. Really good. So thank you, I guess, for giving me a worthy subject."

"Yeah." She snorts. "Anytime you need someone to pour their guts out, I'm your girl. Okay. Well, let's do this."

I lean closer and press play, careful not to brush against her, smelling her signature fresh scent. She blows out a breath and focuses on the screen. I sit on my bed and stare at the toes of my socks on the rug. It's weird to have someone watching you when you're trying to watch something. She doesn't say anything the whole time. I sort of rewatch the whole thing in my mind, smiling to myself when it gets to my favorite part.

"Why did you want to tell your moms this way?" Heaven asks her.

"Because I'm too afraid they won't understand, but I want them to." The way Bethany answers, the little smile on her face, tears lining her eyes, which the sunlight caught perfectly.

I look up at her the second it ends; she's still staring at the screen though. "What do you think?" I ask.

She doesn't say anything for a long while. She looks at

the screen and then down at her fingers, this odd frown playing across her face. She looks confused or maybe a little upset. "It's—it's great. Are you sure Mr. Wei doesn't want you to teach the class?"

"I mean, I'm good, but I'm not that good."

"Yeah, okay," she says, mocking me. "It's pretty perfect. I'm still terrified to show it to the moms though. It's different when I'm just talking to you."

"Just let the video do the talking and then you can go from there. You say a lot here. I'd be shocked if they didn't at least hear you out."

"I'm just picturing the freak-out they are both going to have, especially Teresa. She— Yeah."

"Focus on the best possible outcome instead of the worst. That should help between now and when you show it to them."

"Is that what you do?"

"No." I smile a little, actively thinking about how much it's gonna suck when I see her and Kayden's wedding pictures go down my Instagram feed someday. "But it seems like a good idea."

"True." She laughs and then she lets out a long sigh, looking around my room. She glances at my sack chair. "How are you doing?"

"Good," I lie and then I say the worst thing I could possibly say. "I heard about the big date with Kayden last night." Her eyes go wide and I immediately regret it.

"We don't have to talk about that," Bethany says.

I dig the hole deeper. "We're friends and this was the

whole point. I wanna know if all of my boyfriend effort helped? I think our official breakup date is tomorrow, right? We should at least debrief."

"That is true. Um, Kayden is great," she says. Which isn't like Bethany at all. Bethany never keeps it short and sweet. But maybe this is how she is with me now. I can only see this getting worse from here. "Anyone new catching your eye?"

"Uh, no. Axel really missed me so we're just trying to get that quality bro time in."

"Good." She smiles.

"Well, I'll upload this and send you a private link and you can show it to your moms whenever you're ready."

"You mean when I'm like thirty-four and they are retiring my LA Sparks jersey?"

"How is that positive thinking?"

"You're right. Well. I'll see you later, I guess?"

"Yup." My voice sounds weird and she knows it. She just nods and heads out of my room. I do the polite thing and follow her and stand by the door while she steps into her sneakers. The ones she wore to homecoming. She doesn't say bye. She just gives me a tight smile. I nod back and hold the door open for her. I wait until she climbs back into her car and then I go back to my room. I need to upload this thing and be done with it. When I go back into the kitchen, my Crunchwrap is cold. I eat it anyway.

I feel like a jerk, but I think it's going to be a while before I can be friends with Bethany. I think I might be in love with her.

40
BETHANY
(is dazed and really confused)

have no idea what just happened, but I feel pretty awful.
I barely slept last night and then I made the mistake of
being excited to see Jacob. I knew nothing was going to
happen, but I miss him. So much. He *did not* want to see me.
The urge to just sit in my car is too strong, but I can't just
sit in the rain outside Jacob's house. I don't want to go home
either. Mama T has a game in a couple hours. She's already
at the arena and Momlissa had a bridal party to go to. Sitting in my house alone crying is not what I need right now.
I drive down to the next street and park. Then I call Saylor.
I can't wait for her to text me back.

She answers right away. "Hey, everything okay?"

"Not at all. Where are you?"

"At home."

"Can I come over?"

"Yeah, we're just doing Christmas card things. Come over."

"Who's that?" I hear her dad's deep voice in the background.

"It's Bethany."

"Oh, come on over," Cris says into the phone.

"No, don't— Ow!" I can't tell the twins' voices apart, but Stella is a whole demon, so I know that's her. Scarlett would never.

"You can come over," Saylor confirms.

"I'll be right there." I take my time getting over to their house because no one in Los Angeles can drive in the rain.

Saylor opens the front door of their house before I even get my seat belt off. She's wearing a pair of Christmas pajamas that I'm pretty sure were Cris's idea. "Please tell me you desperately need to dish about Kayden. You left the group text on read all night."

"Ugh, not exactly."

"Booo. Come say hi to Cris and Papa John and then we'll go hide in my room." I follow her into the kitchen. A lot is happening. All of the Fords are wearing the same pajamas. There's Christmas music playing. The smell of hot chocolate is in the air, and there's a really intense assembly-line setup on their island.

"Hey, Bethany," Cris says. "We're just getting our Christmas cards out." She signs a card and then hands it to Mr. Ford who signs it and passes it on to the twins.

"It's the most fun we've ever had," Stella says sarcastically.

Mr. Ford shoots her a look and shakes his head. She grumbles and keeps on signing.

"I love the pajamas," I say.

"We're just getting this week's content out of the way," Saylor explains. "Mom, Bethany needs my emotional support. We'll be in my room for a while."

"Okay, we'll leave you a stack. When you're done, finish signing and then help me stuff."

"Will do. Let's go." We rush up to her room and I feel like I can finally exhale once I flop down into her chair and Saylor practically dives onto her bed. Showing any weakness in front of Stella is a bad idea. "Okay. What's going on? Tell me everything. What happened with Kayden?"

That breaks the dam. My eyes start welling up and tears spill over. "This isn't about Kayden."

"Oh no, Bets. Don't cry. What happened?"

"I really like Jacob," I confess.

"Oh no. The feelings still there?"

"No, you don't—" I have to tell her. This is just getting silly. "The thing between Jacob and me, it wasn't— It was a deal we made."

"What do you mean?"

I tell her everything. About the conversation we had Halloween night and Jacob's idea and how I went along with it. "He felt like he couldn't be himself around anyone and I felt like there was no way I was gonna get over my Crybaby Bethany nerves. But we didn't like each other then. We were gonna help each other. He was gonna help me be more confident with guys like Oliver."

"Okay," she says, clearly concerned that I have lost my mind.

"I mean, I'd never even held anyone's hand, and with Jacob there was no pressure because we didn't like each other."

"But now you do?"

"Yes!" I sob. "I caught feelings for him, but then Kayden—" I can't even finish my sentence. Saylor doesn't push me though. She rushes out of her room and comes back with a fresh box of tissues. She sits on the floor right in front of me and offers me the box. I take like five and try to clean up my face. "We knew we were gonna break up and all of that. And he knew I had a crush on Oliver. But then you said that thing about Kayden being my celebrity crush so he knew I liked Kayden too."

"Oh shit, Bets. I'm sorry."

"No. It was fine, because that was kinda part of the plan. Help me build up my boy confidence. And then last week at the party, like a complete dummy, I told him that Kayden talked to Glory."

"And he ended it, but you really like him?"

"Yeah. I like him so much. And I don't know what to do."

"Okay, first off, that boy likes you," Saylor says just as my phone vibrates in my back pocket. I pull it out and it's a text from Jacob. It's just the link to the video and that's it. A chill runs through me. I know when I'm being shut out. He must really be done with me.

"He sent over the video for my moms. I just came from there. It was so awful. He hates me."

"Oh, can we watch it? After we're finished talking," she adds. "And he does not hate you."

"No, I need a time-out. We can watch it now."

Saylor grabs her computer and I forward her the link. We sit and watch for a few minutes and then Saylor hits pause. "Okay, I don't need to see the rest."

"Why, what's wrong?"

"Bethany. Look at this, please. Look at the screen." I look at her computer and it's paused on the moment Jacob had pulled the still from. One of the last pictures he sent to me before we broke up. "I have known you my whole life and my mother loves a camera more than she loves her own children. This? All of this time, all of this effort, just for you? Just to help you build up the confidence you need to tell Teresa and Melissa what's what? Just for you to be happy? And he edited all of this together after your romance-practice pact ended? And he made you look like the most beautiful person in the world? That boy not only loves you, he *sees* you."

I look at the screen again and think of just how good this video is and how much work he put into it. How he sees me the way I actually see myself, in a way that I'm afraid to admit out loud because I know there's always someone waiting to pat me on the head or shut me down. I'm beautiful and Jacob thinks so too.

"Bets, trust me. He took like four pictures of me when we were together and I never looked this good. This is how he sees you," she says, like she read my mind. Maybe she's right, but what if she isn't? What if this is just another dramatic figment of my imagination? The Jacob part, not how much of a babe I am. What if Jacob just loves the visual medium and I gave him a project to work on? What if he rejects me for real?

"I don't know" is all I can say.

"I can't believe you both did all that. I feel kinda bad that

I made Jacob feel like he was a bad boyfriend. He wasn't."

"I think we were both just embarrassed. It sucked being the only one in our group without someone. I did feel like a big baby."

"You're not and we never think of you that way. But what happened with Kayden?"

"Oh my god. Tell me why it didn't occur to me that his one true love is basketball?"

"Oh no." Saylor laughs.

"Say, he's the nicest. He was so sweet. Came in and talked to my moms. Asked me all these questions. He was sweet after the movie. He kissed me on the cheek good night. But we talked about basketball and basketball-related things. The. Whole. Time. I'd try to change the subject and somehow we'd end up talking about basketball."

"Oh my god. And he probably thinks you were like *oh finally, someone who wants to talk about basketball.*"

"I can't date him. I hate the one thing he loves. We're, like, genuinely incompatible. He is really hot though."

"Yeah, that makes sense. That would be absolute torture. But maybe now you get why I thought Jake and I weren't a good match?"

"No, you're right. I see it now."

"Good. Okay." She stands up again and pulls me up with her. "You're gonna go to the bathroom and fix your face."

"And then what?"

"You're gonna go back over to Jacob's and you're gonna tell him how you feel."

"No, I'm not."

"Oh yes, you are. There's no way you went through a whole literal dating scheme, lied to me about it—which should be illegal—and not even try to go for it with the first boy you truly like." She pulls me down the hall to the bathroom she shares with the twins. I only have a little eye makeup and it's not too messed up, but I do my best to get myself together. I turn back to Saylor when I'm done. "Gorgeous. Go get your man."

"If this fails, I will haunt you."

"Haunt me?" She laughs.

"Yes, I will immediately pass away from embarrassment and disappointment and haunt you for the rest of your life."

"Go. And text me as soon as you two decide to kiss and make up."

I don't argue anymore. I rush downstairs and say bye to the Fords and then I drive back to Jacob's house.

41
JACOB
(gets it right this time)

How come every time the doorbell rings unexpectedly, it feels like there's a murderer at the door? It doesn't help that it's raining harder. I roll off the couch and go check the doorbell camera. It's Bethany, probably back to tell me off. I'm glad she's back though. Now I have a chance to say I'm sorry for how I acted earlier. Yes, my heart is turning to charcoal dust, but I can't take that out on her. It's not cool.

I open the door and feel even worse. She's been crying.

"Hey, I'm—"

She steps past me and just starts talking. "I'm sorry, I had a whole speech planned, but if I don't ask you this now I'm gonna chicken out. Do you like me? Like, actually like me, boyfriend-like me?"

I just stare back at her. "Wait, what?"

"Do you like me?"

"Yes," I blurt out.

"You do?" she asks. She's actually shocked and I realize how badly I screwed up. Why didn't I just tell her?

"Yes. I like you."

"Okay. Good, good. 'Cause I like you. A lot. My speech was way more romantic, but yeah, I like you."

"Good." And then we just stand there, looking at each other, sharing a single brain cell. I should probably say something else. "Um, do you want to be my girlfriend again? For real."

"Yes." She nods. "I do."

"Okay, good. Can I kiss you?"

"If I can hug you first." She steps out of her sneakers and comes farther into the house. And then she hugs me. I hug her back. Her sweatshirt is a little wet, dotted from the rain, but I don't care. "I really missed your hugs. I missed you."

"I missed you too." I pull back just enough to kiss her. She kisses me back. And then she hugs me again. I take her hand and we go to the couch. I can't help but smile when she immediately curls up to my side and wraps her arms around me again.

"I've liked you since homecoming," she says with a watery sigh. I'm pretty sure she's crying again.

"That's when it happened for me too. In the photo booth," I tell her.

She looks up at me, her eyes definitely watery. "Really?"

"Yup."

"We're both pretty oblivious, huh?" She snorts.

"Maybe, but I think we can help each other out. Oh, wait—" I ask her what's her ideal size of comfort hoodie, then run down to the Thunderdome. I come back with a brand-new Ink & Pearl sweatshirt. "Esther said it's not official until I give you a boyfriend hoodie. But then she told me all of mine smell bad. This one's fresh."

"Thanks." Bethany stands up and pulls off her wet hoodie and puts the Ink & Pearl one on. She bunches up the sleeves in her hands and looks down at the logo across her chest. "That's cozy."

I sit down on the arm of the couch and I ask the one question I need an answer to. I'm so glad she's back, but things were definitely different an hour ago. "Not to bring this back up, but um—what happened with Kayden?"

Bethany comes closer and steps between my legs. I put my hands on her hips as she drapes her arms over my shoulders, like we used to. It feels right. It feels good. "I don't know. I just kept thinking about all the boyfriend-girlfriend stuff I still wanted to do, or do again, and I just wanted to be doing those things with you. He's really nice; he's just not my jam." She bites her lips, trying not to laugh.

"I did that to myself, didn't I?"

"You sure did." She smiles at me and then we're kissing again. I can see the final cut of it in my mind. The burnt shards in my chest rolling backward and coming together to form the glowing orb that's now beating in my chest. Bethany's etched her initials on it.

42

BETHANY

(and her moment of truth)

t's a bright, sunny Sunday in December and I decide to take that as a good sign. It's the first time me and the moms are all home, with no post- or pre-game stress. It's time for me to show them my presentation, produced by Jacob Yeun. I almost chicken out three or four times, but we beat Malibu High last night and from the way Coach Miller is just losing his mind over the real shot of us going undefeated and how much I don't want to be a part of it? I know it's time. It feels selfish, but honestly the team will be fine without me. Saylor knows how to rebound too.

But first. The moms.

Jacob offers to come over and provide emotional support. Our first week as a for-real couple, or as everyone else sees it, our first week back together, is pretty great. Saylor vows to keep our weird arrangement a secret. A rumor about a boyfriend-girlfriend pact is not something either of us want going around school. I tell Kayden things won't work out next time I see him and he is really nice about it. Even says he appreciates that I gave him a chance, but he can see how much Jacob and I are into each other.

"Who am I to stand in the way of true love?" he says with

that million-dollar smile. I really hope he finds the right girl for him, a girl who *loves* sports.

I get up early and get started on my moms' surprise breakfast. We're having waffles, with fruit and scrambled eggs instead of bacon, but still waffles.

"This is so nice," Momlissa says, taking her seat at the island. Mama T hands her a cup of coffee and sits down beside her.

"Yeah, this a nice treat, Bets. Thank you."

"You're welcome. So remember I mentioned there was something I wanted to show you?"

"I just wanna know how much it's going to cost," Mama T says.

I open my mouth and close it again, thinking about the cost of kitchen supplies and extremely cute aprons versus how much they've already spent on basketball over the years. "It might be a break-even situation," I say.

"I can handle that."

I exhale and then grab my laptop off the far counter. I try to picture the best-case scenario. They don't disown me. I open my laptop and wake it up as I walk back across the room. I'm so anxious I hit play before I even set it down in front of my moms. I go back and lean against the counter, picking at my own waffle as Heaven's and my voices fill the room. The music Jacob picked is perfect, and having watched it a few more times, I definitely see what Saylor saw. He put this whole thing together so well because he has the ultimate heart eyes, just for me.

Neither of my moms storm out of the room. At different

times they both laugh. When Mrs. Yeun talks about how she wants my recipe, Momlissa nods her head, impressed.

When it's over, Mama T lets out a sigh and shakes her head. There's a little smile on her face. I don't know what it means. Maybe everything I said is so ridiculous, she's thinking about how she can pack me up and ship me off to a twenty-four seven development camp until graduation. She looks over at Momlissa, who is also smirking a little.

"You gonna tell her?" Mama T says.

"Tell me what?" I ask.

"Well, first, I want to say that I am sorry if we ever made you feel any way about your weight. We love you just as you are. Food is great. Having an interest in food, and learning more about it and how to prepare it, is wonderful," Momlissa says.

"Is there a huge but coming?"

"No," Mama T says. "I just want your mother to admit that you are definitely her child." I'm a little confused because I know when my moms are messing with each other, but this is no laughing matter. "Your mom *hated* playing basketball. Hated it."

"What?!"

"I didn't hate it," Momlissa says before she rolls her eyes. "Okay, fine, I hated it, but I was so good I had no excuse to stop playing."

"What did you want to do instead?" My mind is completely blown. My mom could open her own museum to show off all of her basketball-related achievements. I had no clue she felt this way.

"I wanted to be a meteorologist."

"WHAT!"

Mama T just starts laughing. She grabs both their plates and brings them over to the sink.

Momlissa goes on. "Yup. I took this meteorology class in college and I was just hooked. Our teacher was the local station's weatherman and he was the nicest guy. He answered all my silly questions. The girls on my team used to call me Weather Girl."

"Wow," I gasp.

"But I love my job now. I'm a sports journalist and that's pretty cool."

"It is." I smile back at her.

"You still have that email from the cooking school?" Mama T says. I take out my phone and pull it up, then hand it over. I wait patiently as she reads it. Then she hands the phone to Momlissa. They exchange a look and Mama T nods.

"We can go look at their schedule and I'll give them a call. You can start taking classes over there."

"I can?!"

"Girl, you just made a whole *30 for 30* talking about how you don't want to play. I think it would be a little ghoulish of us if we kept you chained to the three-point line."

"I'd like to make a compromise," Momlissa says. "Do you think you can finish out the season? I know it's a few more months, but in the name of sportsmanship, I think it would be nice if you could give your team that long."

"Yeah, of course." The compromise is a great idea. I already feel like a huge weight has been lifted off my shoulders just because I know there's an end. "I just thought you would be angry or give me to Omari."

"Ha," Momlissa says. "His wife is pregnant again. They don't need any more kids." She comes around the island and gives me a big hug. I close my eyes and squeeze her back. Mama T puts her arm around us both. "We're definitely not giving you away. We want you to be happy, Bethany."

"Thank you." I sigh.

"Tell Jacob that was some A plus camera work," Mama T says before she steps back and frowns at me. "I just want to know why you made your granddad's spaghetti recipe for Jacob and his little friends, and we didn't get to try it."

"I'll make it again for you guys. But there's another recipe I wanna try first. You wanna see?"

"Sure." She laughs. I turn my laptop around and pull up Chef Evie's braised-rib recipe.

o o o

I'm still giddy a few hours later after I finish talking things out with my moms. I have to tell Jacob the good news. He's at the skate park. I know that's his special place, but I need to see him now. He drops me the address. I grab my new, but already worn in, Ink & Pearl hoodie and drive over. I don't know what I expected, but it's packed—little kids with scooters, grown people on roller skates, grown people

on skateboards taking turns using the ramps and rails.
Heaven is standing by a nearby ramp. She gives me a nod.
I see Jacob at the top of this ramp looking very focused,
probably not the best time to distract him. I spot Valentina
right away and go join her on a bench. I don't see Axel, but
he's got to be around here somewhere.

"Hey!" I flop down beside Valentina and wonder if she
can tell that I feel different. I wonder if she can tell that I
feel like a new woman.

"Hey. You seem happy."

"I am. I got some good news," I say, just as Jacob skates
over. He's out of breath and all sweaty, but he's never looked
better.

"Well?" he breathes. "How'd it go?"

"They said yes. At the end of the season, I can say goodbye to Lady Minotaurs Basketball and move on to my next
adventure as an amateur chef. A very beginner amateur
chef."

"That's awesome," I hear Valentina say as Jacob pulls me
off the bench and hugs me.

"You did it," he says before he kisses me.

"Nah, *we* did that. The moms were very impressed with
your artistry. The full video presentation definitely sold it."

"And they didn't disown you?"

I shake my head. "Still a Greene."

"Nice." He smiles at me and my insides melt.

I almost kiss him again, but a stocky Black man on roller
skates cruises right over to us. "Is this the Bethany I heard
so much about? I'm Dr. Campbell, Heaven's dad." His voice

is kind and warm, but I see immediately where Heaven gets her fearless personality from.

"Nice to meet you, Dr. Campbell."

"Jake said you don't skate at all."

"No, sir. I do not."

"Well, come on. You don't just come to a skate park to sit around," he says. "Valentina's already got her lessons in."

"And I'm terrible." She laughs. "I like this bench right here, thank you."

"I guess it's my turn, then," I say. Dr. Campbell leads us over to a flat, open area. Heaven and Axel skate over too, to watch.

"You gonna get your kick and push on?" Axel asks.

"I . . . don't know. I guess."

"I got you," Jacob says. "I helped teach Esther how to skate."

"Nah, man," Heaven says. "You film. I'll teach. I'm Missus Steal Your Girl," she sings. I snort a little as Jacob pulls out his phone. Heaven steps off her board, then uses her foot to effortlessly spin it around. She grabs my fingers and guides me into place on the other side of her board. "We're not gonna toss you off the half pipe today, but you're gonna feel the wind through your twists."

I peer over at Jacob, who's already recording on his phone. I wonder if I should have any doubts about trusting his best friend with the safety of my person.

"Okay," I say with a deep breath. "But if I break any-thing, my moms will sue."

"My parents are good for it, trust me. Okay, you're gonna spread your feet and bend your knees."

I follow her instructions and step onto the board. Heaven's a good teacher, but still, I want it to be Jacob holding my hands.

"Okay, we're just going this way," Heaven says, as she starts walking forward. A few times back and forth and I feel less like I'm going to die. I'm definitely not taking up skating soon, or ever, but when Heaven speeds up and starts jogging a bit, I start to get it. I feel the air moving against my face. I can't stop smiling. Even if I have a death grip on Heaven's wrists. We zip back in the other direction, Heaven pulling me along.

"Jacob. Look at me. I'm flying," I call out, giggling like a fool.

"You're a pro, babe!" Jacob laughs. I know he's getting this on his phone, and I know, somehow, he's the only person who can capture just how happy I am.

Acknowledgments

So much has happened since the idea for this book came to be. I'm a different person now than I was then, and I have to thank all of the people who held me together and lifted me up, especially when I doubted my ability to write a story that would do my love for Bethany, Jacob, and all their friends justice.

First I have to thank the meaning in my life, the inspiration, my amazing agent Holly Root. Thank you for helping me find my way again and again. I now have a Holly voice in my head, right next to the voices that sound a lot like my parents. Whenever I have a publishing panic, I can say, What would Holly tell me to do? It's very helpful.

Thank you to the team at Penguin/Razorbill. Julie Rosenberg for smashing the champagne and launching this ship, and Tiara Kittrell for guiding me safely back to shore. And to Casey McIntyre and Simone Roberts-Payne for helping plug all the holes along the way. And thank you Poppy Magda and the whole art team for the gorgeous cover. It's so cute! To everyone on and off every email chain. Thank you. Your work did not go unnoticed or underappreciated.

Next I have to thank my family, who have been the most amazing cheerleaders. Mom and Dad, my brother Clarke, here's something of mine you can finally share with your students. I have to thank my sister-in-law Joanna Ro, my brother-in-law and sister-in-law squared, Jason and Sarah Ro, for always welcoming me into your homes and feeding me. My sister-in-law squared squared, Jen Lim, for the chats and inspiring me to be a little bit more fancy each day. Marley Oh, let's keep making plans to make plans until one of us dies. And the kids! Lucas, Noah, Lindsey, Clara, Josh, Jee-Ah and Jae Young, for inspiring me to be a little bit cooler every day. I have to thank the captain of my research team, Patty Oh, for enthusiastically offering to help me with parts of the story and DMing me about *Bachelor in Paradise*. Mark, Hazel, Zoe, I just want you guys to see your names in print.

Thank you so much to Matthew Kim and Matthew Limb for answering all of my teen-related questions. You're in college now! Sorry publishing moves so slowly. Sal and Liz Perales, thank you for letting me use Axl's name and the Perales vibe in this story.

Oh man, my amazing friends. Ellee Dean (and Porter) and Nick Crawford, thank you for still being here after all these years and inspiring all the warm feelings that the friendships in this book are built on. The Amen girls+Kimmie B, Jenny, Marge, Cathy. You're the best. Kim and Ari, I can't wait to meet your babies. Courtney, Bree, Alyssa. You are also the best. Leona, Liza, Sarah, my Mature Porch Aunties of Greater Los Angeles. Thank you, thank you, thank you.

I'd like to thank all of the young adult authors who have encouraged me to enter this space. What a warm welcome. To Dhonielle Clayton and Zoraida Córdova, you are simply wonderful.

And finally, I'd like to thank you, the reader. I hope this story made you smile.